The Sixties Boys On Tour

To Michael

Best Wishes

The Sixties Boys On Tour

Alan Hammond

Foreword by Dave Berry

This book is dedicated to the memory of sixties teenagers Carol and her brother Rod, who were part of my life, and who tragically died in their teens.

The stories in the book are based on the life, experiences and memories of the author and others. All names of people, places and dates have been changed. Individuals shown in the photographs are not related to any of the story lines.

The band names Modern Edge, The Rubbes and Mod Mania and the composition *Suburban Mod* are not meant to represent any particular bands with these names or any song with this title; they are purely names invented for the storyline of this book.

First published in 2012
Reprinted 2012

British Library Cataloguing in Publication Data

A catalogue record for this book is available from the British Library.

ISBN 978 1 85794 419 8

Silver Link Publishing Ltd
The Trundle
Ringstead Road
Great Addington
Kettering
Northants NN14 4BW

Tel/Fax: 01536 330588
email: sales@nostalgiacollection.com
Website: www.nostalgiacollection.com
Printed and bound in the Czech Republic

Contents

Foreword

I am very pleased to write the foreword for Alan's new 'Sixties' book. I lived in a working-class home in the village of Woodhouse on the Yorkshire-Derbyshire border, and grew up in a house that was generally buzzing with lively music. My Dad was a semi-professional jazz and swing drummer. He was my first introduction to music and he would take me to see all the American bands at Sheffield City Hall in the 1950s.

I was influenced by the wave of American rock and roll music, with the likes of Eddie Cochran and Gene Vincent. My first step as a singer was as a harmony duo with a friend, which included singing Everly Brothers numbers. In 1960 I formed my band, The Cruisers, and what was unusual was that we promoted many of our own gigs. A couple of them I recall were The Leeds Arms at Kiveton and Co-op Hall at Frecheville. The largest place we played at in our early days was The Gaumont, Sheffield, where there were more than 600 people.

At a gig in Doncaster, Mickie Most and Mike Smith, record producers from Decca, came to see us play; they must have been impressed as I signed a recording contract with them. My first record was *Memphis Tennessee* and I had future successes, which included *The Crying Game* in 1964. My biggest-selling record so far was in Europe, with *This Strange Effect*, which was written for me by Ray Davies of the Kinks.

I have toured with the Rolling Stones and many other acts, including the Small Faces, who were always great fun to be with. There was no overnight X-Factor-style success for me. I was one of the original British pop idols, and record sales and fame arrived after several years of hard work touring up and down the country. I really enjoy the sixties tours today. You are working with guys from other bands who you have known for forty-five years.

One of the most bizarre bookings was a pre-Christmas run at a hotel in Usk, South Wales. The hotel booked me for three nights, then I had three days off at the weekend, then returned for another three days. Out of the blue a promoter asked if I would be interested in a one-night show in Hong Kong, then another in mainland China. On looking at the schedule, the Hong Kong show I would be able to do as it coincided with my three-day break. After the third performance in Usk I went straight to bed. A taxi picked me up the next morning for the flight to Hong Kong. I arrived three hours before my performance, did the show, then flew back. I arrived a few hours before the show at Usk. As I checked back into the hotel the receptionist said, 'Hello Dave, have you done much over the weekend?'

Playing today is a real eye-opener for me. I have appeared with Roger Taylor of Queen, Rick Wakeman, Tony Hadley of Spandau Ballet and the late Robin Gibb, among many others. I must have done something right in my long career.

I enjoy performing now just as much as when I first started out in the sixties. I am most grateful to the fans who over the years have given me great support in coming to the shows and buying my records. I can't do it without you, so thank you.

Dave Berry

Introduction and Acknowledgements

First of all I would like to thank everyone who bought my previous books, *The Sixties Boys* and *Sixties Boys Unzipped*. I hope you will enjoy the third and final book of the series.

I have had great fun writing the books and it is an era that I have fond memories of. *Sixties Boys on Tour* takes us into a present-day setting. 'Modern Edge' now have their bus passes! They reform and go on tour again after nearly forty years. They still have the rose-tinted glasses of the sixties, and are now at an age where they can put the world to rights!

Very special thanks to my new publisher, Silver Link Publishing, and especially to Peter Townsend.

Many thanks go to Dave Berry, who has written the Foreword for me. Dave was a sixties superstar, and his book *All There Is To Know* is well worth buying. He is still playing today to full houses and is just as good as ever.

My wife Christine has been a tremendous help and support with all of my books, especially this one. She has used her skills in fine-tuning the manuscript, and added some of her own storylines. I couldn't do it without her.

I have many other people to thank for making this book possible, including my oldest friend Terry Page, who has jogged my memory about the sixties and added his own thoughts.

I am greatly indebted to my good friend John Clifton, who has checked and edited the book and added some of his own memories.

Thanks and gratitude go to Eleanor Roberts, Allan Stanistreet, Roger Curd and Peter Day, who have also proofread the book and have been of great help to me.

Many others in one way or another have contributed to this publication and I would like to thank Steve Clow, *Essex Chronicle*, Mick Phipps, Ray Homewood, Ivan and Jill Bluffield, Pat and Lyn Mitchell, Chris Ross, Grahame Darch, Ron and Joan Saunders, Herby Boxall, Chris Nicholson and Glyn Grainger.

♫ 1 ♫

The phone call that changes your life

It's late at night and you're having your Horlicks, cheese and biscuits and the poxy phone goes. Your heart drops a beat and you know it's trouble. It can't be my parents as they're dead. It's not the wife as she pissed off and left me years ago. It must be the poxy kids. I don't want to answer it, as I know it's either going to cost me or they've broken up with their partners, and want to come back home to live.

At sixty-four years of age it's not an option. No wonder I'm grey. They were nightmare kids and I don't want them back. Thank God, the phone stops ringing and I tuck into my blue cheese again. It rings again. It ain't going to go away; it's got to be answered.

After a ten-minute conversation, I've gone from Horlicks to a large brandy. I'm now lost for words, which isn't like me. This call brings back the emotions of another era when life was simple, uncomplicated and fun. Holding a large brandy and smoking a roll-up, I look in the mirror. I see an old man with a fat gut, hair coming out of his nose and ears, smoker's cough and clothes from Primark – what a bleedin' mess.

After my third brandy I shed a tear and remember when I was someone. The bloke on the phone wants me to return as that person – some chance!

Three days later I've left my Romford flat and headed to Ilford. I find the building, and climb up three flights of stairs. I'm knackered and have to stop to get my breath back. I have a quick puff on my inhaler before I walk into the office. On the door there's a plaque: 'Wayne Brodie Enterprises'.

Sitting at the desk is a lad about thirty years old with a mop of ginger hair, and dressed like a Mod with a target tee-shirt. He looks up and says, 'You must be Nick Sheldon?'

'That's me. So what's all this about, Wayne?'

'Your band Modern Edge was one of the best Mod bands around in the sixties and your big hit *Suburban Mod* is still a classic. I'm in the process of putting together a Road Show of that era; it'll be countrywide and I want your band to be the headline act.'

I'm lost for words and have another puff on the inhaler.

'You've got to be kidding! We haven't played since the mid-seventies and I don't even know where the others are as we've never kept in contact. It's over thirty-five years ago, don't forget.'

'I appreciate it's a bolt out of the blue, Nick. Have a think about it – I'll give you a list of proposed dates and the type of money you could be on as a taster. I need to know within two months before I finalise the tour.'

When I got home to the cold empty flat, I wished I had a partner to talk to. My marriage finished years ago due to me playing with various bands all over Europe and getting up to no good. It was my own fault. I had two kids with my wife Helen.

Tracy, the youngest, is thirty-three and a full-on Essex girl with her spray tan and monthly wax. Her favourite TV programme is *The Only Way Is Essex*. She's just had a new pair of tits that make Jordan's look like tennis balls. Her role models are Kerry Katona and Cheryl Cole! She's got more mobiles than BT and is a shareholder in Costa Coffee, where she spends most of her time with her mates.

Her husband Mick works his bollocks off to keep up with it all. It's fortunate he's a CID officer, so he's always busy! They've got ten-year-old twins, Zacharias and Clinton. Where do they get these names from?

My son Rob, the eldest, is thirty-five, works in finance and lives with Zoe. They have one girl, Jade, who's a precocious little shit. At eleven years old she runs the house. If she doesn't get what she wants she swears and uses the F-word more times than Ramsey. No wonder Rob goes down the gym every day. Sometimes I think he's batting for the other side – he's always in the beauty parlour having his nails done and his body hair ripped off. He's got more moisturising cream in his bathroom cupboard than Boots. It doesn't help that they live next door, so I'm always on call.

When they were young they were a pain in the arse. I still have trouble today coming to terms with them after all the grief they gave me and Helen. They look at me like some old fart that's never had a life. Little do they know I was once a pop idol and experienced things that they could only dream about. After our band Modern Edge broke up I played with various other bands up until 2005. Now I just do a little bit of gigging on my own at small venues like the British Legion. It sounds a bit sad but it suits me.

My best mate in the band was Steve, and together we wrote *Suburban Mod*, which still brings in a fair amount of royalties and keeps me in beer and fags. As I've mentioned, I don't know where any of the other lads are. The only guy I keep in touch with from those days is Des. He was our roadie and driver. In his youth he was a real rascal and was the sixties equivalent of Arthur Daley or Del Boy. I still see him nearly every day, and we often have a beer at the Queen's Arms – sorry, now called Ziggies – what a name to call a bleedin' pub! It was where all the lads used to meet back in the early days.

I now have a decision to make. Do I want to trace the guys from a band who haven't played together for years or do I let sleeping dogs lie and just remember the great times we had together?

While I'm dreaming of the sixties there's a knock on the door and my daughter storms in with her two noisy brats.

'Dad, can you look after the twins tonight, and can you lend me three hundred quid? I need a tyre for my 4x4.'

This is what some kids are like today when it comes to their parents. I have three words for it: 'Use and abuse'.

Wouldn't it be nice if they first asked you how your day had been, *then* mugged you for the money? I think I want to escape back to the sixties and remember when I had a smile on my face and enjoyed life to the full. Decision made – find the guys who were part of the happiest times of my life and see whether we can turn the clock back. Before the search begins I'd better take you back in time to 1964 when our journey began.

♫ 2 ♫

The Swinging Sixties

My best mate, Steve, lived down the same street as me. We were inseparable. We only had one thing on our mind: girls. Life was great – dances, parties, music, Double Diamond, Woodbines and your own motor. Mine was a Ford 100E. What more could you ask for at seventeen years of age?

At school we had a really good music teacher, Mr Thomas. All the teachers seemed to be Welsh in those days – would you want to work down a coal mine? He taught Steve and me to play the guitar and after many hours of practising we started up a band with another school mate, Tony, who played the drums. We called ourselves Tony and the Mustangs, playing mainly at youth clubs.

Steve and I packed the band up when we left school at fifteen, but we would still have a jam with Tony now and again. One night we went down to our local coffee bar, La Nero in Hornchurch. Tony was playing that night with another band. We got talking and agreed we should start up another group. That was the beginning of Modern Edge, me on lead guitar, Steve on bass guitar and Tony on drums.

We needed a singer. One night I helped out another band with a gig. It was a posh bird's 21st birthday, and she wanted to sing a number. She was bleedin' dire and within ten seconds of her singing all the guests went to the bog. Her boyfriend got on the mic to help her out – now, he *could* sing, and that's how we found Rick. He was one good-looking guy, and girls would throw themselves at him. Mind you, we caught a few of them.

At the beginning we'd just do covers from bands like the Small Faces, Who, Hollies, Kinks and Beatles. We were enjoying every minute of it; we played coffee bars, dance halls and youth clubs. We were crumpet-mad and most nights we were at it. It certainly was the Swinging Sixties for us.

We were a Mod band and dressed in target tee-shirts or Ben Sherman and Fred Perry short-sleeve shirts. With our Sta-Prest trousers and winkle-pickers we looked the part.

1964 was the year of the Mods 'n' Rockers knocking shit out of each other, mostly at holiday resorts. We were at Brighton when it all kicked off, the resort a backdrop for the film *Quadrophenia*. It was a wild time, and we had plenty of punch-ups with Rockers dressed up in their black leather jackets and tight jeans. They rode motorbikes, which included Triumphs and Nortons, while the Mods rode their Italian scooters, Lambrettas and Vespas. The Rockers used to call these hairdryers.

As the band progressed we started to write our own material. Drugs were now coming on the scene: Blues, Purple Hearts, Black Bombers, and the rest. In the early days we were happy with a pint of Red Barrel or Double Diamond. Drugs unfortunately had a disastrous effect on the band later in our careers. As we were getting more gigs we decided to go full-time – we were now seventeen years of age.

Rick's Dad became our manager. He invested some money in the band and we went into a studio and made a demo, *Suburban Mod*. The first tour of many was in the South West of England where I met Anita, a girl I've never forgotten, even after all these years.

When I was in Devon I badly needed a haircut, so I went to a hairdressers in Dawlish and Anita cut my hair. In those days it was unheard of for a girl to cut a bloke's hair. She was a special lady and we got very close.

Over the next few years we had an on-off relationship, which I messed up big time. There weren't too many towns in Britain that we didn't play. We even played on the Greek island of Rhodes – what a great time that was. We were on the road for three years and the parties we went to were legendary.

It all came to an end in 1966. Even though we were having a great time, we were making no money, so we disbanded. Our last show was in Harwich, Essex. After the gig a bloke came up to me and asked if we had any tapes of the band. All we had were a couple of demo vinyls of *Suburban Mod*. I gave him one and thought nothing more of it.

A week later Steve and I took two birds down to the coast at Walton-on-Naze in an old Vauxhall Victor. We had the radio on listening to one of the pirate radio stations. These were ships broadcasting just outside British territorial waters; two of the most famous were Radio Caroline and Radio London. While we're having a snog and a grope in the motor our record came on over the airwaves. What a shock that was. The guy we gave the vinyl to was a DJ on another boat called Radio North Essex, and that started an unbelievable journey for the band.

After the record was played the listeners bombarded the radio station to find out where they could buy it. Because of that, the band reformed within a month and was signed up by a record company in January 1967. The record made the Top 30 and the sky was the limit. We played at some top venues around the country and in Holland. Mind you, we had problems on the way with Rick's Dad. He was supposed to be managing us, but ripped us off financially. He then got arrested for a couple of robberies and got banged up for three years. From being the next best young thing in the music industry we went tits up.

Rick left the band for a short while as he had to sort out his Dad's business affairs. We recruited Ray, who we'd met on the road when he was playing for another band. He turned out to be a right good signing for the group. He fitted in well and the band moved forward once again.

It's all looking tasty then the shit hits the fan. First, our record company kicks us into touch, then Tony, our drummer, starts puffing and popping for England – he's hooked on drugs.

We'd done a lot of shows in Reading for a big dance hall promoter called TJ. The venue was one of the top places to play and he liked us and we liked him.

One night he got another record company to come and listen to us. Before the gig we had a word with Tony about his drug-taking and how it was affecting his playing. We wanted him to realise that we had another chance tonight to get a recording contract. We asked him to focus on his playing and not how many purple hearts he could get down his throat. He got a cob on and walked out on the band. We didn't see him again for years.

TJ got us another drummer for the night and, lo and behold, the record guy liked our music. Within a few weeks we got a record deal and the show is back on the road. We got another drummer, Billy from Barnet, North London. He used to play in Ray's band, but he wasn't the long-term answer. I remember a gig in Devon. He was knocking the shit out of the drums and I said to him, 'Are your family Apaches?'

'Whatcha mean by that?'

'I thought you were sending feckin' messages back home to them in Barnet.'

TJ became our manager. The company he represented was a really good outfit – not once did they rip us off. We had a great working relationship with him. He must be in his late seventies now and I'd love to know if he's still alive.

Tony's younger sister Penny was a fair drummer. It ran in the family – their father was a drummer in the 1950s and taught them both how to play. Tony had gone off to meditate and ended up on a drugs charge in the Far East and was sent to prison.

Rick rejoined the band as a keyboard player and part vocals, so we were now a five-piece. We offered Penny the job as our drummer and she accepted, so by 1968 we were on a roll. For the next few years we made records and toured all over Europe and beyond.

We weren't one of the mega-bands but we had a good following, especially with the Mods, and our records sold well.

Unfortunately one of the band members put Penny up the duff. To this day I don't know which one it was. I've got my suspicions, but we'll leave it at that! With Penny sprogged up we needed another drummer, and as luck would have it Tony was back on the scene. He was out of jail and had cleaned up his act, so he came back on board.

We were not just a band but also great mates, and we rarely fell out, except when Tony got into drugs. We were always there for each other. What helped was that none of us were married while the band was in existence.

We played hard and partied hard. We did arenas, theatres, festivals – you name it, we played it. However, it couldn't go on for ever, and after a show in Holland we agreed the band had run its course. There was no animosity or friction, and on the flight home it was agreed that after we'd fulfilled our outstanding obligations that would be it.

Our last gig, funnily enough, was at Reading where TJ had arranged for the record guy to come and hear us play.

Reading was special to me as this is where Anita now lived and worked after leaving Dawlish. She owned a hairdressing salon with her best mate, Jenny, who at the time was going out with Steve. The four of us had some great times together, but with our lifestyles we couldn't say no to what was on offer! It had all ended in tears and to that day I regretted it. She was the real deal, and I had let her slip through the net. I often wondered where she was now and what she was doing.

The band said their goodbyes and we went our separate ways. We kept in touch for a few years, but as time passed we saw less and less of each other and the Christmas cards finally stopped coming.

Steve, I recall, went over to Australia with Jenny. I think she wanted him to get away from me and the pop scene, with all its temptations. We were a double act and I can't blame her for that – we did put it about a bit.

Rick sang with various bands, then disappeared off the radar. Somebody said he'd done a runner from an East End gangster who didn't want his daughter hanging about with him. He'd gone abroad to escape his threats. Ray reformed his band, Bad Brakes, the group he'd played with before he joined us. They had moderate success but then, like a lot of bands, they disbanded.

The last time I'd heard from him was well over twenty years ago. He'd got married to this country girl from Suffolk and had a smallholding breeding dogs, which I gather were greyhounds. That would suit him, as he went out with a few!

Tony went back to taking drugs while playing with other bands. To kick the habit he went into a monastery in North Wales. Whether that cured him I don't know. I hope it did because he was the leader of our first band and a great lad. No one knows where Penny is – that's a right mystery. She had a little boy called Robin. She never did let on who the father was.

I've now got two months to find a few old boys and try and put our band back together again.

♫ 3 ♫

Hunting for old pop stars

I don't understand Twatter or Twitter, and Facebook is alien to me. I've still got a Betamax video and a mobile with a battery as big as a brick, so you can see that I'm a lost cause! Anyway, none of it's any good as I haven't got a computer and I don't want one. But I know someone who has.

On the way to the gym, my son Rob drops Jade off. She's brought her laptop with her.

'Right, Grandad,' she says, all cocky like. 'Who're we looking for first?'

'I thought we'd start off with Tony. He's got an unusual surname, and all his family were local people. I'm sure there'd still be some family members around the area.'

'Well, what is it then?' she says impatiently. 'I've got a Wii party with my mates in a couple of hours and then we're off to McDonald's for lunch.'

I'm looking at her like she's on another planet. I'm thinking to myself how have we made these little monsters?

'His surname is Minster, spelt M...'

'I know how to spell it, Grandad. While I'm on the search engine, you make us a cappuccino, and make sure there's plenty of chocolate on top?'

As I disappear into the kitchen I think of the Camp coffee my mum used to give us when we were kids. I gave her a Lidl's special while she was on the laptop looking like she'd done it all her life. Thinking about it, she probably had. An hour later she says:

'Right, Grandad, I've had a hit. You wanted old people like yourself, but the only one I've got on a site from this area is a woman in her thirties with that name. She's allowed me onto her page and I've told her who you are looking for. She's emailed me back and given you her phone number, which is unusual, so she must have some info for you.'

'That's great Jade, you're a star.'

'I know, and it's only going to cost you a McDonald's.'

As I dig a fiver out of my wallet she says, 'No, Grandad, a McDonald's for all the girls!'

It was with trepidation that I rang this mobile number. Her name was Linda and I explained who I was and my reason for calling. She listened intently and suggested I'd better call round and see her.

The next day I found the flat in a nice part of Harold Wood. As the door opened there was this well-dressed slim girl who had an air of authority about her. As we entered the lounge it was like a reunion of Modern Edge. I was gobsmacked. There were photos of the band on the wall. Linda made some coffee and we sat down. I was just going to tell her why I was here when she took a deep breath and butted in.

'I'm sorry to say Nick that my father Tony died a year ago from a heart attack.'

'What!'

'Yeah, it was quite sudden, even though we knew he had a heart problem and diabetes. As you can imagine, the whole family was devastated, especially as his sister Penny died six months previously.'

'Penny's dead as well? I don't believe it!'

'Yes, I'm sorry to say she had a bad time with breast cancer, which she finally succumbed to. Penny and Dad spoke very highly of you and the other members of the band. He did try to find you a couple of times.'

'I wish he had, but I must admit I've kept a low profile over the last few years. What about your Mum?'

'She left Dad years ago – band life wasn't for her. Dad was a bit of a lad, as they say, and that didn't suit her.'

'What was her name?'

'Alice.'

'Alice! She wasn't from Norfolk, was she?'

'Yeah, she came from Great Yarmouth. Did you know her?'

'Yeah, I think so.'

'She remarried again and I see her quite regularly.'

We continued our chat for another hour and I found out that Linda was an accountant. I'm sure this had made Tony a proud father.

As I was leaving, she said, 'By the way, I'm sure Penny's son, Robin, would like to meet you. He's continued the family tradition – he's a drummer and plays in a local band.'

Thank goodness he doesn't play guitar, I said under my breath!

'Did Penny get married?'

'No, she stayed single and devoted all her time to her son.'

We said our goodbyes and it was quite a sad journey home knowing that two great friends and band members had died. I did have a little smile to myself when Linda told me that Tony's wife, Alice, hadn't liked the band life.

We first met Alice at a gig in Great Yarmouth. Tony met her after the show. Later we found out that no band member was safe when they played Yarmouth. They called her Slack Alice and she certainly put it about.

That night I went up to my local and had a beer with Des, a real live wire back in the sixties. He got up to all sorts of things and used to cultivate his own weed in his greenhouses. He and his old man used to have a car repair business. They were real sharks and were renowned for the term 'cut and shut'. To the uninitiated this is welding two different motors of the same model together. He was one of our roadies – now called a guitar technician!

Des walked into the pub. He was the same age as me, hadn't worn too well and was struggling for breath. I suppose thirty fags a day hadn't helped. We made a good pair. I told him about Tony and Penny, and like me he was totally gutted. He was quite close to Tony in the early days and it was a real blow for him, hearing the bad news.

We both went outside for a smoke under a canopy, which had been erected for us smokers. Some wanker had slit the plastic roof, and while we're puffing away the rain was pouring through. Des, looking at me like a drowned rat, pulled a face and said:

'What's it all coming to? I used to come in this pub, have a few pints, a fag, chat up the barmaid and all for under a fiver. Now the barmaid can't understand English, and I've been chucked outside to have a smoke and catch me death in a feckin' leaking igloo. There are more chemicals in the beer now and I've got to pay nearly four quid a pint to get poisoned. What's happening to the world, Nick?'

'Des, my son, the world's moved on but unfortunately we haven't. We're still sixties boys at heart.'

'Yeah, and proud of it. It was the best time of my life. Make me feel better and tell me more about getting the band back together.'

We had a few more beers and I explained about the promoter getting in touch.

After hearing about Penny and Tony, I wasn't keen to continue the search for the others. But Des wouldn't have it, and was adamant that getting the band back on the road would be just what we needed. He wanted to get involved and help find the others. It clinched it for me when he said:

'Just think how many thousands of people bought your records and came to watch you play. There's a big sixties revival going on now and

I bet you there's plenty of fans out there who remember the band and would pay to come and see you play.'

'It sounds great, Des, but that was many moons ago.'

'Put it another way, Nick. We're in the autumn of our lives and the winter is nearly upon us. The highlight of the week for me and you is when you play up the Legion and I come and watch. We have a few pints, a Chinky afterwards and go home to an empty house with nobody to cuddle up to. Don't you want to go back to when you were somebody and relive that golden era? You've now got an opportunity to turn the clock back. Let's find the other lads and see where it leads us.'

Later that week I had an appointment for some test results and I was now on my way to the hospital. The old flow was now a drip. Not like when I was younger, when I could piss over a wall. I knew it was bad a few months ago. I went to see a band and, as you do, visited the loo at half-time. There were four of us over sixty having a leak – well, trying to – while the younger blokes were coming in and out and having a jimmy in seconds. We were in there so long the management brought us in a cup of tea each!

The previous week the doctor had shoved his fingers up my bum and told me my prostate was a bit on the large size and I needed a biopsy to be safe. A few days later I'm in his hands. I'm shitting myself and all through the procedure a nurse is holding my hand.

If anybody has had it done you know what it's like. He puts this thing up your arse and starts. I can only describe it as like a click of your fingers as he takes samples from your prostate. I had eleven clicks altogether. The nurse, seeing my anxiety, kept saying, 'Only seven more to go, Mr Sheldon – you've been really brave.'

She's treating me like a kid, and she was spot on.

As I waited outside the consultant's room for my results I was thinking of all the worse scenarios. My life was flashing by – I was going to make a determined effort to pack up smoking and get fit. I was in panic mode. It was half an hour past my appointment time and I was getting really stressed out. It was now an hour and I was feeling like I was going to kick his door down.

Suddenly it opened and the doctor said, 'Sorry to keep you waiting, Mr Sheldon. Would you please take a seat over there?'

I knew from his body language it might be bad news.

A few days later I was having a coffee with Des round my place before we went to watch the Hammers playing Manchester United – lambs to the slaughter comes to mind. There was a knock on the door. Standing there was Jade with her laptop. She strutted in, threw me a sachet and said, 'Could you make me a coffee, Grandad? I can't stand that rubbish you drink.'

Then she said, 'We need to talk.'

'How much is it going to cost me, Jade?'

'You're OK, Grandad, this is free. Our form teachers have set us a project. We've got to make up a scrapbook of the sixties with an emphasis on the music of the era. When I was looking on the computer a few days ago you mentioned a band you played in. I want to Google it and see what comes up.'

'What's a Google?'

'It's a search engine.'

'What's a search engine?'

'Grandad, leave it to me. Right, what's the name of the group?'

'It's Modern Edge.'

Her little fingers worked at speed and suddenly hit the right spot.

I was totally overcome and lost for words, as was Jade, who for once in her little life was totally silent as she read the data and looked at the photographs that had appeared.

'Faaackinell, Grandad, you're a star.'

'Language, Jade! Where'd you get that from?'

'Aunty Tracy, Grandad.'

We all looked at the screen and for me it was quite a moving experience. There was loads of information about our band and photographs. Fans had put messages on the various sites recalling some of the gigs we did. It appeared to me that there were still lots of people out there who remembered us.

Des said enthusiastically, 'I told you, if ever there was a reason to get this band back on the road, this is it. They would come out in their droves to see you play again.'

Next day Des and I went about finding Steve, Rick and Ray. Des had been doing a bit of digging about Ray, and suggested we go greyhound racing down Romford. He was going to ask a few faces if they knew if Ray was still breeding greyhounds. We backed four losers and asked lots of people about Ray, but no joy.

We stayed for the last race and, reading the card for the runners, noticed there was a dog in trap six called 'Top Twister'. Something clicked – we used to call Ray that. He could dance a mean twist back in the sixties. I looked for the owner and trainer's name on the race card, but neither was there. We went to the parade ring where the dogs were being led around by the kennel maids. As the trap six dog passed I shouted out to the girl leading it, 'Excuse me, luv, who named this dog?'

She looked at me as if I was mad.

'I know it's a stupid question.'

'If you really want to know, my boyfriend's Dad gave it to us. He retired a while back and I now train his greyhounds.'

'What's his name?'

'Ray Walker.'

Bingo – we'd found Ray. He lived just outside Ipswich.

Next day Des and I set off up the A12 in Des's beaten-up old Fiesta. We thought we would surprise him. We eventually found his place. It was massive. As we drove up the winding driveway I'm thinking to myself Ray has struck lucky here. We parked next to a BMW and a 4x4.

We rang the bell and the door was opened by a woman about our age. She was done up to the nines and looked a right snob. She turned her nose up at us and sarcastically said, 'Can I help you?'

'Is Ray in?' I said.

'You know Raymond – I don't think so.'

'As it happens we do. Is he in?'

'No he isn't – he's golfing today.'

'When's he back?'

'Look, he's not here. I've got two guard dogs so don't get any ideas.'

'We ain't bleedin' burglars, luv,' pipes up Des.

'You look like it, and don't you swear at me, you horrible man.'

The door slammed in our faces. End of conversation.

'I was impressed with that, Des.'

'Cor, what a stuck-up cow.'

As we went back down the drive we saw a bloke of about fifty tending the garden.

'Stop the motor, Des.'

I got out and said to the bloke, 'Could you give this phone number to Ray when you next see him?'

'Of course I can. Didn't get a lot of joy from fancy pants, then?'

'Is she always like that?'

'Yeah, old bag. Ray's as good as gold – I'll make sure he rings you.'

♫ 4 ♫

Mods, Rockers and Brighton

That night I was playing at a social club in Dagenham. I still used my Fender Telecaster that I bought back in '67, and a Vox AC 30 amp. I play all the sixties numbers, as most of the people who go there are my age. To earn an extra few bob I had a CD done and I knock that out for ten quid. I sell quite a few of them when I go to the various clubs. There's a few Modern Edge numbers on it, and the rest are covers.

I'd just finished singing a number by Dave Berry called *The Crying Game*, which ended the first set. A few people came over to buy the CD, including a dyed blonde lady about my age; she looked like she'd seen a bit of action in her earlier life. All through the second set she had been staring at me.

When I stopped playing, she came over and said, 'I was wondering where I knew you from. I looked at that CD cover with a photo of you in the sixties, then it all fell into place.'

'You've lost me, luv.'

'You didn't say that, Nick, when you used to get me in the back seat of your Ford Cortina over Upminster Common.'

Bells are now ringing and the memory is trying to go back over forty years ago.

'It's Mandy. Me and my mate Viv used to go out with you and Steve.'

'Mandy! I don't believe it!'

We had a quick chat and a couple of laughs and she said, 'I only live around the corner. Come back for a nightcap, and we can talk about old times.'

We went back to Mandy's council flat and while she made the coffee I recalled the fun we had together.

Mandy and Viv were Mods and dressed really smart. They had Twiggy hairstyles and always wore the latest fashions. They did like a good time, and they could certainly show you a good time. They were the female equivalent of me and Steve. If they were short of a bit of male company they'd give us a bell and vice versa. This worked on and off for years. It was a great arrangement and we did rattle the cage with them.

As I watched her making the coffee, I noticed that, like me, she hadn't worn too well. Her dyed blonde hair was now falling out. Her legs had a bad case of varicose veins and she was well overweight. She once had a figure to die for and was always in demand with the blokes. It was sad really that both of us were once hot stuff, but now every day above ground was a bonus. Over coffee we reminisced about the Swinging Sixties and what we all got up to. Mandy had equalled her Mum in being married three times, and had six kids, but was now living on her own.

Her Mum was a real goer and the classic was when she was with this bloke in bed and he had a heart attack. When the ambulance men turned up she said to one of them, 'I didn't know I was that good.'

Mandy's mate Viv, who went out with Steve, was now a pillar of respectability in Brentwood. She was now a Councillor, had five kids and only one husband! They still see each other and when they meet up the conversation always goes back to when they were teenagers.

It was now time to leave and head home. Well, that's what I thought until Mandy said with a grin, 'Shall we go back to nearly fifty years ago when I first met you down Romford High Street, and see whether we can still find a bit of passion, but not in the back of a Cortina this time?'

As we undressed I didn't know who had the biggest gut. We're standing there with nothing on looking at each other. We both burst out laughing. We looked like a road accident waiting to happen.

Later the next day I got a call from Ray. It was great to speak to him again. We had a long chat and arranged to meet in a week's time as he was off to his villa in Spain for a few days. I didn't say too much about reforming the band as I still wasn't a hundred percent sure it was the right thing to do. Ray's off to Spain and I'm making my way to the local Poundland store to get a few things with Des – I know which I'd rather be doing.

The last time I went abroad was with a band in the late nineties. We played to five thousand revellers at a stadium in Denmark. Tonight I'm playing to about fifty in an Old People's Home in Epping. How the mighty have fallen. We're having our pot of tea and two slices of Marmite on toast in a cafe after our shopping expedition when Des comes up with a little gem. I should've thought of it myself.

'Steve will be getting his half of the royalties from *Suburban Mod* so someone has got his address. But trying to get it with all the data protection crap that's about today could be a nightmare.'

'That's a great shout, Des. I'll ring Wayne and see if he can help.'

Later I gave Wayne Brodie, the promoter of the Road Show, a bell.

I updated him with our quest to find the band members and asked him whether he could help to find Steve's address. He said he'd use his contacts and come back to me.

Within two days Wayne had given me an address in Brighton. Funnily enough, this is where Steve and I got involved with the Mods 'n' Rockers scene back in 1964. We were a couple of scallywags then and we'd had some right laughs.

As we headed South in Des's Fiesta we were worried about whether the old banger would get us there. It was a typical Des motor, oil pissing out of the engine and more smoke coming out of the exhaust than fifty chain-smokers. We were both looking forward to seeing Steve again.

Meeting up with people you knew from another era doesn't always work out. Hopefully this wouldn't be the case with Steve. Before we looked for the address we had a bit of grub in a cafe on the seafront.

This is where it all happened in the sixties. It brought it all back – the day when Steve and I had sat in this very cafe in May 1964 with two girls. What a great weekend we had with them. It's terrible when you think to yourself, I wonder if they're still alive?

We found Steve's address and pulled up outside the semi. I had butterflies in my stomach. Stupid, ain't it? I pressed the bell and after a few seconds a woman of about forty opened the door. She had a hard-looking face and looked like she wouldn't take any prisoners.

'Sorry to trouble you. Is Steve in?'

I knew immediately I'd hit a raw nerve. In a strong London accent she spat out her reply. 'No he ain't. Who are you then?'

'Nick Sheldon. I used to play in a band with him when we were younger.'

The touch paper had now been lit and she was on a roll.

'So you're the famous Nick he's always going on about. Do you know it's almost like I know you. He's never stopped talking about that poxy band, Modern Edge, and the things you all got up to.'

She looked at Des, screwed up her face up at him and snarled, 'Where do you fit into all this?'

'I'm Des...'

'So you're Des, the jailbird who's always thieving.'

'That's a bit strong, missus.'

'You're probably both like him, living in the past, thinking you're still pop stars.'

'Do I take it Steve doesn't live here any more?'

'Not after I found him in bed with my younger sister.'

Des looked at me, laughed and said, 'Nothing's changed with Steve, then.'

The rocket's now been launched and she loses it and gets personal.

'Do you think it's funny, you stupid old git?'

She suddenly lurched forward and tried to lamp Des one. It was now getting out of control. She looked stronger than us – it was time for a quick retreat.

'Have you got an address for him before you kill us?'

She went back into the hallway, pulled out two big black bin-liners and threw them at us.

'These are his clothes and tell him he'll be hearing from my solicitor. He's got a room in Harry's Bar on the seafront where he attempts to sing and play guitar most nights.'

The door slammed shut and we were off to the seafront and Harry's Bar. Listening to her was like going back in time. It looked like Steve hadn't changed his ways – he was still putting it about.

Harry's Bar wasn't the most salubrious of places. In fact, it looked a right old dive. Mind you, I've played in plenty of these places. There was a poster of Steve on the window advertising that he was playing tonight. Somebody had put some work into the photo as he looked about thirty instead of sixty-three. Des and I decided we'd pay him a visit later to hear him play.

We're back at the cafe having some grub and enjoying a bit of nostalgia when the poxy mobile goes off.

Life is back in the shit lane. It's the hospital and I'm back there tomorrow for more urgent tests. Seconds later, the phone rings again. It's Tracy, and she wants to borrow more money as she now needs two tyres. I turn the phone off and wish I was back in the sixties when we only had pigeons to communicate!

Later that night we sat at the back of Harry's Bar with about fifty others waiting for Steve to appear. As he enters, and walks onto a small stage with his acoustic guitar, my thoughts go back to when we were kids, living down the same street. I was now looking at a guy who'd worn well and still had that edge about him.

'Christ, Nick, where'd he get that shirt from? He looks like a canary. I hope he can sing like one?'

'Yeah, it's a bit bright, Des. He won't get knocked over wearing that. Hang about – he's starting the first set.'

Steve started strumming and singing an old sixties number by

Donovan, *Sunshine Superman*. After a few bars Des laughed and said, 'Nothing's changed then – he still can't play a six-string guitar and sing.'

'I always told him to stick with the bass – he was good with that. I hope Donovan's not in town. He'd jump off the pier listening to this,' I said.

We listened to Steve playing some more old numbers until he finished the first set. While everybody clapped we heckled him. He couldn't see who it was, as we hid at the back. We gave him plenty of stick until he lost it. He was on a mission now as he came over to sort us out. As he clapped eyes on us, he stopped, looked and scratched his now thinning white hair. He looked at me hard like and said, 'Don't I know you from somewhere, mate?'

'You should do, you plonker. I've only known you nearly sixty years.'

'Nick! What're you doing here?'

'Nothing much. I thought I'd just pop in and see whether you want to join my new band, Modern Edge.'

Steve and I embraced and Des said, 'Don't I get a kiss then, Steve?'

'It's not Des, is it?'

'The very one, my son.'

'Christ, guys, it's good to see you both again!'

Everybody in the pub must've thought it was a gay bar as we hugged each other.

'Look, I've got to do this second set and then we've got a lot of catching up to do.'

Within a few minutes I was on stage with Steve playing his spare guitar and knocking out old favourites like we used to. It felt like it was only yesterday instead of decades ago. We had a great jam and finished with *I Can't Let Maggie Go* by Honeybus. Afterwards the three of us went up to Steve's room above the pub with some cans.

He went through his life since I'd last seen him. When the band split up he went over to Aussie with Jenny, but she got homesick and left within a few months. He met up with Rocker Big Al over there. Al was a roadie for us in the early days, and was a good mate.

I first met Big Al playing schoolboy football for the district team of Hornchurch back in 1957. He played in the same team. The next time I saw him was a few years later when Steve and I went down to Brighton on the May Bank Holiday weekend in 1964. This is when the Mods 'n' Rockers trouble kicked off. On the way to Brighton a bunch of them were knocking shit out of each other by the roadside. We were Mods but we drove down in my Ford 100E.

As they were beating the crap out of each other, two of the Mods' girlfriends, Maureen and Wendy, were looking on and were not impressed. Being gentlemen we offered them a lift to Brighton! We stopped at a roadside cafe and as we left the blokes they were with drove in on their Vespas and Lambrettas. Seeing us, the six Mods started to give us a good hiding. Then a dozen Rockers turned up on their motorbikes, one being Big Al. We both recognised each other, they sorted the Mods out, and I took his phone number. Later on that year he joined us as a roadie for one of our tours and brought his dog Sampson along. It was a big old beast, and took no prisoners.

Al was now managing a well-known Australian band. They'd lost their bass player and Steve had stepped in. He played for them for a number of years touring the Far East. Steve met a girl over there who was on holiday from Germany and, when she went back home, he followed her. He joined an English band based there and played the American Air Force bases around Europe. After breaking up with her he met another German girl, Petra, and married her. They had two boys but within a few years had split up and divorced. He came back to England, joined another band, and met and married Karen, who'd just chucked him out. He now lived in this dingy little room with no money, just his guitars.

I said to him, 'Your missus is a bit feisty! She didn't like us and I've got a couple of bags of your gear in the motor.'

'Rottweiler comes to mind,' he laughed.

I asked him about Jenny. He hadn't heard from her for many years. He did say Anita had got married to her previous boyfriend, Simon, after she split with me. I remember him having a go at me about seeing her behind his back. He was a real plum-in-the-mouth bloke. Steve said he went on to become a millionaire. I'm well choked up now to know she's married. Sad, ain't it? Did I really think she was still waiting for me after all these years? I told Steve my story.

After I'd finished he said, 'It's great to see you both but you haven't just come to talk over old times.'

'No you're right, mate. I'd better get the bad news out first. I'm sorry to say both Tone and Penny have died.'

There was a deathly silence and I could see Steve was upset.

'I'm really sorry to hear that.'

'They both died in the last eighteen months.'

'I don't believe it, Nick. We had so much fun together. I'm really upset about that.'

For a few minutes we said nothing until Steve spoke.

'How did you find this out, Nick?'

'A promoter got in touch with me about reforming the band and going on tour again. I tracked Tone's daughter, Linda, and she gave me the bad news.'

'He had a daughter then.'

'Guess who his missus was?'

'Surprise me.'

'Only Slack Alice from Great Yarmouth.'

'Christ almighty, not her? I gave her one as well.'

'I didn't know that. Did you give Penny one?'

'I'm not going down that route, mate. But why do you ask?'

'Well, as you know Penny had a boy called Robin – he's now in his late thirties. Linda reckons he plays a mean bass guitar.'

'Don't plant that one on me. I seem to remember you had the hots for her as well.'

'There is some good news. We've tracked Ray down in Suffolk and we're seeing him in a few days. It looks as if he's had it off, looking at the size of his place.'

'I'm glad he's still breathing, after the bad news about Penny and Tone. I can't get my head around it that they're no longer with us.'

We talked a bit longer until Des butted in.

'It's great to hear about what we used to get up to, but are you on board for a reunion, Steve?'

'Too right I am! Just got to sort a few problems out with my beloved and I'll be down to Essex in a couple of weeks time. The only problem is I've got nowhere to stay and I've got no readies.'

'Don't worry about that, Stevie boy – I've got plenty of room since the old man died.'

'Des, don't take this personal, but has it had a clean since I was last round there?'

'It's like a new pin. Nearly all the animals have gone except a family of rats who just won't leave. But I've got that in hand.'

'What do mean?'

'Well, the four cats and three ferrets – they should see them off!'

With Steve on board, Des and I set out to find Rick. Before that, another pint of blood had to be taken, and more tests at the hospital. I'd got a feeling that there was bad news coming my way. I'd just have to deal with it if it happened.

My family was still at it. Rob had a problem with his mortgage and muggins had to bale him out, yet again. There was a bit of good news. A song I'd penned many moons ago was now being used on a poxy dog advert, so there'd be a few bob in royalties coming my way.

Des and I went to a cafe that had been run by the same family for many years in our quest to find Rick. They were and probably still are involved in villainy. In the old days many a job was planned over a plate of egg and bacon. The head honcho is Sammy, who's in his seventies. A well-built man with silver hair, he has these piercing eyes that look right through you. He still serves the teas to the punters. He's done more porridge than Quakers, as have his four sons.

Rick's family were criminals back in the sixties. His Dad, who'd been our manager, got caught hijacking lorries and got three years. His brother, Mickey, had caused havoc in the banking world by relieving them of their cash and had spent a fair amount of time behind bars.

Rick, as far as we knew, was never involved in villainy. His only crime was trying to give one to the favourite daughter of a well-known face. Hence him having to disappear over to Spain to escape.

We were here to have a chat with Sammy to see if he knew where Rick was. I knew one of Sammy's sons, as I used to go to school with him. Des used to look after his motors and I gather helped with a few getaway vehicles in the past. As we entered the cafe we noticed it was full of blokes with bent noses and no necks.

Sammy still looked a handful, even at his age. On seeing us he shouted out loud in a strong cockney accent, 'Christ, you two are a sight for sore eyes! How's the old man, Des?'

'Unfortunately he passed on a few months ago.'

'I'm sorry to hear that, son.'

'Your Dad was the best car ringer in South East England. What about when he got done for them dodgy MOTs? What was it? Oh yeah, the prosecuting brief said he would've had to issue a passed MOT every half an hour every day, including Sundays, for a whole year to cover the passes he'd given out in four months.'

'I remember that, Sammy,' I said. 'And what did your old man say Des? Bleedin' admin error! Can you believe it?'

'Well, it was, Nick.'

All the punters in the cafe fell about laughing.

'What can I get you, lads?'

'Two eggs on wholemeal toast twice and can we have them lightly poached and sunny side up, please, Sammy?'

'You are taking the piss, Des?'

After our breakfast we called Sammy over to our table.

'Sammy, I want you to cast your mind back to the late sixties and early seventies. There was a family called Brady who were at it round about that time. Do you know anything about them?'

'Why do you want to know, Nick?'

'We're trying to find a guy about our age called Rick. He was one of the sons.'

Sammy pondered for a moment. 'Yeah, I came across that family a couple of times. There were two brothers. One of them was Mickey and he was out of Ilford. The other had a transport business in Brentwood. Can't remember his name but I know he had a randy little son because he was after Carol, my youngest. I soon warned him off. He didn't fancy a sawn-off down his pants.'

Des looked at me and we both laughed out loud.

'What's funny about that?'

'So it was you that he did a runner from? You must've put the fear of God into him – he pissed off to Spain to get away from you.'

'So that's who you're looking for! Why do you want him?'

'We've got a chance of putting our old band back together, go on tour and earn a bit of wedge. He was our keyboard player and singer and we need him back.'

'I remember that band of yours, Nick. You were quite a star turn. My Carol might know.'

'That would be brill if she did.'

'She's done well for herself. Had three kids, they all work up in the City, and her husband's as straight as a die.'

'That must be a first for the family then, Sammy...'

'Des, I've still got that sawn-off upstairs.'

'Only kidding, Sammy.'

'She's round here later with the grandkids. If you come back later she might be able to help you. Now on your bike – I've got punters to serve.'

When we got back to the cafe Carol was waiting for us. She was a bit younger than us. Her clothes were modern and well cut.

'My Dad says I might be able to help you guys.'

'I'm Nick and I'm looking for an ex-band member of ours.'

'What was your band's name?'

'Modern Edge.'

'Bloody hell, that brings back memories. I bought all your records.'

'We're looking for our singer, Rick.'

Sammy joined us at the table. 'Don't you remember – that's the bloke

I sent packing. I'm glad he didn't get his hands on you.'

'You must be joking, Dad! He was the best-looking bloke around. We had a right good time together.'

'What? Don't tell me you, you had…'

'Sex, Dad? Yeah – he was good at it, as well.'

'My little girl, with him…?'

'Dad, get real – this was forty years ago. I'm sorry to say, Nick, but I have no idea where Rick is. The last time I heard from him was in the seventies. He was going through a bad patch and asked for some help. I'd just got married and told him I'd moved on and couldn't help him.'

'That's a pity.'

'You know his Mum's still alive?'

'No, I didn't.'

'I know that because my middle son's wife works at a nursing home in Noak Hill. A while back she got talking to her and she mentioned her son once played in a famous band in Romford. Of course, me being local and a sixties girl she told me all about it.'

'That's great! You wouldn't have the address?'

I rang the nursing home to make sure she was still alive, as Mrs Brady would now be in her nineties. We were told she was quite poorly. After we explained who we were and what we wanted, the matron said we could visit. On our way there Des and I stopped off to get her some flowers. We recalled the days when we would go round to Rick's. His Mum made the best bread pudding you ever tasted. I knew her very well – she was a nice lady.

We were shown her room. She sat in a comfortable chair looking out of the window across the lawns. She was very frail and had a red shawl over her shoulders. The nurse went over to her and said gently, 'Vera, there's two nice young men come to see you.'

She looked up, smiled and beckoned us over to her while the nurse sat at the back of the room. We pulled up two chairs next to her and she placed her bony hand gently into mine. In a whisper she said, 'I don't get many visitors so please tell me who you are as my eyesight is fading.'

'I'm Nick Sheldon. I played in a group back in the sixties and seventies with your son Rick. We used to come round to your house and scoff all your bread pudding.'

She looked at us puzzled like, and after about twenty seconds she replied, 'Modern Edge.'

'That's it, Mrs Brady – what a memory you have!'

'And say again who you are.'

'I'm Nick, who played guitar.'

'I remember you. You were a nice boy.'

She pointed to Des. 'Who's he?'

'This is Des. He used to help with the band.'

She gave a weak smile and said, 'He was the naughty one.'

With a laugh Des replied, 'I must be public enemy number one from Brighton to Romford.'

The nurse, noticing that Mrs Brady was getting tired, said, 'I think we'll have to finish in a minute.'

'OK – I just want to ask one final question.'

'Make it quick if you don't mind.'

'Mrs Brady, we want to contact Rick just for old time's sake. Do you have his address?'

There were tears in her eyes as she said, 'I haven't seen him for a while. The home will have his address. Tell him I love him. I would so much like to see him again. I don't know how long I've got.'

I gave her a kiss on her forehead and she squeezed my hand one last time.

The lady in the office gave me Rick's address. She mentioned that Rick was a regular visitor up until about eighteen months ago. She indicated he had his own problems but wouldn't expand on this. The address was in Wisbech, Cambridgeshire, which was a bit of a hike. We thought we'd see Ray first before the long journey to the Fens.

♫ 5 ♫

Good news and bad news

I had to go to the hospital again, and while I was in the waiting room one of the consultants came out and called out, 'Mr Sinclair.'

There was no response and he went back into his room. Five minutes later he was out again, looking annoyed.

'Is Mr Sinclair here yet?'

The bloke who's sitting next to me happened to look up at the consultant. He shouted out to me really loud, 'What's that doctor saying?'

So I shouted back, 'He wants a Mr Sinclair.'

'Oh, that's me.'

He got up to go over to him, and the doctor met him half way and said, 'Why didn't you answer me before when I called for you?'

'The reason I'm here, Doc, is because I've gone bleedin' deaf.'

There was good news and bad news. My prostate was not cancerous but they did say that one in five biopsies can give a false reading. So not out of the woods yet. The bad news is I'm diabetic and I've got to take tablets every day for the rest of my life. My diet is now a priority. Living on your own and microwaving crap out of a packet is not good news. I need to get on the plot and find a nice lady who can cook healthy food, do a bit of housework and washing, and still likes a rumble!

I'm on my way to meet Ray at a pub in Chelmsford. Des had a bit of business on so he couldn't join us. I recognised Ray as soon as I walked into the bar. He looked a million dollars with his deep suntan and designer clothes. I looked like a bag of Murphy spuds compared to him.

'It's great to see you again, mate.'

'And you, Nick – it's been a long time.'

We hugged each other and you could feel the friendship was still there.

Ray told us what had happened to him when the band disbanded. He reformed his previous band, Bad Brakes, with the original line-up. That lasted a couple of years, then they all went their separate ways. He then fell on his feet big time when he met Claire, whom he married. Her family had pots of money, and owned and trained greyhounds. They also owned a lot of rental property. Her Dad died suddenly and Ray took over the running of the family business, Claire being the only child.

He also had his own portfolio of companies, employing over fifty people. Ray said, without being flash, that he was a millionaire and that life was great. Well, nearly great, as he and Claire lived in the same house but did their own thing. He'd got a couple of sons who were also involved in running the family businesses, which allowed him more time to play golf. After I'd told him what I had got up to after the band split he said, 'I'm really pleased you've got in touch, but there must be a reason after all this time. By the way, how did you find me?'

'Des knew you were into greyhounds and we went racing one night and there was a dog named 'Top Twister' in the last race. We used to call you that after we saw you twisting away at that holiday camp we played at in Weymouth.'

'I remember that well. We had two birds from up North. Afterwards we went back to their place, a ruddy tent.'

'Don't tell me! We had two nights with them. The first night we heard this earth shovelling noise coming from under my air bed.'

'That's right, Nick, and the next night there was a loud bang like a bomb going off, and your airbed burst and a mole stuck its head out. The girls ran out of that tent like their knickers were on fire!'

'What great times they were! Anyway, I've had a call from a promoter who's putting a Mod tour together. He wants us to reform Modern Edge to headline it.'

Ray couldn't get his words out quick enough.

'Count me in! It'll be great to be back on the road with the boys again. Have you found anybody else yet?'

'Well, there's some bad news. Both Tony and Penny have died.'

'That really is sad news. What happened?'

'Tone had a heart attack and Penny died of cancer.'

'We were all so close back then. We were like a family as we travelled the world and played music. It was a magical era and I often reminisce about those days. What happened to Penny's son?'

'Robin is a singer in a group! As it happens he's got all your movements on stage!'

'Don't go there, Nick. Did he find out who his father was?'

'I know Robin's middle name is Ray.'

'You're joking! Please tell me you're winding me up.'

'It's still a mystery who the Dad is. But I would think it's close to home.'

'What about Steve – any news on him?'

'I tracked him down to Brighton and he's well up for it.'

'That's great! Just Rick to find now.'

'I've got an address in Wisbech. I was going up there with Des in a couple of days.'

'Des is still about then?'

'Yeah, he's a good lad and wants to be involved in the band.'

'It will be like old times with him on board. I'll tell you what, would you mind if I come with you? We can go up in my motor.'

'Of course I don't mind, Ray. Rick will be well surprised when we turn up on his doorstep. By the way, you can breathe easy. Robin's a drummer – but he still looks a bit like you!'

It was like travelling with royalty as Ray drove this monster 4x4. It was a top-of-the-range job and had all the bells and whistles on it. Ray put the stereo on and Modern Edge came over loud and clear.

I said, 'I knew they'd put some of our records on these CD compilations you get now. I didn't know there were so many.'

'I've also taken them off some of our records, which were vinyls. I've got my own recording studio at home and I still play around a bit with music. I've made a copy for you and Des. They're in the glove compartment.'

'I suppose you've got a gym and all…'

'Of course, Des – you look like you could do with a workout.'

We came to the outskirts of Wisbech and looked for the road. For some reason it wasn't on the satnav so we stopped the motor and asked a community policeman. Well, two of them. They're like bailiffs – you only ever see them in twos. But even they didn't know where it was. We asked a Farmer Giles type who pointed us in the right direction. We went down a dirt track that seemed to be going nowhere and stopped outside what I can only describe as a shack. It was a hovel, definitely pre-war – but which one?

We were having doubts about whether this was the right place. The three of us went up a path overgrown with weeds. The knocker on the door was so rusty it wouldn't move.

Des knocked on the wooden door and got a knuckle-full of splinters. No answer, so Des gave it a kick. We could hear a shuffle and the door opened. The bloke who stood there was like a scarecrow with a thin gaunt face, sunken eyes and a month's growth. His clothes were rags, and his grey hair matted. He was in a state.

'Sorry mate, we've knocked on the wrong door.'

We walked back up the path when the guy said, 'No you haven't, Nick.'

We stopped and slowly turned round and faced Rick. Where had that good-looking bloke gone, with black wavy hair, the smart dresser and a twinkle in his eye?

'Rick, mate, I'm sorry but…'

'Yeah, it's been a long time, Nick, and yes, I'm a mess. I won't invite you in. I'm too embarrassed at the state of the place.'

'We're not worried about that,' said Des.

'No, I've still got some pride left. It's good to see the three of you.'

With a weak smile he looked at Ray who was dressed like an advert for Savile Row and said, 'I can see you've done well for yourself, Ray.'

Trying to make a joke of it, I said, 'Are you saying Des and I don't look smart in our Primark clobber?'

Rick suddenly came towards us and hugged us.

'You don't know how good it is to see you guys again.'

We went to the nearest pub where Rick explained how he'd landed up living like this.

'When the band called it a day I did some session work, which paid well. I then met Carol. Her dad was a right nasty piece of work. He threatened me with a shotgun if I didn't pack her in, so I took the hint and pissed off to Spain.'

We started laughing and Rick said, 'What's funny about that?'

'I'll tell you later,' I said.

Rick continued.

'Anyway, I joined a band over there and played all over Spain and had a great time. After a couple of years I came back to England joined another group and played the cruise circuit around the world. It was a great experience and life was sweet. Then, as you do, you meet a bird who wants you to do a nine-to-five job, which like a twot I did. Serving in a poxy shop was not my idea of fun, so I was off again. My Dad died suddenly and that really had an effect on me. I moped about for a couple of years but fell on my feet again after joining an ace band from Lincolnshire. They were a good bunch of blokes and I was with them for five years.

'At one of the venues I met Angie, who was a terrific girl, so much so I married her. I'd saved up a few bob so I bought a music shop in Cambridge. We both worked hard in the shop and for the first time in my life I wasn't chasing skirt and was well contented…'

Rick started coughing and we had to get him a glass of water. Then he continued.

'Angie later found out she couldn't have children and after that she started getting more and more depressed. This went on for a good few years. I tried everything to help her but it didn't work. Whether Angie meant it we'll never know.'

'Meant what?' I said.

'She took an overdose and died.'

'I'm so sorry,' said Ray.

'From then on it was a downward spiral. The business fell apart, debts were piling up and I lost everything. That's how I ended up in this khazi in the middle of no man's land. Then it got worse.'

'How worse does it get then, mate?' says Des.

'Well, you've been in prison, Des – you know what it's like.'

'What did you do?'

'I got eighteen months for nicking a load of booze from a warehouse. I should've known better. My Dad got put away for the same thing. I got out a couple of months ago and I'm trying to get my life back together again. Anyway, that's my sorry tale. So how did you track me down, and why?'

I told him about Carol and now he knew why we started laughing when he was telling us about the shotgun. He was very subdued when we told him about our visit to his Mum.

Des said, 'I appreciate all the grief you've been through, Rick, but not seeing your old Mum for a long time, that's not like you.'

'You're right. I couldn't tell her the reason why I hadn't visited her was because I'd been in prison. Since I've been out I can't face her. She'd be devastated after what she went through with my Dad. It also doesn't help that I haven't got a motor.'

I told him why we wanted to find him. He was well up for getting back together again, but was worried because he hadn't sung for well over ten years and might have lost it. I told him about Tone and Penny. He was well choked. I explained about Steve, then he asked, 'What about Penny's son, Robin?'

'Oh he's doing all right. He's playing keyboards and singing in a band. In fact, his voice sounds a bit like yours!'

'You're joking, Nick!'

'No mate – he's even got your black wavy hair.'

♫ 6 ♫

Hot to trot

Ray was turning out to be a real top man. He took Rick out of his hovel and put him in one of his flats until he got himself back on his feet. He also gave him a motor that enabled him to see his Mum again. I contacted Wayne Brodie to tell him we were up for the tour, and he was delighted. Ray, being a businessman, was going to sort out the contract and all the money issues with him. We arranged to meet with Wayne the following week to finalise the tour details.

It was great when Steve travelled up from Brighton. We all met up at Ziggies, the first time in donkey's years. It was like we'd never been parted. The wind-ups between us were great and the chemistry full on. There were, of course, lots of other matters to be sorted out, which we discussed.

We needed a drummer, somewhere to practise and a van. None of us had the necessary kit to play large theatres. There was money to be laid out and, apart from Ray, none of us had much of that. The most important factor was, could we still play together and recreate our sound? Other than Ray, who was as fit as a butcher's dog, none of us could climb a flight of stairs without getting puffed out.

Somehow we had to get fit in readiness for a grinding tour across Britain. Pints of London Pride and Benson & Hedges were not the answer. As mentioned, Des wanted to be part of the tour, and said to us, 'Leave the transport to me. I'll pay for the van. I can also be your driver.'

'Of course you can be the driver, but you're more than that to us, Des, you're a mate. We want you on the tour anyway,' said Steve, 'but we're not having you pay for the van – that's not on.'

'Look, my Dad left me a lot of money. There are no other family members to leave it to, so I ain't short of lolly. I've still got a yard that I rent out and I've got lots of other irons in the fire. It's not up for debate. I've still got plenty of contacts in the motor trade. Leave the van to me.'

A drummer was the top priority, and I reminded the lads that Penny's son really was a drummer. They all breathed a sigh of relief, but we all knew that somebody around the table was probably Robin's father.

With a grin, Ray said, 'I'm still in touch with Billy. I could give him a bell – see if he's up for the drumming job?'

'Get real, Ray!' said Steve. 'That's why we've all got bleedin' hearing aids because of the racket he used to make!'

It was agreed that Steve and I would go and see Robin and find out what his drumming was like and if he was available. We wanted to keep it in the family and it would be a nice touch to remember Penny and Tony with Robin as our drummer. We were getting quite reliant on Ray to get the band up and running. He suggested that we rehearsed round his place. He had an empty barn and a gym where we could attempt to get fit. That'd be a laugh – within a few minutes he'd probably have to dial three nines for an ambulance.

I rang Robin and he was happy to meet up with us. Linda, Tony's daughter, had contacted him to say we might get in touch. It was with trepidation that Steve and I turned up at a little semi in Collier Row. As he opened the door we both eyeballed him to see if there were any resemblances between him and any of the band members. He showed us into the dining room and introduced us to his wife, Sonia. She made us tea, then went into the garden with their two young children.

We wondered if Penny had ever told him who his father was, but this wasn't mentioned, thank God. He told us that he worked in a record shop, but unfortunately he was being made redundant in a couple of weeks as the shop was closing down. Lots of people now bought on-line and that had affected their business. He spoke about playing for a local band, and that's when I asked the question.

'We're going to reform Modern Edge and go on tour across the UK. We're looking for a drummer and we thought we'd have a chat with you as we'd like to keep it in the family.'

'I don't know what to say, Nick. You've taken me by surprise. I know all your numbers. When my Mum was teaching me she made sure I could drum to them all. In fact, the band I play in do a few of your numbers. We're playing this Saturday in a pub at Barkingside if you want to come and have a listen. I've got no job offers coming in and the mortgage has got to be paid.'

'The money on offer will be half decent,' I said.

'Look, guys, come and listen to me play. If you think I'm good enough, I'll have a word with Sonia and we'll take it from there.'

Rick's flat was not far from Ray's place in Ipswich, which we now nicknamed 'The Ponderosa'. Ray really worked on Rick to get his self-esteem back. He got him working out in his gym every day and made sure he got regular meals. The change in him through Ray's kindness was amazing – he was getting back to his old self. He insisted he didn't want charity, and did some odd jobs around the place. Rick hadn't sung or played keyboards for a long time, so Ray took him into his studio and put him through his paces. Once we had the drummer in place we were going to spend a week at the Ponderosa to do some serious rehearsing. Ray had enough bedrooms to put us all up.

Ray had done the business with Wayne and we now had the dates and venues where we were appearing. We were playing all over the UK at some great theatres. There were a few days off in between shows, which would be needed. The money was good and it would certainly go a long way to supplementing our pensions.

There were two other well-known bands and a couple of solo singers on the tour. We knew some of them, but how many of them were original band members we didn't know. Before we started the tour we needed a warm-up gig in front of a live audience.

Ray had got in touch with a theatre in Romford and booked a spare night, paying for it with his own money. We didn't believe it, but he'd got his own PA, Liz, and she was now liaising with the theatre regarding the selling of the tickets. Ray's thoughts were that Modern Edge was once a well-known local band and he was going to tap into our fan base. He was going to do this using the internet, radio, local papers and any other form of publicity that would put bums on seats. He'd even set up a website for the band, and we were interested to know what kind of response we would get from it.

With the current sixties revival going on around the country he was pretty sure he could pull it off. Just one problem – we hadn't played a chord yet, and what would happen if that magic wasn't there any more? We'd be well and truly in trouble.

Being with Steve again was just like the old days as we got ready to go out and hear Robin play. But it wasn't Old Spice aftershave I put on, but Intense, which my daughter bought me for Christmas – with my money! We still felt like a couple of the chaps as we entered the pub. Christ, what a shock! We looked like fish up a tree, as they were all youngsters. They looked at us like we were from outer space. We got our pints and disappeared into a corner a bit rapid.

Robin's band came on later, and his drumming was spot on. His technique reminded me of his Mum's and Tony's. They were really good drummers and he was definitely following in the family's footsteps.

Within a couple of days Robin had squared it off with Sonia and he was now part of Modern Edge.

We had a real bit of luck locating some kit. We trawled a few shops and couldn't believe that an old mate owned one of them. His Dad had owned the business, and when he died, Terry had taken it over. Terry was a good lad and he'd lost none of his humour as he looked at Steve.

'Christ, Steve, you look like an advert for a care home. Who wheeled you in here – matron?'

We had a right laugh and got our own back on Terry when we reminded him of his band. They had played the same circuit as us in the sixties. They were called Terry and the Tanks, so called because his surname was Sherman. You couldn't make it up.

We told Terry what we were looking for and he took us into a side room piled high with amps, speakers – you name it, he had it. We wanted the gear to be authentic sixties. He came up with three standard Vox AC 30s and a Wem bass amp. We added some Marshall speakers and a Farfisa compact keyboard.

The only problem was that after the tour the kit probably wouldn't be used again, so we needed to strike a deal with him. He was as good as gold and we rented the kit from him at a sensible price. It was agreed that Des would pick it up when he got hold of a van. Des said he'd located a vehicle, which he was getting checked out and done up. Everything was now in place. Just the burning question – could we still play?

It was now the first week of rehearsals. I picked up Robin first, then Steve. He'd settled in well at Des's house, who'd really made him welcome. Des was going to drive the new van, which we hadn't seen, up to Ray's tomorrow. He was picking up the kit from Terry's and Robin's Ludwig drum kit today.

As we were going down the A12 Steve's mobile rang every few minutes. His ex-missus in Germany was after him for some money she reckoned he owed her. The current one in Brighton also wanted her share. If that wasn't enough, one of his sons, Karl, was on the earhole too.

'That's it – I've had enough of all of them!'

And with that he winds the window down and lobs the phone out into some undergrowth, shouting out, 'No bastard can get hold of me now!'

'Do you feel better for that, mate?'

'For the first time in my life, Nick, nobody knows where I am. It's a great feeling.'

We arrived at the Ponderosa and Ray and Rick greeted us. Rick had definitely turned the corner and was looking really good. Neither of them had met Robin, so over coffee we all got to know each other. Ray's missus, Claire, had gone off to their villa for a couple of weeks so we were ready to get the show on the road.

That night we had a good drink and the memories came flooding back. Ray got us up early and we were in the gym for a good work-out. I've never heard so much coughing and heavy breathing in my life. Sweat was dripping off us, except for Ray and Robin, who were both fit. The phone went. It was Des to say he was only a couple of minutes away. We all made our way to the large courtyard to see what heap of crap Des had got us.

We looked up the driveway and Steve said, 'How much did we drink last night, because I'm sure I've just seen a red London double-decker bus!'

'I know satnavs play up a bit, but this is taking it a bit too far,' said Rick.

As it gets closer, there's Des in the driving seat with a busman's hat on. Ray says with a laugh, 'Who does he think we are – feckin' Cliff Richard and the Shadows?'

The bus comes to a halt and Des jumps out.

'Awesome, ain't it?'

It's the first time I've ever seen all the lads lost for words. Standing in front of us is this red bus with blackened widows and Modern Edge plastered all over it. Still no words are uttered as Des takes us on a guided tour.

On the upper deck it's got a couple of bedrooms, toilet, shower and a television room. It's decked out to a high standard in black and red leather, and the fittings look gold-plated. On the lower deck there's a couple of sofas, a walled television, stereo and DVD. It also boasts a small fitted kitchen.

We all sat on the sofas totally gobsmacked. Ray, who was looking after the finances, said to Des, who had a smile like a Cheshire cat, 'Des, what've you done? We'll have to work years to pay for this beast.'

'Nonsense! This posh bus company went tits up and I've bought it off the administrators for a steal.'

'But we're going to need a bleedin' fuel tanker to follow us around.'

'Ray, I might look a bit of a prat but I've factored all this in. I've worked out from the tour route you gave me roughly how much diesel we're going to need. Even after all that I'm still going to make money when I sell it after the tour. It's already on eBay and I've had two offers, one from the USA and another from Dubai. I'll drive and sleep in the bus and you guys can travel in comfort and just concentrate on the gigs.'

He got up from the sofa and put the stereo on. What a sound, as Eric Clapton echoed around the bus.

'I'm impressed, Des,' said Ray. 'In fact, so impressed that I think you can run the band's finances.'

We explored the bus and had to admit that it was a bit special. I could see us having some fun as we criss-crossed the country.

Ray had some style. He'd organised a couple of guys to unload the kit from the bus and set it all up in the barn. To top it, he had a catering company on site looking after all our needs for the week. With the amps and speakers set up we were ready to see whether the magic was still there. Just before the first chord was struck Robin, with the biggest grin I've ever seen, said, 'It's nice playing with my Dad in a band.'

He then slowly and deliberately looked at each of us for a few seconds and started laughing. I can tell you now, the morning session was chronic as we all wondered whether it was our son playing drums. We had to find ten songs to play for the tour and another ten for our first date.

The first two days of rehearsing was like we all had Alzheimer's, except for Robin, who was a helluva drummer. After the third day we're thinking it isn't going to work, and we discuss pulling the plug. As we're having a coffee, Ray's PA, Liz, turns up. A well-preserved lady in her forties, she had striking dark hair and immaculate make-up. The body language was telling me she was doing more than just looking after his paperwork.

'Do you want the good news or the really good news, Ray?'

'I don't understand, Liz.'

'Ticket sales for the show have gone through the roof. The publicity has really paid off. The theatre has come back and said the following night is free and they reckon they can fill that night as well. Wayne from the Mod Tour has got in touch to say the tickets for all the venues are on sale and are selling like hot cakes.'

'That's all good news, Liz,' said Rick, 'but at the moment we can't put a song together. In fact, we're crap.'

'Why don't you play a number and I'll give you my opinion.'

We all looked at her as if to say, we've got about one hundred and fifty years of music experience between us and she's going to tell us what's wrong?

'OK, we'll do that, Liz,' says a creeping Ray.

I thought, oh yeah, keep her happy and he'll get his end away tonight.

So we did what we were told and played one of our B sides from a record we recorded in 1969.

After we'd finished, she said, 'Because you haven't played together for such a long time my impression is that you're trying too hard to outdo each other on the individual parts of the song. Another thing – you're all so intent on getting it right that the fun has gone out of it. There isn't a smile between you. I bet when you went on stage before, you had a few drinks to relax you. Anyway, I've got to go Ray. I've left some letters in your office to be signed. Oh, by the way, somebody's parked a red bus in the courtyard.'

After a few bottles of wine we got into it and it was sounding a lot better. The only way to crack it was to keep rehearsing until we got it right, so we stayed an extra week at Ray's. We also agreed to the extra night at the theatre in Romford.

Liz was starting to get more involved with the band. She said we needed a make-over from top to bottom. First stop a hairdressers she knew in London. As we walked in, the young staff looked at us as if to say, Christ, there's a Saga coach just turned up.

We were taken straight to the wash basins, as you could tell they wanted to make sure there was nothing escaping from our hair. The young juniors started washing it with expensive shampoo, a bit different from the Sunlight soap we used in the sixties. The girls then gave us what's called an Indian head massage. That was magic, and I could've stayed there all day.

After that it was over to the stylists, who could hopefully take a few years off us. They knew we had played in a well-known group in the sixties and we got talking to them. The young girl who was cutting my hair innocently said, 'My great-grandma used to buy your records!'

Talk about feeling an old codger! To be fair to her, she gave me a good haircut and it definitely made me feel a bit younger. From the hairdressers Liz took us to a clothes shop nearby that specialised in Mod gear and flashed Ray's credit card yet again. We bought the Ben Sherman shirts, Levi jeans and baseball boots. We didn't want to look like we were trying to be eighteen again, like some sixties bands do today. I went to a theatre a while back and saw one of those bands. The music was good, but the band wore these leather trousers that were so tight they looked like John Wayne when they walked.

After our make-over we met up with Robin and Ray to have some pictures taken of the band by a professional photographer. Wayne wanted some for publicity posters and for the merchandising desk after the show.

The next day we were all having a coffee when Rick said with a laugh, 'We're all suited and booted and nowhere to go. Our lives have gone from Sex, Drugs and Rock 'n' Roll to Yeast-vite, Cocoa and Zimmer frames!'

'You're right. We have no ladies in tow and we need to put ourselves about,' said Steve.

'*Last of the Summer Wine* comes to mind at the moment,' I laughed.

Just then my mobile rang. After struggling to get it out of my pocket, as you do, I answered it. Great news.

'Would you believe it? That's randy Mandy I met a few weeks back.'

'Not Viv and Mandy fame?' said Steve.

'The very ones! She and Viv have bought tickets for our gig and, to top it all, Viv is having her sixtieth birthday party at her place in Brentwood and all the band is invited.'

'That Viv was a right goer back in those days,' says Steve. 'She always wore the full kit, none of those horrible tights. I wonder what she looks like now?'

'After five kids, probably not too good,' I said. 'Mind you, she could still be wearing stockings – but probably support ones now.'

'Brentwood was where I used to live when I was a teenager. I did put it about round there. I wonder if there'll be anybody there I'll know?' says an excited Rick.

'Yeah, probably loads of your kids.'

'Don't go there…'

Des was a bit quiet and I said to him, 'What's wrong, mate?'

'I'm not a band member so the party is off for me.'

'Leave it out, Des! You're one of us – where we go, you go.'

Ray and Robin weren't coming to the party, so it was just going to be the four of us.

♫ 7 ♫

Essex girls do like a party

The four of us now looked the part after our complete make-over. We walked up the driveway of a large Georgian house on the outskirts of Brentwood and knocked on the door. We could hear a Small Faces number blaring out. The door opened and standing there were Viv and Mandy, both wearing hardly anything. As it happens Viv had a fair figure for her age and looked good. Steve licked his lips – I could see there was going to be trouble. Mandy was Mandy – it was all hanging out, but in all the wrong places.

'We've been waiting for you guys,' said an excited Viv.

As we walked into the lounge the other forty or so guests, all dressed up in sixties gear, gave us the once over. Most of them were women, so it should be a good night.

'It's great that you could come to my birthday party bearing in mind you're going on tour soon,' says Viv.

We felt like we were in a goldfish bowl as everybody was staring at us. That soon changed when the drinks started flowing and Mandy and Viv grabbed Steve and me for a dance. Viv's husband looked a bit of a non-event, but he was keeping a close eye on his wife as Steve was all over her.

Rick and Des were soon amongst the ladies and it was the start of a great night, or so we thought. When you're our age you feel a bit of a dingle dancing about like you're still a teenager. So for me it's always the smooch, which suited Mandy's varicose veins! While the two girls went to refill their glasses, Steve was in seventh heaven with Viv. He was beaming as he said, 'She's a tasty bit of stuff, Nick. I think I'm in love.'

'Steve, if I could have a pound for every time you've said that I'd be a bloody millionaire. We're not kids any more, mate.'

Mandy came back and I said to her as I was watching Steve slobbering over Viv, 'I thought Viv was happily married?'

'Well, she is, or was. I think, with your band getting all this publicity about the tour, she's reliving her youth. With Steve being an old flame and now a bit of a celeb, I think it's gone to her head.'

'That's bad news. Steve doesn't need any encouragement when it comes to reliving his past. He still thinks he's eighteen.'

Rick was now full of confidence and back to his old self. The lady he was with seemed nice and he was twisting away like a two-year-old to a Kinks number. Poor old Des always ended up with something different. She was short and dumpy. The tattoos on her arms and legs were a bit off-putting and, with her arse bulging out of hot pants, not a pretty sight!

Other people were turning up at the party, which was now in full swing. A couple came in and the lady looked familiar. She was a good-looker and the trouser suit with matching shirt and tie looked great on her. She had a second glance at me and you could see her mind ticking over. While her partner, who looked well fit and much younger than her, went to get some drinks, I slid over to her like the original lounge lizard.

'Sorry, don't I know you?'

With a laugh she said, 'That might have worked at the La Nero coffee bar in Hornchurch when we were sixteen, Nick, but it's a bit old hat now.'

'Diane, I can't believe it's you – you look great!'

'Don't let my partner hear you say that – he gets really jealous. In fact, he's coming back with the drinks now.'

I made myself scarce as I'm too old for a punch-up. Diane was one of my first girlfriends and we saw a lot of each other when we were younger. Her brother Pete helped us get our first record contract. She was one of the gang we knocked about with when we were putting the tanners in the jukebox.

Steve was now on a collision course with Viv's other half. I pulled him away from her and had a quiet word. 'It's all going to kick off in a minute, so give it a rest.'

'She won't leave me alone, Nick!'

'Oh, bollocks Steve, you don't need any encouragement. You're like a dog with two dicks.'

I shoved a beer in his hand and told him about Diane. He wasn't interested and went back to Viv, who was lapping it up. Mandy came over to me and she was now well tanked up on rum punch. One of her breasts had popped out of her low-cut top. She got hold of it with both hands and replaced it in the heaving bra.

The party had now moved into the garden and the drink was flowing freely. I saw Des go into the potting shed at the bottom of the garden with tattoo Lil – I'd hate to think where else she's tattooed. Rick was now holding hands with his latest flame and feeling like a teenager again. Later Des reappeared from the potting shed. He could hardly walk. He found the nearest chair and plonked himself down while Lil went to fetch the drinks.

'You look a bit knackered, mate.'

'Tell me about it! It was like a tsunami – she just engulfed me. My teeth are still rattling. I had a hip replacement a couple of years back – after this I'm going to need the other bastard done.'

'She looks a handful. You were lucky to get out alive, mate.'

'What do you think of her, Nick?'

I screwed my face up. 'Grim reaper comes to mind. A couple of weeks of her and we'll be having a whip round for a wreath for you.'

We both burst out laughing.

I wandered about keeping out of Mandy's way. Diane's partner was having a laugh with another bloke so I went hunting for her. She was having a chat with another lady. She saw me hovering and came over.

'How did you know it was me, Diane?'

'I live in Hornchurch and your band has been plastered all over the local newspapers and on the radio. In fact, I'm coming with a few of the girls to see you play on the first night.'

'How long have you been with your toy boy?'

'Do you think he's a bit young, then?'

'It's the short trousers that give it away.'

'Oh shut up, Nick, he ain't that young. I've been with Neil a few months. I lost my husband a couple of years ago. How about you, Nick?'

'How long have you got?'

'It's like that, then...'

'I'll tell you what – how about a meet to talk over old times?'

She starts giggling and says, 'Nick, you're losing your touch.'

'What?'

'It's taken you twenty minutes to ask me out. The old Nick would've taken about twenty seconds.'

Suddenly a dark shadow covered the proceedings in the shape of Neil, and he wasn't happy as he snidely said, 'Who's this old boy then, Di?'

Looking uncomfortable and scared she replied, 'This is Nick – we go way back.'

'Is that right?' he said menacingly. 'Well, Nicky boy, it's time for you to piss off and go back to your nursing home.'

With that he grabbed Diane's hand and pulled her away. I couldn't believe it – what a prick! She seemed petrified of him and that really upset me. If I'd been younger I would've put one on him. She didn't deserve that – she's a nice lady and he was well out of order.

I'm having a nice cold beer sitting outside in the garden when the inevitable happens on all fronts. Steve and Viv have just come out of the potting shed. Her husband clocks it and goes ballistic. He picks up a spade and is chasing Steve around the garden like a madman. Then the husband of the lady Rick was with arrives to pick her up. He isn't impressed seeing Rick's arm around his wife. And to top it all, Mandy, after licking the bowl of rum punch dry, is giving me verbals about me not taking enough interest in her. The only one who's escaped from the Essex girls is Des – he's so knackered he couldn't have run if he'd wanted to.

As we quickly make our escape, Rick says, 'Christ, lads, we're in trouble after just one party. What's going to happen when we go on tour?'

♫ 8 ♫

First show, Romford

The first night at our Romford gig was a nervous affair. We were allowed into the theatre early. Ray had brought the two lads with him who had helped us set up the gear before, and they went to work straight away. The manager confirmed that most of the seats were sold for both nights, so we were making some money. Once everything was set up we started rehearsing. It didn't start well when Robin, who had a wicked sense of humour, said on the first number, 'Right, Dad, let's go.'

We all instinctively turned around and looked at him, grinning like a silly kid. On the road with him, thinking he could be your sprog, was not good for the blood pressure. There were other pressures tonight with lots of friends and relations coming. Stupid really, when you think that between us we'd done thousands of venues and we were uptight about this one. I was still well upset about Diane, and I was hoping I would see her tonight to have a chat.

All the thoughts about tonight went out the window when Des turned up looking really smart with the lady he met at the party. Tattoo Lil – real name Ruth – was about fifty with long dark hair that trailed half way down her back. The clothes she wore were odd – charity shop comes to mind.

What mattered most was that Des and her seemed to get on well. He had never got married. He was engaged loads of times, but most of the girls gave him the elbow, which was a shame as he's got a heart of gold. Unfortunately he's a bit scruffy with feet at ten to two, a long neck and even longer nose. The kids at his senior school used to call him Pinocchio. So to see him smart with a smile on his face was nice. After a good rehearsal it was nosh time.

As we made a move to go, Des said, 'No need to go anywhere. Ruth has rustled up some grub for you.'

A couple of cooler boxes were brought into the dressing room. Ruth took charge and was handing out all the goodies. The food was out of this world. It was all homemade, from quiche to chicken and ham pie, followed by cherry crumble and washed down with flasks of coffee.

After the feast Des said, 'How was that, lads?'

'Tiptop compliments to the chef,' said Steve, still licking all the plates.

'That was very thoughtful of you, Ruth,' said Ray.

'That's OK, guys, my pleasure.'

We all stopped and looked at her. We'd never heard her speak before. Her voice wasn't like her body – it was really sexy and she'd a smile that lit up the room.

'I'm glad you liked it,' said Des. 'I've got a suggestion. Ruth has offered to come on tour with us. We've got "The Mother Ship"...'

'Hang about, who've we got?' said Steve.

'That's what I've called the bus.'

'This ain't *Star Trek*,' I said.

'Anyway, Ruth is happy to do all the cooking and washing on tour. There's plenty of room on the bus for her.'

'That's really nice of her,' said Ray, 'but hasn't she got a job?'

'I've been a full-time carer for my Mum for the past five years. She died three months ago and I need to get my life back. Money's not important as she left me enough not to worry for a while. To come on tour with you guys and, of course, Des would be doing me a favour. Hopefully I can make sure you're well looked after, bearing in mind your ages.'

She burst out laughing when she realised what she'd said.

'Sorry, I didn't mean it like that, guys.'

'As it happens you're spot on, Ruth. We do need looking after and you can start now. How about some more grub tonight?' said Rick with a laugh.

'All taken care of. There's another couple of cooler boxes in the car for later.'

'I think you've just been hired, Ruth. Welcome aboard – you're now part of Modern Edge and you'll be looked after for your troubles. You'll be on wages just like us,' said Ray.

All of us were up for Ruth coming on board and it made Des one happy bunny. We were later to find out what a great girl she was, and it taught me never to judge a person on first impressions.

Two hours before the show we did our last sound check. The sound engineer from the theatre knew his stuff and it was all systems go. Mandy and Viv somehow got in the dressing room and that was just what we didn't want. Steve was on Viv's case in seconds and Mandy was now bra-less and causing mayhem among the band. Poor old Robin had his wife, Sonia, there and she must have been thinking, what's he going to get up to while he's on tour? She wasn't impressed. There were more people coming in and out of the dressing room than Paddington station. With an hour to go I put my foot down and kicked everybody out except Ruth and Des. Peace reigned again and we could now concentrate on the music.

I popped outside for a smoke. The theatre was filling up and the nerves were kicking in. I had just had my last drag when Diane and a couple of her mates came into view. She left them and made her way over to me.

'I'm really sorry, Nick, for what happened at the party. I felt so embarrassed.'

'That's OK. I'm more worried about you. Things aren't right, are they?'

'They could be better.'

'Where's the thug tonight?'

'He's gone to a boxing tournament with his mates.'

I looked closely at her and I could see bruising under her make-up.

'Don't tell me he's hitting you.'

'Look, I'm going to have to go. Hope the show goes well tonight.'

'Diane, give us your mobile number and I'll ring you tomorrow.'

'I can't do that. He'll kill me if he knows I'm talking to you.'

'Here's my number. Get in touch. We really need to talk.'

We could hear the buzz from the audience as we were about to go on stage. We hugged and wished each other luck. Robin had gone really quiet as reality kicked in that this was about four hundred and fifty more people than he'd played to before. I looked at Rick, who'd just put this black pork pie hat on. You know when a member of any band has a hat on he's nearly always bald.

'Christ, Rick, you like a wide boy down the market with that on,' said Steve.

'Look, you ain't a coot yet so give it a miss, mate,' said Ray.

'I thought I looked cool in it.'

'What do you think, Ruth?' I said.

'It's about as good as those hot pants I wore at the party.'

Any tension we had was gone as we roared with laughter. The hat came off and we were ready to rock 'n' roll. It was a short distance to the stage and as we arrived there was a roar from the crowd. Steve and I picked up our guitars while Rick got behind the keyboards and Robin sat behind his drums. Ray took the Shure mic off the stand and looked at Robin, who hit four beats and we went straight into our biggest hit, *Suburban Mod*.

It was a great night even though there were a few bum notes and some senior moments with lyrics.

Next day we were all bubbly and couldn't wait for the next performance. But life has a way of kicking you in the bollocks when things are going well. Sadly, later that morning Rick's Mum died. He was devastated. Losing your Mum is tragic enough but, what made it worse, he was now the only family member left alive. We thought of cancelling, but Rick wouldn't have it. He felt he couldn't play but wanted us to continue.

Diane rang me later and said she wanted to talk. I was meeting the other band members at the theatre at about 4 o'clock, so I suggested she come round to my flat a couple of hours before.

As I made Diane coffee, I could see sadness in her eyes. We sat down and she poured her heart out to me.

She'd been happily married for thirty-five years when her husband had a sudden heart attack and died at their home in Swindon. Being a Hornchurch girl she decided to come back to her roots and bought a little bungalow. Later she met this bloke Neil, who was in his early forties. Neil was a fitness instructor; he also worked the doors at various clubs.

For the first three months everything was fine. When he moved in it all changed. He was treating her place like he owned it and was telling her what she could and couldn't do. When she rebelled he started hitting her and she was now frightened shitless of him. Her brother, Pete, who I mentioned before, a big help with our band in the early days, lived in America and she wanted to visit him. Her passport suddenly disappeared and he was now demanding money from her. She had nowhere to go as she had no kids to help her and Pete was a long way away.

I made another coffee and said, 'I'm really sorry, Diane, that this is happening to you.'

'When you've been happily married for so long and you lose your soul mate you've nowhere to turn.'

'What about the police?'

'I've thought about that. Unless they lock him away he'll come looking for me and he can be very violent, Nick.'

I met the lads later and we did an hour's rehearsing. After that it was pandemonium in the dressing room. Viv burst in with more on show than Lady Gaga. Steve couldn't help himself – he was all over her like a rash. He said, 'Viv, you look more beautiful than ever now.'

'Do you think so, Stevie?'

I'm trying not to be sick as they're pawing each other. Then Liz shows up. She's married as well, and there's Ray nibbling her ear and whispering sweet nothings. Robin's only been with the band one night and he's chatting up the theatre manager's wife, who's lapping it up.

Then the odd couple turn up in the shape of Des and Ruth. They're so loved up I'm thinking they'll be off to Gretna Green, never to be seen again. Ruth is now my favourite lady, as she's brought in some more homemade grub. Her gala pie and sausage rolls are far more important to me than women with baggage.

Des and I went out for a fag about half an hour before the start of the show. He could see I had things on my mind and said, 'What's wrong, Nick – nervous about tonight?'

'I wish it was that easy.'

I told him about Diane, who he knew well, as she was one of the group we knocked about with when we were younger.

'The world has changed, Nick – hitting women in our days was taboo. When I saw her at the party she looked really nice and I thought she'd worn well.'

'Not like us, Des,' I said with a laugh.

We missed Rick and it told. The crowd seemed to like us and the old buzz was there again. We had a little problem with Robin, and after the first set we had to have a word with him. He now thought he was a rock star and his drumming was all over the place. Instead of concentrating on what he was doing, he kept looking at the audience and giving silly grins and exaggerating his stick movements. Steve summed it up well.

'Robin, if we wanted a grinning baboon we would've gone to a zoo. Keep your mind on the job – remember this is a job and like any business P45s can be given out.'

He still thought it was a huge laugh and said, 'OK, Dad.'

That was it. Steve flew at him – I thought he was going to lay him out.

'I've had enough of you! If you think I'm your Dad get a DNA test done. If I am, you'll cop a right-hander. Mess about any more you'll be out of the band, pronto, understood?'

Robin looked for support from us. There wasn't any. He was now feeling isolated and he knew we meant business.

Ray added, 'And another thing – you've got a lovely wife and kids and if we see you messing about with any other women you're off the tour.'

Calling the pot black came to mind when Liz came in and planted a smacker on Ray's lips. Robin now knew the time of day and it was up to him to shape up or be shipped out.

When you're on tour for a long time and living in each other's pockets you all have to try and get on. It's not easy and you can fall out with each other, but it has to be controlled – if the gap is too big, trouble sets in. After Robin's bollocking he had to be lifted up and as we made our way back on stage Des put his arm on his shoulder and quietly said, 'Listen to what they say, Rob. They've been all over the world and they've more experience than other bands dream about. Just drum, keep your head down, and you'll be fine.'

The second night was a success and we now felt we were ready for the tour. After the show we all decided to go out for a drink. Not a good idea. I just don't understand the youth of today. The street we visited had a row of bars and clubs. All you could see were youngsters pissed out of their brains. Young girls flashing their knickers and showing their arses, blokes staggering about or fighting each other; others lying on the floor paralytic and spewing up everywhere. They call it anti-social behaviour. I'd call it something else! In the corner of the street was a small coach, which I gather they call a Booze Bus. Unpaid volunteers manned this through the night to tend those who were under the influence or had been injured in some way. Blue lights were flashing everywhere. I couldn't believe what I was seeing. When I was a teenager we liked a drink, but this was not enjoying yourself, surely? We didn't hang about and left the area to find somewhere else to drink where we didn't feel so threatened.

Wayne had been in touch. We'd had national coverage in newspapers and music magazines, and most of the venues were now full. Before the tour everybody was meeting up for a full rehearsal and to meet the tour manager, the boss of the show. We kept rehearsing as much as possible – you can never do enough. Robin had now come into line, so that little problem was now hopefully sorted.

We went to Rick's Mum's funeral, and after they'd laid her to rest he said, 'The only family I've got left now is you guys.'

I was now seeing Diane when I could and we were getting close. She was taking a chance as Neil was on her case. He was now using her credit card like it was his.

Just before the tour I got an early morning visit from Diane. She had heavy bruising to her face. Des was with me at the time and he was really shocked at the state of her. She was crying – something had to be done. Des got his mobile out and took a picture of her face.

'This has got to be sorted, Nick. Can you disappear for a couple of days, Diane? Tell that arsehole Neil a long-lost aunt has died in Manchester and her solicitor wants you to go and see him about some money she's left you in her will.'

'I don't understand, Des…'

'You will. Do what I say, please.'

'You can stay with me. He doesn't know where I live,' I said.

Des was now on a mission. I got into his motor and we headed for Sammy's cafe. As we entered Sammy took the piss and said, 'Twice in a month – you must like my sausage sandwiches.'

'Sammy, can I have a quiet word in private.'

'What's all this about, Des?'

We went to a back room and all three of us sat around a table while Sammy's missus, Eve, brought in some tea. I was thinking how many times she must've done this for Sammy's dodgy associates.

'What's on your mind, son?'

'Sammy, how many times have me and my Dad helped you out with iffy motors? Remember that Triumph 2000 we souped up for you? It left the Old Bill standing when your team did that bank job.'

Sammy went from being jovial to a look that clearly indicated we'd crossed the line. 'Too much information. Remember the saying – careless talk costs lives.'

'I understand, Sammy. Sorry, but we need some help and…'

'Are you trying to say I owe you, son?'

'Look at this photo on my mobile.'

Sammy took a look and screwed up his face. 'Not nice. But what's this got to do with me, Des?'

'This lady is a close friend of ours. In fact, she was a friend of Wendy, your eldest, when they were teenagers.'

'Cut to the chase, Des, spit it out.'

'Her partner is knocking the crap out of her and thieving money hand over fist. We want him sorted.'

'Whoa, whoa, just stop right there. I'm not rent-a-mob.'

'I wouldn't normally ask, but this girl is desperate.'

'Why don't you sort him out yourselves?'

'If we were his age we would. He's in his forties, a bouncer and a fit bastard. We have trouble doing up our shoelaces.'

'Sammy, we're happy to pay.'

'That won't be necessary. I need to think about this. Give me all the details about him. If he's working the clubs he'll be on my radar. I'll give you a bell when I have an answer.'

That night Diane stayed with me and it was great talking over the good times we had had at the La Nero coffee bar with our friends, and the dances we used to go to.

'Sometimes I wish I could go back, Nick, when life was fun, and the friends we had were real mates, who would never let you down.'

'Tell me about it! What about Alec with his Lambretta in 1964? He was king of the Essex Mods, and his scooter had so many mirrors and lights on it he could hardly ride it.'

'I haven't seen him for a long time. I used to fancy him.'

We had a long walk down memory lane and enjoyed each other's company.

The next morning I got a phone call from Des. Sammy wanted to see us. I met Des and we went over to Sammy's. He was very businesslike as we went into his back room again.

'Your friend Diane has fallen upon a nasty piece of work. The word on the street is he wants a chunk of the security scene. That's my domain around here. He wants to make a name for himself, a wannabe gangster. He's been rattling a few cages and upsetting a lot of people. In fact, you've done me a favour bringing him to my attention. I must be slipping not knowing about him.'

'Not you Sammy, surely?' laughs Des.

'Don't take the piss, son.'

Then he made a statement that sent a chill down my spine.

'Within a few hours this will be put to bed and your friend won't have any more problems with him. Give me her address where he's staying.'

Alarmed, I shouted, 'You ain't going to kill him?'

'Feck me, son, what do think I am, a gangster? No, we have more subtle ways to deal with the likes of him. You stick to music and I'll deal with the real world.'

When I got home Diane was in a panic. Neil had been leaving threatening messages on her mobile. I told her not to worry as hopefully it would be sorted soon. Her mobile was getting calls from him until about 4 o'clock, then it just suddenly stopped. Had Sammy sorted him out? What if they'd gone over the top and taken him out for good?

A couple of hours later my mobile went – I nearly jumped out of my skin. I answered it.

'Job done,' said Des. 'Diane won't have any more trouble from him. She's free to go home.'

Diane wanted to stay with me that night, but we did go back to her place for a quick look round.

As she put the key in the lock she held me tight and we both went slowly into the hallway. I was shitting myself as much as she was. She went into the bedroom and all his clothes had gone. As we went around the house all evidence that he'd ever lived there had vanished. On the kitchen table was her passport and a wad of cash. There was a note. I recognised Des's writing. A locksmith was coming tomorrow at 10 o'clock to change the locks. In the lounge a new pot plant was on show. As we made our way into the kitchen, Diane screamed out.

'What's wrong, Diane?'

'Look, blood's dripping out of the fridge, Nick!'

I'm stupidly thinking to myself, surely they ain't put his feckin' head in there? I gingerly pulled the fridge door open, then started laughing.

'It's only a dripping beetroot.'

Diane went home the next day, the locks were changed and she went back to normal living. I saw her nearly every day until the start of the tour. I wanted to take our relationship further but she'd made her mind up she was going off to the USA to stay with her brother for a while. Maybe when I was back off the tour and she returned from the States we could pick up again.

After speaking to Des about what happened, I thought he was more than a bit involved in Neil moving on. Sammy's name was known far and wide within the criminal fraternity in so far as you didn't mess around with him and his associates. Once it was pointed out to Neil that Sammy was taking a personal interest in Diane's welfare, he vanished off the scene.

The changing of the door locks and flowers were all Des's idea, which was a nice touch. The money, Des said, came from when they tipped this Neil upside down and gave him a shake after he'd been to his bank – must have been some shake! I did ask about Sammy, who had all this power but was still serving teas in his cafe.

Des remarked, 'His power and respect have been built up over fifty years. People are still frightened of the name and, with his four sons carrying on the family tradition, he's happy to take a back seat and play in his cafe.'

Now all I wanted to do was play music and forget about the Sammies of this world.

♫ 9 ♫

Golden oldie tour

Today we were off to Dartford to meet the other bands and the people connected with the tour. After the meeting it was a run through of the two sets we'd be playing at the venues.
Wayne, the promoter, greeted us and we sat down with him and one of the other bands. We knew the group – Mod Mania – well as we'd been on the circuit with them back in the early seventies. What was very unusual was that three of the four band members were in the original line-up.

The wind-ups started straight away. The bass player, Reg, was wearing this terrible syrup. Rick said to him, 'Is that a Terry or a Brucie you've got on, my son?'

'It's started already then, touring with you lot! I don't think I can stand it.'

They were a good bunch of lads and we knew we'd have some fun with them. They'd had chart success back in those days.

The solo singer, Johnny D. Freshman, turned up. He'd put a bit of weight on. He had been the lead singer with Terry and the Tanks – it was Terry, of course, who had got us the amps. His nickname was Dinky, because if he didn't get his own way he'd throw his toys out of the pram. The band was so fed up with him that they told him to sling his hook and he went solo after that. He did have a good voice and was a character. Steve wound him up straight away.

'Dinky, I'm impressed how much weight you've lost since we last saw you.'

'Do you think so Steve? I'm on this special diet. I think its working.'

'Yeah, what is it – a steak and kidney or beef and onion?'

'Oh, piss off – least I can sing! You used to play bass like you'd got boxing gloves on.'

All the wind-ups stopped when Tammy, the girl singer, entered the room with a bloke of about seventy. She wasn't the best singer you've ever heard, but she had a figure like Kate Moss. Somehow she'd stayed slim and at fifty-seven was still gorgeous. She was a real Mod when she sang on the circuit with us, and still had that Mary Quant look about her today. Ray, being the horny little bastard he was, had sampled the fruits with her back in the seventies. We did a tour with her in Scandinavia and they got close.

All bubbly, she said, 'Hi, guys, have you missed me?'

'Ray missed your tits,' I said.

Looking embarrassed, she quickly said, 'Oh, by the way, this is my musical director, Herbert – he's also my partner. He'll be having quite a bit of influence on the tour.'

Under his breath Wayne murmured, 'Like feck he will...'

Her partner made us look like young bucks. What she saw in him I don't know, with his dour face and old-fashioned clothes.

While we were waiting for the other band to show, Wayne said that this was the first big tour he'd put together and he had a lot at stake, financially.

'Why are we the headline act?' I asked.

'My Dad said you were a great band back in the Mods 'n' Rockers days, and with the other acts we've got from that era he thought it would make a great tour. You'll meet him later.'

The other band, The Rubbes, were late turning up, and what a shock for Wayne and us when they showed up with their manager. Two brothers were at the heart of the band when it was formed in 1966. We didn't know them, but I gather they were a bit wild, always getting into trouble, a bit like us. We were now looking at a tribute band, as none of the original members were in the line-up. They didn't look right for a sixties tour – more like a 'Take That' tour. They were much younger than us and punters would soon rumble they'd been sold a pup.

Wayne went ballistic, marched their manager into another room and tearing into him. He thought he was at least getting one member of the original band. What I reckoned happened was that the brothers who owned the rights to the name didn't want to play any more, so they farmed the name out and were now on an earner every time they played.

I felt sorry for Wayne, but that wasn't our problem. The hall had been set up and we were now going through our paces in playing the sets. The Rubbes would open up first, then they would back Dinky with his songs. Mod Mania would close the first part of the show with their set. The second set would open with Tammy, backed by the Rubbes.

As the headline act we would finish off the evening and hopefully send the punters home happy. The Rubbes had been told in advance what numbers they would be backing the two singers with and, fingers crossed, they would've sent them a CD with their interpretation of the songs. Hopefully Dinky and Tammy would like what they heard and it would all work well. The Rubbes went on first and for some reason while they were plugging in they pulled a curtain across the stage.

Everybody involved in the tour was there. Wayne, still boiling, was waiting for the first chord with bated breath. The curtain opened and there stood the two grinning long-haired brothers playing their guitars with a couple of other wrinklies. What a wind-up! The bastards had substituted their sons, nearly giving poor old Wayne a heart attack. The brothers and the other two group members had really got the tour going with a giant wind-up!

We'd have to watch out for this lot. They played their first set and were top drawer, as were Mod Mania. Dinky had lost a bit of power in his voice but it was still acceptable. Tammy wasn't ready, so we played our set, which appeared to go down well. We were feeling pleased with ourselves when we heard this booming voice shout out from the back of the hall.

'That was crap! Get them off the stage and pay them off!'

I thought I was hearing things, but he said it again. I wasn't having that, so I jumped off the stage and went to the back of the hall to have it out with him. As I reached the back there stood this horrible big snarling Doberman. I took a step back, then I knew who it was.

'Big Al – it's got to be you!'

Out of the shadows came a bloke of our age, well over six feet looking like Wild Bill Hickok with his long hair and droopy moustache.

'Christ, what're you doing here?'

As I went to shake his hand the dog growled and showed its teeth. Big Al shouted out, 'Leave him, Sampson!' The dog obeyed immediately.

I hadn't seen him for over 40 years. Steve had met up with him over in Australia, and as mentioned played in a band for him. We sat down with Al and had a long chat and asked him what he was doing here.

'You're looking at your tour manager. Wayne's my son and I've come out of retirement to help him out. So you'd better not give me any trouble or Sampson will sort you out,' he said with a laugh.

We only knew him as Big Al. What a shock to know he was Wayne's Dad! Al's trademark when touring with bands was that he always had a tasty dog with him. It meant we always got paid and, with the dog in the van overnight, you never got your gear nicked like we nearly did in Torquay, when two guys attempted to break into the van.. Sampson (Mark 1), who was just as big as his present dog, tore them apart. Al told us he named all his dogs Sampson, as it reminded him of the first dog he had. After our chat we were now really looking forward to the tour with Big Al and all the other acts.

There were a few things to tidy up before the fun began. The most important was to run Diane to Heathrow Airport. She was off to see her brother in LA. We'd got quite close and it was nice to see her looking happy after the experience she'd suffered. Her former partner was now off the map. I did ask Des what had happened to him.

'Don't ask, but all I'll say is how would you like to live in Hull?'

With all the medical conditions the band had, we had to make sure we all had our medication and this is where Ruth came into play. She had qualified as a nurse and had worked in hospitals for ten years. She put all our names, and all the tablets we had to take each day, on an A3 chart, including Des and Big Al – he was on eight a day. We'd more bleedin' tablets on the bus than Superdrug. You have to laugh. When we went on tours before all we stocked were johnnies, Woodbines, whisky and pills.

The big red bus, now known as the Mother Ship, was now being kitted out by Des and Ruth, who would sleep on it. We'd been booked into Travel Inns and, hey, some Premier Inns, which was big time! All our favourite CDs and DVDs were put on board and, with a fully loaded stock of food, we were ready to hit the road. The amps, speakers, drum kits and other gear were being transported independently in a lorry, all insured.

Wayne was so impressed with our authentic sixties amps, speakers and other kit that we'd got from Terry that he used them for the other bands as well, and picked up the tab for the lot – what a result! If you looked at the lorry you wouldn't give it a second glance. It looked a heap of toot, but mechanically it was sound. The logic was that, if you had a lorry looking like this, it was unlikely to be broken into.

My family, seeing their meal ticket going away for a few weeks, wanted to get their last orders in before I went. First that little treasure Jade turned up with the sweetest smile, like butter wouldn't melt in her mouth, and said, 'Grandad, I'm sure you're aware that while you're away it's my twelfth birthday. Please don't think I'm being too forward for asking, but what can I expect as a present from my favourite Grandad?'

I felt like saying feck all, as the cheesy grin on her face covered what really was a little two-faced, know-all brat. I said with a straight face, 'I've booked you in for a course of Botox, as you are my special little Essex girl.'

'Really, Grandad, that's all us girls talk about! Wait till I tell them!'

She gave me a big kiss and ran out of the room as happy as a duck on a pond. There was I thinking she'd taken it hook, line and sinker. Later that day her mother, Zoe, phoned me up and said, 'Dad, Jade thinks you've lost the plot about her birthday present. She'll stick to her normal £100 and suggests that you have the Botox as you've got more cracks on your face than the coalition.'

We both laughed our heads off.

Then it was my daughter Tracy's turn.

'The twins are being picked on at school because of the size of their noses. They won't go to school so the only answer is to get nose jobs for them. Could you help with the cost of it, Dad?'

'You are winding me up, Tracy?'

'No, I'm deadly serious. I've told Mick to do as much overtime as possible, because if they don't get it done it could lead to them having mental problems.'

I lost it. 'Mental problems? You've got the mental problem! Ten-year-olds having nose jobs? Get real, will you? You've been under that sun lamp too long – it's frazzled your brain!'

'I can't believe you've just said that to me, Dad. You know how much I suffer with my nerves.'

'You get on my poxy nerves all the time! Thank goodness I'm getting away from it all!'

She slammed the door, dislodging some plaster, got into her 4x4 and gave it some welly up the road.

Later I gave husband Mick a ring and asked what was happening.

'Don't worry, Dad, the twins don't want to go to school, so they came up with the nose excuse. They'd rather stay at home and play on their Play Station. They're little arseholes – next week it'll be they've got big ears. Anyway, I'm glad you rang. Des Smith is a mate of yours, isn't he?'

'Well, yeah – why do you ask?'

'One of the faces is missing off his manor and there's a suggestion that foul play could have taken place. Des's name came into the frame.'

'Des? You're having a laugh! He's not a gangster. You're on the wrong track there, Mick.'

I quickly got off the phone thinking, bloody hell, I hope Sammy didn't come up with a long-term solution for that Neil. It was time to get out of town quick – thank goodness we're off on tour tomorrow.

That night Ray took us greyhound racing. The first two races we lost our money. On the third race, Ray said, 'There's a dog in this race I fancy called "One Eyed Bill"...'

'Hang about,' I said. 'It's a stupid question, but has it only got one eye?'

'Well, yeah, but…'

'You want us to put our money on a one-eyed dog?'

'It's in trap one, so it's worth a few bob.'

'Did you make any money greyhound racing?' said Rick, taking the piss.

'Trust me. Look, as long as it's in trap one he'll see the rail and he'll fly.'

'What if he was in another trap?' said Steve.

Ray started laughing and said, 'He'll end up in the feckin' High Street.'

Ray said that, a few years back, he owned a greyhound that won a lot of races. It was a black dog, but had a distinctive white paw on his left front leg. It was well known as a fast dog. One day with his son he took it to an illegal flapping track, which was on a piece of marsh land. Before he went he painted the white paw black so nobody knew who the dog was.

It was an early-morning race and his dog won with ease. He had a good bet on it and won a few bob. As they rounded the dog up, his son said, 'We better get going, Dad. The black dye is coming off his paw because of the wet ground.'

They ran back to their motor faster than the greyhound.

♫ 10 ♫

Dodgy satnav

The first venue was Brighton, which some say was one of the capitals of the Mod movement. We all met at Des's yard where he'd parked the bus. He jokingly said, 'I've just put a grand's worth of diesel in it!'

We were now ready to jump on the Mother Ship and make our way south. Des had this stupid hat on and looked like Reg Varney of *On The Buses* fame. He jumped in the driver's seat and we all got on board. As we moved off we couldn't help ourselves as we sang out loud, 'We're all going on a summer holiday!'

Big Al wanted all the acts to be at each venue no later than 2 o'clock, which was sensible, so we left early to make sure we were on time. Des said we'd go the country way to Brighton, and put the satnav on. It was all in poxy German and all we could hear from the cab was this Heidi bird! So Des had to keep looking at the map. The bus was comfortable, coffee was flowing courtesy of Ruth, and Genesis was coming over loud and clear from the CD player. Through the tinted windows we were enjoying the Sussex countryside on a perfect May day.

All was well until the B road became a lane and then a dirt track with a great big bridge looming up in front of us, which we had no chance of getting under. The bus stopped and Des got out of the cab looking really stressed out.

'I don't know how to say this, lads, but we can't go forward or backwards.'

'What do you mean?' I said.

'Well, we can't get under the main railway line from London to Brighton, that's for sure. And trying to reverse a ten-ton bus to the next junction would be a challenge.'

'Des, that's why we told you to buy a satnav, so we don't have these problems,' I said. 'Where'd you buy this one from – a cowboy?'

'Well, as it happens I bought it off Ronnie.'

Alarm bells rang immediately, and I lost it.

'Not Ronnie! We all know he's nicknamed "Conner Ronner".'

'He's all right.'

'Oh, leave it out, Des – he's a feckin' crook. Don't you remember when he tried to sell the band some amps and guitars way back? He said the amps were Vox and the guitars were Fenders. When we opened the boxes they were Vex amps and Fonder guitars. They were Japanese copies – they couldn't even spell the names right.'

'Do you feel better after ranting and raving, Nick?' said Steve, laughing his head off.

'We'd all better stop laughing as we're supposed to be at the theatre in an hour's time,' said a worried Ray.

Then, bless her, Ruth said, 'How about a nice cup of tea, lads?'

Do you remember when you were younger and your Mum would say the same thing if there was a problem. And you would say under your breath, 'I don't want to ever get like that.'

While we're having our tea and looking like spare pricks at a wedding a tractor pulls up behind us. A young guy in his thirties jumps out of the cab and comes over to us and says with a grin, 'Dodgy satnav, lads?'

'Yeah,' says Des.

'Well, you're not the first bus to come down here. The very early ones were useless – they were all out of sync.'

'What did I say, Des? That Ronnie's tucked us up again, and it's in poxy German too.'

'What's the height of the bus?'

'Sorry, what's your name?' asks Des.

'Justin.'

'It's thirteen foot, give an inch or two.'

'Yeah, that could be a problem.'

'I ain't driving this thing underneath there on a wing and a prayer and bringing the bridge down on top of me.'

Time's marching on and nobody has a clue what to do next. Then Justin says, 'I can see you're a band – where are you tonight?'

'The big theatre in Brighton. We're on a Mod tour – not your era,' I said.

'I've seen it advertised all over the place around here. Tickets are a bit expensive.'

'They'll have to be with the damages we're going to have to pay out if we carry on like this,' I said.

'I'll tell you what I'll do. Give me ten minutes and I'll be back and hopefully I'll drive the bus underneath it. Don't worry – I've got a Class C licence.'

'What's that?' says a bemused Des.

We all look at him gobsmacked.

'I'll drive it but I want two tickets for my Mum and Dad for the show tonight. They were both Mods and were at Brighton when it all kicked off back in the sixties.'

'You're on,' I said.

He took some details of the bus, and ran off. Within a few minutes he was back.

'I've just been home and Googled it and got the measurements of this model.'

We all closed our eyes and prayed. Justin got into the cab and confidently levelled it up and went straight through without a hitch.

Des looked dumfounded as Justin jumped out and said, 'Go up there about two hundred yards, do a left and in minutes you'll be on the main Brighton road. Where do my parents pick the tickets up from?'

'We'll leave them at the box office under your name,' I said.

As we were leaving I said to Ruth, 'I could do with a nice cup of tea.'

We arrived two hours late and Al was not happy. He took us into a side room and tore into us.

'We might be mates but I'm telling you now, don't mess me about. You're not kids any more and I expect you to be on time. I won't be saying this again. Your sound check is in half an hour, so get your arses in gear and make sure you give me a performance tonight that warrants the money we're paying you.'

We were pretty gobsmacked with the bollocking, especially at our age. We wouldn't normally take shit from anybody.

As we were licking our wounds Des came into the dressing room looking sheepish.

'I'm sorry about today, lads. I've just gone out and bought a new satnav. Now I'm worried about the TV, CD and DVD players. I bought them off Ronnie.'

He rushed out of the room as a shoe nearly took his head off.

It was a good-size auditorium and we were pleased that the performance had sold out. We did the sound check, which was fine, but there was trouble in the camp when Perry of the Rubbes stormed in and started swearing.

'What's up, mate? Somebody nicked your Zimmer frame?'

'You can bugger off, Rick. Least I ain't got a hole in my head where there used to be hair and a brain.'

Then the other brother, Frank, said with hatred in his eyes, 'I ain't backing that scrubber Tammy and her geriatric partner. He thinks he's the tour's musical director.'

Big Al, not looking happy, bounces in and says to Perry and Frank, 'Because of you two she said she isn't going to sing tonight.'

'That's lucky for the punters then,' says Frank. 'They won't have to put ear plugs in.'

Al gives us a look that said 'disappear', and we did. We didn't know what was going down with Tammy, so we kept well out of it.

With about an hour and a half to kick-off we helped set up the merchandising desk as Al had more important things to worry about. There had already been one casualty this morning. The girl who was running the desk for the tour never showed. She'd phoned up and said she'd met this famous footballer, she was in love and he didn't want her to go. I wonder if his wife knew? So Ruth was our new sales lady and she revelled in it.

Merchandising is a key part of any tour and for groups like us it's good bunce money. Wayne was plugging his glossy programme. It gave the punters a breakdown of the artists, complete with photos of them. Everyone else had their CDs to flog – we were the only band without one. But we did have a result as we had some of our records on a CD compilation. Ray had trawled the net and found a pallet load of them gathering dust in a warehouse. He bought the whole lot for 25p each, and we were knocking them out for a tenner. With photos to sign and other memorabilia it was a good earner. It did mean that after every show we had to be at the desk signing and selling, which of course none of us minded.

♫ 11 ♫

Glastonbury to Salisbury

All the sound checks had been completed and we were an hour away from the first night's show at Brighton. What was amazing was the numbers of scooters and sixty-year-old Mods outside the theatre with all the gear on. It's a great feeling to think people still remember those days with affection and they're coming to hear you play. The miniskirts and Mod tee-shirts were out in force, as were the winkle-pickers. There was a real party feeling about it. On a lot of these tours you get more women attending than blokes, and tonight was no exception.

The girls like to come with their mates and they really know how to party. I think women are much more nostalgic about the past than guys. The merchandising desk was busy and Des was giving Ruth a helping hand.

Steve and I went outside for a smoke – so much for packing it up. We got a few smiles from the ladies, which is always nice – it starts the night off on the right foot.

Wayne had computerised images of sixties events flashing on a screen at the back of the stage before we played – a great backdrop.

A packed crowd were all waiting for the first act and the Rubbes didn't disappoint. They were on top of their game and having fun, as were the audience. After their set they stayed on stage to back Dinky. How he got into those leather trousers I'll never know. He was bursting at the seams as he pranced around the stage singing his rhythm and blues stuff. He looked like a demented chicken.

After his set it was the turn of Mod Mania – a class act, and the crowd loved them. The only down side was Reg's wig, which seemed to have a mind of its own as it slid about on top of his head as he played his bass guitar.

The first set finished, and Wayne and Big Al were happy that it had gone well. After the twenty-minute break it was Tammy's turn. We weren't about when she did her rehearsal at Dartford, so we were looking forward to hearing her sing. This wasn't the case with the Rubbes, whose mood changed significantly from the euphoria of playing their own set to backing her and 'Lurch', their nickname for her partner, Herbert. Tammy looked gorgeous in her outfit, short and tight. Rick and Ray were already sniffing around her.

After a great opening it all started to go downhill. Lurch was wearing this dinner jacket and bow tie and sat behind this big Hammond organ. To the right of him the Rubbes were ready to back Tammy.

She came on stage to enthusiastic applause, mostly from the blokes. From the wings we looked on and I could now understand why Perry had the hump with Lurch. First of all, Tammy sang quite raunchy music. So where did the dinner jacket come from?

The final indignity for the band was when Lurch started to conduct the band with one hand whilst playing the organ with the other. It looked bizarre, and the band weren't happy. You could see from the crowd that they thought it looked odd for a show like this. Tammy's singing was fair but her biggest asset was her arse as she wiggled it about. On her last number we went back into the dressing room to get ready for our set.

We were just leaving the room to go on stage when the Rubbes came in. Perry was spitting feathers.

'That feckin' Lurch thinks he's at the proms the way he's conducting us with his white baton. We haven't got a clue what he's on about. He looks like a poxy copper on point duty!'

We couldn't stop laughing as we went on stage to a great reception. You'd have to have played in a band to know the feeling being on stage and playing music to a packed theatre. Where Tammy was the bloke's favourite it looked like the girls were now having their say as they really got behind us.

What a night! All those memories of yesteryear came flooding back as we played the sixties numbers that we were renowned for. With a couple still to play the crowd were up on their feet with a lot of ladies dancing in the aisles. Like us, they were reliving their youth. We finished the last number but they wanted more, and they got it. After the final number all the artists came back on stage and together we played *Twist and Shout*.

We gave our final bow to the audience and it was straight to the merchandising desk to sell our wares. Some of the women were like excited teenagers as they chatted to us. It was a great feeling, especially as we shifted a bit of gear as well. At the end of the night we were all knackered and went straight to bed. In our prime it would have been off to a party!

The first night had been a great success, but the Lurch problem wasn't going away. He was making a nuisance of himself with the other musicians, including us. He was trying to tell us how to play and was now becoming a real pain in the arse. Rick had a quiet word with Tammy about him, but she blanked him. He was staying and that was that.

Big Al knew this couldn't go on – something had to give. The next night at Southsea went well, but Perry was now on a crusade to oust Herbert, and was starting to lose it. Eventually it came to a head, but not in very nice circumstances, although there was a funny ending. After the show Perry blew a blood vessel in front of everybody and started shouting at Big Al.

'If you don't get that wanker off the tour we're off home. I'm not having him waving that feckin' thing at me every night. If he does it once more I'm going to stick it right up his arse!' And with that he collapsed on the floor in a heap.

For a second we thought he was messing about and just laughed, but not so. We quickly got Ruth, who was our registered first-aider on the tour, and she immediately called an ambulance. We were all stunned at what had happened, and there was no fun that night.

Early the next morning Perry's brother Frank rang from the hospital. It was good news. Unknown to us Perry had a pacemaker and the battery needed changing. That wasn't why he collapsed – he'd just fainted – but while he was there they checked the battery and found it needed replacing. He would be back on tour in a week's time. So the Rubbes needed a temporary lead guitarist, and Al asked me to fill in. The other boys in the band were happy for me to take his place for the week.

Next night it was Hove, and Dinky came out with a classic as he said to the audience, 'Playing here makes me feel great. I'm the only person in Hove who's got his own hips.'

When it came for us to back Tammy I could see why Perry had the hump with Lurch. As she was going through her paces he was waving his baton just a few feet from my face.

After the show I said to Al, 'You know, you're going to have to sort this out.'

The final nail in the coffin for Lurch came when one of the local papers reviewing the show said, 'I didn't know if I was at an André Previn concert or a sixties gig.'

Next day Al dug out Tammy's contract and he was in luck. There was nothing nailed down about Lurch, and as far as he was concerned he could out him, which he did. Tammy sulked and said she wasn't singing any more, which got a cryptic comment from Ray.

'Well, she doesn't anyway.'

So Lurch with his Hammond organ was rapidly dispatched back to the local bandstand at Eastbourne. As soon as he was out the door Rick was all over Tammy. It didn't take long for him to worm his way around her and show her another baton!

Perry came back with his new Duracell and the fun started straight away.

'Nice to you see back, mate,' said Steve. 'We've got a new name for you and your band.'

'Go on then.'

'Perry and the Pacemakers.'

The whole crew fell about laughing.

We were now on our way to the South West. We were chilling out watching the TV when Steve happened to look out of the back of the bus and noticed that a white van was following behind us. A few minutes later it was still there. Steve shouted out to Des, 'We have got a licence for this television?'

'Why'd you ask?'

'I'm sure there's been a TV detector van following us for about three miles.'

'Are you sure?' said Des. 'I thought they were off the road now.'

'Take it from me, it is one, I should know. I got done a year ago. One of these poxy vans was outside my house.'

Suddenly the bus goes into overdrive and Des is driving like a maniac. We're hanging on for dear life as he swings the bus round every corner. He then shouts out, 'Hold tight!'

We've come to a roundabout, which he takes us round three times. He suddenly does a left and the TV van goes the wrong way. He puts his foot down again and we've lost him.

After we've picked ourselves off the floor, Rick shouts, 'Des, wouldn't it be safer to buy a licence?'

Somehow we ended up at Glastonbury, which was well out of our way. Then the bus started to play up. We pulled off the road on to a piece of ground so Des could have a look at it. No wonder it was playing up – he'd shot it to pieces trying to be Lewis Hamilton. Steam was coming out the radiator and oil was dripping from the sump.

Steve went over to Des, whose head was buried in the engine, and said, 'We're not in the AA then?'

Two words were uttered, the second being 'off'.

After about half an hour Des stated the obvious.

'It looks like we're here for the night. I'm going to have to ring round and get a mechanic out.'

That was handy, stuck in the middle of nowhere. The only good news was that there was a pub up the road. We felt guilty as we trooped up there, especially as Ruth had made us a nice dinner before we went. She was staying with Des, as was Robin, so he wasn't on his own.

When we walked in the locals thought the Glastonbury Pop Festival had started early. Hearing our London accents they took a step back and checked their wallets were in a safe place. It was quite a busy pub with most of the drinkers being our age. They must have had music from time to time as there was a small stage at the back of the bar. We went on the scrumpy and after a pint we're all as happy as Larry. This stuff is so strong they could use it as rocket fuel. We're now very talkative and the landlord finds out we're in a well-known band. Not one to miss an opportunity, he says, 'Do you fancy playing a few numbers, lads?'

So it was back to the bus to pick up a couple of guitars. Des had found somebody to work on the bus, so hopefully we could push on tomorrow morning. I didn't know what they used for communication around there, but the pub was filling up.

The landlord had a couple of amps and mics so we were ready to party – and did we have a party! The scrumpy was flowing as the landlord topped our glasses up. The pub was now jam-packed and we were flying. What a night it was! Rick and Ray were singing their hearts out while Steve and I were on fire playing numbers we hadn't played for years.

How we got back to the bus I don't know. We were wrecked as we fell into it, but we didn't show our arses or beat anybody up! Des mumbled that the bus was fixed, but we were out for the count and just fell asleep where we could.

The next morning I woke up first. I had a mouth like a cesspit and was dying for a leak. With a pounding headache I just couldn't be bothered with finding the toilet so I went outside. I was just going to start when I looked up. We were surrounded by what I would call New Age travellers and their scruffy old vehicles. I was gobsmacked, even more so when a girl walked by and said, 'Good morning!' I put my willy away and rushed back into the bus.

What had happened was that a number of these travellers had seen us and thought there was a camp here.

With thumping headaches and feeling sick, we made our way to the next gig. The problem with the bus wasn't major, so it had been an easy fix, thanks to the mechanic who came out from Bridgwater.

♫ 12 ♫

Being a teenager again

Our next gig was at Salisbury, Wiltshire, and we were up for it. It was all going to happen here and the mickey-taking and laughter was going to be non-stop.

First of all we were sitting in the Mother Ship waiting for one of Ruth's special meals when she said to Des, 'You've got to do it. Come on, Des, be brave.'

'I don't want to do it, Ruth. How many times have I got to tell you?'

This went on for about ten minutes until Robin said, 'For Christ's sake whatever it is, Des, just do it! You're giving me a right headache.'

'Come on, Dessie, do it for Ruthie.'

'I'm not some kid, Ruth.'

'Well, you're acting like it. Just do it and get it over and done with. I've been asking all day for you to do it.'

'Just get off my back.'

Ruth was just a few minutes away from putting the spaghetti bolognese on the table when Des, who was now in a temper, got up from his seat, grabbed a plastic bag with something in it, went into the toilet and slammed the door.

A few minutes later Des was shouting to himself, 'Stay still, you bastard!' Then there was a moment of silence before he started up again. 'I've bloody had enough of this! I ain't chasing this about any more!'

We're now tucking into our pasta delight when he comes out of the toilet, slings the bag on the floor in a temper and takes his seat at the table.

'That's it, Ruth – don't ask me again. I ain't doing it.'

In the middle of a mouthful of spaghetti, Rick says, 'What are you up to, Des?'

'If you must know, I've been chasing a bleedin' six-inch turd around the pan.'

Everybody stopped eating. Rick was now turning green.

'What he means,' says Ruth laughing, 'is he needs to get a smear of faeces put onto a card so he can send it off to a laboratory to be checked out. What the dickhead has been doing is trying to spear a turd around the pan with an applicator to get a sample, instead of wiping his arse and taking it off the toilet paper.'

We couldn't stop laughing. I really couldn't take the rise because I'd attempted the same thing when I got my test kit through the post. Des then picked up a piece of garlic bread and started munching away.

'You have washed your hands, Des?' I asked.

'I didn't use my hands to catch it.'

It seemed all of Salisbury was coming to the show. The theatre was packed to the rafters. Looking out at the audience it was about three to one in the favour of the ladies. It was all happening behind the scenes. Steve had crept into the dressing room where Mod Mania were while they were having their sandwiches in another room. Reg had taken his wig off and hid it in his guitar case. On a previous occasion somebody had nicked it for a laugh. Now Steve gave it a good helping of itching powder, then crept out again.

Then it was Perry's turn, as Big Al, who was also the compere, introduced the Rubbes to the audience as Perry and the Pacemakers. After their set it was Dinky's turn. As the tour progressed he seemed to be putting on more weight. It finally told when he jumped up in the air and his trousers split up the back. What was even funnier was that he wasn't aware of it. As he was bouncing about on stage there was a nice pair of red and blue pants on show – not a pretty sight. What a great laugh, as Mod Mania followed Dinky. All our eyes were on Reg's syrup. He was trying to play his bass guitar while scratching his head. The more he scratched the more the wig moved. On their final number it was nearly over his forehead. He wasn't happy as he came off stage – he knew that one of us had doctored it.

We were now on both bands' hit list and they were looking to get us back – and they did. Tammy as normal opened the second set with backing from the Rubbes. Her voice tonight sounded like she had a frog in her throat. As Steve said, 'More like she's had something else in her throat!'

Finally we came on. Tonight we were on overdrive and the crowd responded. They were dancing in the aisles after the second number. We were really having fun and we had our first 'runner', as we called them. One of the women jumped on the stage and grabbed Ray. Security in the shape of an old boy of about eighty had to come to his rescue. Most of the people who work at these venues are volunteers and he was one of them. After the song Ray and Steve had to help him off the stage.

It was a magic night and it got better later when we were at the merchandising desk. Two very nice-looking ladies got talking to Steve and me and suggested perhaps we could meet them the following morning for coffee. We had a day off before our next date at Barnstaple, so we thought why not?

Denise was in her late fifties and had a strong Wiltshire twang. She was well dressed, had a trim figure and her light brown hair was immaculate. Mary was near enough the same age, slightly plumper, but again well dressed, her main feature being an enormous pair of breasts that you couldn't take your eyes off. As we sat down for coffee in a nice, olde worlde beamed building, Steve got in first and sat next to Mary. As he scoffed a toasted teacake and slurped his cappuccino he said, 'This is very pleasant – I could get used to this.'

'Both of us saw you play here back in '64,' said Mary.

'Yeah, three and sixpence to get in, if I remember,' says Denise.

'Hope you enjoyed last night.'

'We thought it was fantastic and we had a ball. It brought back so many happy memories for us, Nick. You made us feel young again.'

'That's what we try and do, Denise. We love playing the old numbers and having fun.'

'Nowadays it's just miserable husbands and kids who only want you for what they can get out of you.'

'Don't tell me about kids, Denise. I could write a book on the subject.'

We sat and had a chat with them for about an hour. It appeared that their husbands had got into their woolly jumpers and tweed trousers a good few years back and were now only interested in bowling. I got the impression that the fun in their lives was at an all-time low. As it happens they were two nice ladies and we enjoyed their company.

Out of the blue Mary said, 'Would you like to come back to my place for a bit of lunch?'

She hadn't got the last word out when Steve jumped in and said, 'That would be very nice, but what about your husbands?'

'Don't worry about them – they're bowling in Chard. They won't get back till late.'

Within minutes we were in Mary's Toyota Yaris. We arrived at a little village just outside town. Her house was at the bottom of a leafy lane. It was like a military operation as she said to Steve and me, 'Get your heads down – don't want any nosy neighbours asking questions.'

We flew into her driveway and were quickly ushered into the house.

We were shown into a spacious lounge that had class stamped all over it. It was unreal, as normally it's the blokes who do the ducking and diving.

The CD player was switched on with music from the Hollies. In our day it would have been the grey and maroon Dansette with a vinyl! While the ladies went into the kitchen I said with a laugh, 'There's got to be a catch here, Steve. We can't be this lucky.'

'It's like being teenagers again.'

The girls had touched up their make-up and they came back in with a bottle of champagne and four glasses. That was soon dispatched followed by another. The four of us were laughing and joking about our teens, then it all went quiet for a second.

Then it just happened. Mary got hold of Steve's hand and without a fuss led him upstairs. Denise came and sat next to me. I caught a strong whiff of Opium perfume as she kissed me. Well, it was all systems go after that as we made our way to another bedroom. Why I don't know, but I was a bit embarrassed as I took my clothes off. Then I couldn't get my baseball boots off. She had to pull them off for me and was greeted by Essex white socks full of holes. She laughed, then stripped off to her underwear.

To say it was pleasant was an understatement. It was a very enjoyable senior moment, apart from the Steve thing. When we were younger he was always very vocal whenever he was having sex. He was the town crier this afternoon! Mind you, Mary was quite vocal, especially when she shouted out, 'I ain't doing that, Steve – that's disgusting!'

It was all going so well and I thought I might have seconds when the shit hit the fan. When a lady who talks quite posh swears it doesn't seem to have an impact, but it did this time.

'Feckin' hell – Cyril and Arthur have just driven in!'

After that all hell let loose. Steve was pushed into our room holding his clothes while Denise got dressed quickly and joined her mate downstairs.

She said, 'You two just keep quiet, and don't say a word.'

Steve thought it was hilarious, quoting his favourite Laurel and Hardy line.

'Another fine mess you've got us into, Stanley...'

However, it wasn't funny as we both got dressed and held our breath. The two husbands were in the house and talking loudly.

Cyril, Mary's husband, said, 'I see you've enjoyed some champagne today, dear. Four glasses? Who's been round?'

As quick as a flash Mary said, 'It was Maggie's birthday today. She and Peggy came round for a celebratory drink.'

'I bet!' said Cyril. 'I reckon you've got two blokes hiding upstairs. Shall we check, Arthur?'

Steve looked at me and the blood drained from our faces. There was laughter downstairs and it looked like it had been said as a joke. We had now been in this room for an hour and we were both dying for a pee.

Steve reminded me that this had happened to us before on tour when we went back to a girl's house in Bournemouth in the sixties. On that occasion the girl's parents came home and we had to jump from a bedroom window. We had both landed in a bleedin' great fish pond and got half drowned. Suddenly the door opened and Mary put her finger over her mouth and indicated that we should follow her. Slowly and quietly we were led down the stairs. We could hear laughing and joking coming from the conservatory. Mary let us out of the front door and we quickly made our way up the path.

Suddenly there was a loud shout from behind us. 'Who the hell are you?'

With that we bolted up the drive as he shouted, 'Burglars, burglars! Call the police!'

I've never run so fast in my life. We both collapsed about two hundred yards up the road and hid in some bushes. When the coast seemed clear we phoned Des and he came and picked us up.

I got a phone call from Denise the next day. She said the men didn't call the police. Mary explained to Cyril that we were Jehovah's Witnesses and she had sent us packing when we came to the door.

As the tour moved on Robin was starting to get really moody, and his drumming was not as good as it should've been. We knew the signs. His uncle, our ex-drummer Tony, had been on drugs. Robin was also getting mouthy and winding everybody up in the band about who his father was. It appeared that the talking-to by Steve before the tour had still not got through to him. It didn't help when he gave all the band members Father's Day cards.

As you get older you get less tolerant of people, and being tired as well doesn't help. He was now becoming a pain in the arse and it was all going to kick off again soon.

On the tour he was pally with the drummer of Mod Mania, who was about his age. They would go out to clubs together and we were sure they were smoking weed and popping pills. We couldn't prove it but we were on his case. There was no way we were prepared to go back to the bad old days when Tony was doing drugs.

One of the venues on the tour was quite an eye-opener. Normally when you arrive you have a walk around the place. Steve and I sat outside a coffee shop in this rural town and couldn't help noticing what a run-down place it was. It looked like a war zone with lots of shops boarded up and litter everywhere. I know it seems sad, but we like to 'people watch', and that's what we did over our coffee. What was really surprising was the number of people under forty on mobility scooters. Were they playing the system or were they genuine? Young girls with loads of kids, tattoos and smoking roll-ups seemed to be everywhere. There were blokes roaming around with hoodies, baseball caps and a pit bull type of dog in tow. Some looked so thin – you could see drugs were involved.

With the foreign languages being spoken as well it was a real eye-opener. I suppose this is the New England – what else is there to say? There were three hundred people coming tonight, all paying eighteen quid. It didn't make sense.

♫ 13 ♫

Dora and her Angels

The tour was settling down nicely and most of the time it was fun. It was great travelling from place to place on the bus. It had a spare bedroom so we could get our heads down whenever we wanted.

We were on our way to Manchester after having done a gig in Coventry. The spare bedroom door was locked, so we took it as read that Rick was in there, as he hadn't shown for breakfast at the digs. Half way down the motorway he must've woken up as there was a fair bit of commotion. He was either talking to himself or there was someone else in there. Then this bird of about fifty comes out of the room with a shagged-out Rick following her. She had more studs on her face than a pair of football boots. She was rough, and what a gob!

'You've got to get me feckin' back to Coventry, Rick! My old man's going to miss me when he wakes up!'

She was ranting and raving and we tried to make ourselves scarce, which is a bit hard on a bus. Ruth tried to talk to her but she was having none of it. We pulled into a service station and Rick took her off for breakfast. Within a minute he rushed back and shouted out to Des, 'Get it in first and let's get off quick!'

We shot out of the car park to get back on to the motorway. As we're doing so we got stuck behind a lorry that was having trouble. Rick looked back and could see this bird running like Usain Bolt behind us.

'Des, get your foot down – she's catching us up!'

'I've got nowhere to go, Rick – this lorry is hardly moving in front.'

'Des, do something – she's going to kill me! Look at her! She's off her head!'

We all looked back. She was one angry lady.

Steve shouted to Des, 'It's now or never! She's in touching distance!'

With that Des gave it the gun and drove over a flower garden, across a pathway and onto the slip road leading back onto the motorway.

'That wasn't very nice, Rick, leaving that poor girl stranded,' said Ruth.

'Poor girl? She's an animal!'

'Have you seen that advert, Rick?' says Ray.

'What are you on about?'

'You should've gone to Specsavers.'

'Leave it out, Ray. You've had some dogs in your time.'

'Rick, there's a lady present!' says Des.

'Sorry, Nick!'

The mickey-taking continued all through the day. It was Ray's birthday, so Ruth baked him a cake and made a fuss of him while the rest of us wound him up about his age. It was a birthday to remember as we played Manchester that night. It was a great venue and another sell-out. After the second song we asked the audience to sing 'Happy Birthday' to Ray, and suddenly a lady about our age got up from her seat and shouted out loudly, 'I wondered where you'd disappeared to, Ray!'

The crowd went silent and so did we as she had another go.

'Don't you remember? Your band played the Corn Exchange in 1972. After the show you took me out, and well, this was the result of it.'

A tall girl in her thirties stood up next to her Mum and they both walked towards the stage. Ray went white. He looked like he was going to collapse. You could hear a pin drop as they mounted the stage and eyeballed Ray. Security did nothing as they wanted to hear what Ray was going to say.

'You haven't got a lot to say for yourself, Ray. This is Jill. Say hello to your daughter. You've missed all her birthdays. I had to bring her up all on my own with no help from you.'

Ray was gobsmacked. He said meekly, 'Hello Jill.'

As soon as he said that the other guys on the tour came and joined us on stage and sang 'Happy Birthday'. They'd done Ray and us up like a kipper, the bastards! As soon as the crowd knew it was a stitch-up the whole theatre roared with laughter.

What a performance that lady gave! After the show we found out it was Big Al's missus and his eldest daughter. We were well and truly mullered – we weren't as clever as we thought we were. We took some terrible stick off the other band members after that.

Dinky was a randy little bastard and whenever he could he'd get his leg over. We did two towns quite close together. At the first one he'd met a lady and was going to see her the following night, so he was full of himself. However, he wasn't quite the stallion he thought he was, as he took some Viagra before his spot on stage. As soon as he'd finished he was going back to the hotel next to the venue to meet her. I've never laughed so much as when he went on stage that night. As I mentioned, he wore these tight trousers on stage and the Viagra kicked in. It was like an elephant's trunk as it got bigger and bigger. He could hardly walk on stage, let alone jump up and down. We were crying as he tried to shield it from the punters. A hack from a local newspaper, reviewing the show, wrote, 'It was a hard act to follow.'

Poor old Dinky had the piss taken out of him for the rest of the tour.

The next night, at the show in Newcastle, Steve and I met a couple of ladies and they invited us out for lunch at a local restaurant the following day. It was quite posh so we tried to behave. We'd ordered our main course, and the veg came on separate plates. Steve, who likes to think he's a bit of a gourmet, said out loud on seeing the veg, 'I do like a bit of minge.'

Well, the two ladies and the other people in the restaurant didn't know where to put their faces. It all went quiet until Steve said, 'What's wrong?

'You prat, its mangetout, not minge!'

My turn next. We had the meal and I was asked by the waiter, 'Would sir like coffee?'

'Yeah, a catheter of coffee would be nice.'

The two girls and Steve looked at me and burst out laughing.

'What's the joke?'

Steve got his own back. 'Going to shove it up your willy then?'

'What're you on about?'

'It's a cafetière, not a catheter.'

That night we were in Sunderland and the atmosphere was electric. It was going to be a hell of a show. The Geordies – sorry, Makems – gave the whole team on the tour a really warm welcome and it was one of the best shows we played.

The next morning we all got back to the bus by 10 o'clock, except Robin. Carlisle was a bit of a trot so we couldn't hang about. Des rang Robin's mobile but it went on to voice mail. We waited till 11, but he still didn't show. We were really annoyed, as it showed disrespect to Big Al and us. We left for Carlisle without him, trying to think who we could get to replace him at short notice, as he was now becoming a liability.

When we arrived at the venue we found out that Mod Mania drummer, Danny, like Robin, was also on the missing list. I had a word with Reg, and he was just as hacked off as we were. Their drummer had only been with the band for a few weeks. Reg said he thought he was also on drugs, and he was in the process of looking for another drummer once the tour had been completed. When Big Al found out they hadn't arrived, and learned of our suspicions that they were heavily into drugs, he went loopy. He pulled us and Mod Mania together and tore into us.

'What the hell's happening here, lads? The tour was really going well and now we're short of two drummers. To go with that, you now tell me they could be on drugs and are probably as high as a kite somewhere.'

As Al was getting wound up, so was his dog, so we moved to the other side of the room to give him a wide berth.

Suddenly the door burst open and Robin and Danny stood there looking like death warmed up. Before they could say anything Al threw us all out the room and started tearing into the two of them, with Sampson barking and growling – it was all going off.

After Al's tirade, and the bollocking we gave him, we had no more trouble with Robin for the rest of the tour, other than that he still kept calling each of us Dad. Sooner or later that would have to be sorted out, as to which one of us was his father.

We had a few days off before the next venues. Rick didn't come home with us – he and Tammy were doing their own thing and were going to meet us at the next gig in Southampton. It appeared that Lurch was history and Rick was now in the frame.

On the way home we diverted through London because of an accident on the motorway. We were driving along Victoria Embankment when some brainless old boy standing at a bus stop jumped out in front of us. Des just about stopped the bus in time. An angry Steve shouted out, 'What're you doing, mate? We nearly killed you!'

It went straight over this bloke's head. He said, 'Is this the bus for Blackfriars?'

It all went a bit pear-shaped when we arrived back home. Des had finally taken his bowel screening test and now had an urgent call from his doctor about the results. So we had lost our driver and the bus. Des had an offer he couldn't refuse on it, and sold it for big money.

He felt guilty about it, but we didn't blame him as it was a good deal for him. He didn't let us down and hired out a minibus, which had plenty of room. We were more concerned about his health, as was Ruth, who'd now become a permanent fixture in his life. They were made for each other and we hoped he'd found some real happiness for the first time in his life.

As soon as the family knew I was back home they were on the earhole. They were queuing up for a handout, so I kept well out of their way.

There was some good news on the band front, however. The record company had been in touch and they were bringing out a CD, *The Best of Modern Edge*, and it would also be available on iTunes, whatever that was. It appeared that the tour and all the publicity about the band had done the trick.

Steve was staying with me for a few days. He felt he had been at Des's long enough. When the tour finished he was going to look for a flat near me.

Meanwhile Ray's love life was in meltdown. Liz's husband had got wind that he was shuffling more than papers with her; so it was not a happy time at the Ponderosa.

Robin went home to his wife and kids and hopefully enjoyed their company more than the pills he was popping.

I didn't realise how tired I was and slept for nearly twenty-four hours. After the big sleep it was now time for a bit of action. But where do you go? There are no nightclubs for sixty-year-olds. Pubs don't really cater for wrinklies on the pull, so it was a buzz to Mandy and Viv. They were up for it, so we were seeing them that night.

I then received a phone call that could change our lives again. Wayne Brodie wanted an urgent meeting. We thought there was a problem with the tour or we'd messed up in some way. As Steve and I sat in his office we felt like there was a bollocking coming our way. Wayne came in with his dad, Big Al, and Sampson looking meaner than ever. His daughter served coffee and Al started the conversation.

'First of all, the tour so far has been a great success and your part in it has been a big plus – so much so that promoters have been in touch with us about booking you for future gigs. We're not your management so I'll give you a list of who's interested.'

We were taken aback. As far as we were concerned this was a one off tour and we would then all go our separate ways after it finished.

Al added, 'If you did want to go on the road we'd be very happy to manage and promote you.'

Mandy and Viv were eager to see us. Viv had now left her husband and was living in Rush Green, Romford. They were full of themselves and acting like a couple of ladettes. We took them out for a meal and while Mandy was giving some hammer to a rump steak and chips she said rather too loudly, 'Do you know what, Nick, this is the first time you've ever taken me out for a meal? Usually it's one drink and then you're trying to get my knickers off.'

I didn't know where to put my face as the other diners in the restaurant started sniggering.

'And you can stop laughing, Steve,' says Viv. 'You've never even bought me the one drink.'

They were like a double act. Once upon a time it would've been Steve and me leading the way, but these two were definitely in charge. They wanted to know all about the tour and what we'd been up to. Steve looked at me as if to say, it's like being grilled by the missus. They'd filled their stomachs and put back three bottles of wine between them when Viv said, 'Do you want a nightcap?'

We got a taxi and it was back to Viv's place. As we jumped out of the taxi two blokes a bit younger than us and looking a bit handy came over. They weren't happy.

One of them said to Mandy, 'Where've you two been? I thought we were going out tonight.'

'Well, you thought wrong.'

The other bloke then had his say. Looking at Viv, he said, 'Yeah, what's going on? It was all arranged we'd meet down at Zags night club.'

'We didn't go because we don't fancy you two any more, so on your bikes,' said Viv.

I looked at Steve and we both stepped back a few feet.

'I left my partner for you, Viv.'

'Well, I hope you've still got her phone number.'

This didn't go down too well and they started on us.

One of them said, 'Are these our replacements then? They look like old farts to me.'

There's a time to stick up for yourself and a time to let it go over your head. We chose the latter and were off, as it looked like it was going to get nasty.

What a night that was! We were supposed to be chilling out before the next part of the tour.

We had two nights at Southampton, a nice theatre. As we drove away in the minibus to the venue we made it quite clear to Robin that we didn't want any more drug issues, and if there was he'd be on his way home. He was still an irritating little shit as he still wouldn't stop calling us all Dad, although one of us probably was.

We'd had a band meet a couple of weeks back to discuss it. After a few beers we all agreed that we did all sleep with his Mum, so it was still a time-bomb ticking. She was our drummer and we were with her all the time, so it was unlikely it was anybody else.

We got there in plenty of time for the first show. We told Robin to disappear for half an hour as we had business to talk about. We discussed what Big Al had said about promoters contacting them about us doing more shows after the tour. All four of us were up for it. Robin was not in the frame, so we were on the lookout for another stick man. Once the tour had finished we would put a plan together that suited all of us, then have a chat with Al.

All the acts met up again and were ready for the last part of the tour. Dinky had shagged himself to death on the first part of the tour and it was showing. The bags under his eyes were now so big it looked like his bollocks had swapped places. Mod Mania's Reg had bought a new syrup – it looked like an Afghan rug after a sandstorm. The Rubbes turned up late, putting Big Al and his brute of a dog in a bad mood. Steve took the rise out of Perry as he rushed into the theatre.

'You want to connect that pacemaker to your watch, Perry.'

It was all good fun as we got ourselves ready for the gig.

About an hour before the show I popped outside for a fag. Lots of people were arriving at the theatre. It amazed me that the music was still so popular and people would pay good money to come and watch us play. As I walked back into the theatre a voice called out my name.

'Hi, Nick.'

The voice sounded familiar. I turned around and couldn't believe who was facing me. I was stunned. Even after all these years I would recognise her anywhere.

'Anita! I don't believe it's you! You look amazing.'

She started laughing and said, 'Still the same old chat-up lines.'

'What're you doing here?'

'Jenny and I have come to watch you and Steve play. And before the sap rises, we're both happily married.'

'Jenny's here as well? Steve will be really pleased to see her. Look, I've got to go now. Can we meet for a drink after the show?'

'Just a drink, Nick, that's all. We're staying at the Holiday Inn. We'll meet you there in the bar.'

'Christ, the Holiday Inn! We're at Joan's B&B.'

Steve couldn't believe that Jenny was here. Like me with Anita, he'd enjoyed a close relationship with her and still had fond memories of their time together. We were acting like a couple of teenagers and were getting all excited about meeting up with them later.

Just before the gig it all kicked off. Dinky lived up to his name and threw his toys out of the pram. He now thought he was the star of the show and wanted to come on last in the second set, which was our spot. Big Al told him in no uncertain terms that he was a support act and was lucky to be on the tour. He started to get stroppy with Al, but when Sampson showed his teeth he agreed that perhaps he'd misjudged the situation, and of course he was very happy to sing in the first set.

Then not two minutes later two big blokes entered our dressing room and asked for Ray. Ray tried to duck down behind a cabinet but to no avail. One of them gave him a big brown envelope and growled, 'Make sure you read this, Mr Walker.'

And with that they went.

Then there's Rick. He's now had enough of Tammy and is in the process of giving her the elbow. She's not happy and starts screaming at him, using every swear word known to man, or, in her case, woman. Robin says 'Dad' to us one too many times and Steve lamps him one across the ear. Ray undoes his envelope and – surprise, surprise – Mrs Walker's solicitor has issued divorce papers on him. What a great start to the Southampton show. But, as they say, the show must go on.

The Rubbes opened the show and gave their usual tight performance. They were followed by Dinky, who forgot the words on his first number and slowly went downhill. Mod Mania finished the first set, and they were spot on.

At the start of the second set Tammy's voice was a bit strained. I suppose after volleying Rick for an hour something had to give. Then it was our turn. Steve and I had shot back to the B&B during the first set and put our best gear on. We couldn't disappoint the girls tonight so we were looking the biz. We'd told Rick and Ray about meeting Anita; they of course knew her and Jenny well from the old days.

In our act we always mentioned the 'Summer of Love' in 1967, then went into *A Whiter Shade of Pale* by Procol Harum. Just before we started the number Rick had a word with the audience, and Steve and I were not happy.

'We have two special guests with us tonight. Would Anita and Jenny like to stand up and introduce themselves?'

The lights went on and the two girls, looking very embarrassed, stood up.

'This number is for you girls from Nick and Steve,' says a sniggering Rick.

If I could've got hold of him there and then I would've taken his head off. The lights went off and we went into the number.

After the show I tore into Rick. 'What did you have to do that for?

We're meeting them later. They'll be well unhappy after what you did to them.'

'Bollocks, Nick, where's your sense of humour gone?'

Then Big Al walks in and has a pop at Rick. Al doesn't like anything that is not prearranged with him. Even a simple thing like Rick's comment he's not happy about. Rick was not flavour of the night.

Steve and I raced round to the hotel to see the girls. When they'd stood up in the theatre they'd looked delightful. They'd worn really well and our hearts were beating like a couple of silly teenagers as we sat in the bar.

After two pints and waiting for an hour Steve said, 'I know how a spare prick at a wedding feels now.'

We waited another half an hour but they didn't show. Being stood up at sixty-four years of age is not good for the ego. We went to reception and tried to explain who we were looking for, as we didn't know their surnames. The girl looked at us like we were a couple of babbling old fools. She was probably right.

The next afternoon we went to watch a football match just outside Southampton. Now I think I've seen most things at football matches, but this was a first. The game was a semi-professional league game. It was a good standard of football and there were a few hundred people watching. We stood behind the manager of the home team. He was in the technical area shouting out instructions to his players. One of the home-side players nearly killed a pigeon with a shot that sailed high and wide over the stand! Another ball was used and the game continued. The ball that was kicked over the stand was found and placed on the side of the pitch between the two opposing managers' dugouts. These balls cost a lot of money and are gold dust to teams in the lower leagues, so you don't want to lose one.

Suddenly an eagle-eyed spectator shouted out to the home manager, 'I've just seen the opposing manager pick up that ball and sneak it into his kit bag.'

The home manager shouts out to the other manager, 'That's our feckin' ball you've just nicked!'

Rather sheepishly he took it out of his kit bag and kicked it to the home manager, who turned round to us and said with a big grin on his face, 'He thinks he's clever, but he's not as clever as us. We played his team three weeks ago at their place and we nicked two of their balls.'

The tour progressed from town to town and we were still having great fun. It was really tiring, but the adrenalin always pumped when you went out to play. Robin was a permanent pain in the arse and we couldn't wait to ditch him when the tour finished. He kept throwing in the father thing all the time. When we were playing back in London, Steve, Rick, Ray and I got well tanked up one night in this seedy pub. A geezer we got talking to said he would take him out for five grand. We could only muster a couple of hundred!

Word came through from Ruth that Des had been diagnosed with bowel cancer. We were gutted. Des was one of us. He was having treatment and Ruth was looking after him. We spoke to him most days after that while on tour.

We were now playing on home territory when we played Clacton-on-Sea, and what a laugh that was! It was one lady's birthday, and her mates came out in force to celebrate it. I've seen most things from Essex girls, having lived in the county all my life, but this was extreme and scary. Now, we're talking about women in their sixties, not teenagers. They were wild and taking no prisoners.

We'd got to the venue quite early, so the band had a walk along the prom with Dinky. It was a toss-up whether we got Dinky a wheelchair. He was now so fat that he waddled down the prom like a pregnant duck. We'd just got to the pier when we met the women dressed up in nothing more than bras and knickers – well, that's how it looked. They were well tanked up and everybody was giving them a wide berth.

Then one of them, Dora, the birthday girl, recognised Dinky and shouted out like a fog horn, 'Faaackinell, girls, it's only Johnny D. Freshman!'

With that the girls smothered him with kisses and pushed their tits into his face. We stepped well back. They were well rough and with gobs to go with it.

Then Dora says, 'We're coming to watch you tonight, Johnny. You don't remember me, do you?'

'I can't put a name to the face, luv.'

'Godzilla,' Steve muttered under his breath.

We roared with laughter and stood back another few feet, leaving Dinky at their mercy. Then Dora, with a glint in her eye and a grin on her face, said:

'Johnny, you must remember me. It's Dora, Lowestoft 1969. You were lead singer with Terry and the Tanks. I came and watched you play at the holiday camp I was staying at. After the show we went back to my chalet and spent the night together. You must remember that!'

We'd never laughed so much in all our lives when she said that.

You could see him trying to come up with the answer. Then he hit the jackpot.

'Of course, Dora, how are you? You look really great!'

It was so false, we all rolled up. Dora was sixty going on seventy. A failed weightwatcher, the lines on her face looked like a map of the Underground. She did have quite nice boobs, which gave her two out of ten.

'We're all coming tonight, Johnny – perhaps we can meet up afterwards.'

Dinky was on the back foot now and wasn't quite quick enough to find an excuse.

Ray said, 'He'll be well chuffed with that, Dora. If you wait for him outside the stage door after the show he'll be there.'

'Let's make it a party!' said Dora. 'I'll bring the girls and you lot can join us.'

When we got back to the theatre we had the usual sound check. After that the band, minus Robin, had a chat with Big Al. The four of us agreed that we wanted to continue with the band and to take up Al's offer to manage us and arrange the bookings. He said he would draw up a contract for us to look at. About a month after the tour he would line up some venues. We needed a drummer and some more numbers under our belt, as we would be playing two-hour shows.

With all Ray's domestic problems he was looking to rent a house with enough room for Steve and Rick to stay. Ray didn't seem too worried about his missus and the pending divorce. His sons didn't go a lot on their mother so they were on his side, and they would still run his businesses. He said he'd put a lot of money away so she couldn't get her hands on it. He was more worried about Liz's husband, who was now on his case. Ray had tried to back off from Liz a bit, but couldn't help himself, as she stayed over at a lot of the venues. We thought he was also having a little flutter with Tammy. Rick didn't care about that, as the lady who had taken over from Ruth on the merchandising stand was now the love of his life. We didn't have the heart to tell him that she was Big Al's sister!

There was a good feel about tonight, until Dora and her Angels turned up. They were outrageous. They sat in the front row with everything on show singing loudly *Johnny Remember Me*. All the boys from the bands were now checking their gear on stage every few minutes to get an eyeful, all except Dinky, who was now paralysed with fear at the thought of what the night could bring. And he would not be disappointed.

Everyone was now in their seats waiting for the show to start. Dinky and Tammy had swapped sets so Dinky would come on just before us in the second set. Normally it was during the second set that people got up and danced in the aisles or in the front row next to the stage. Not tonight. Dora's Angels got up from their seats as soon as the Rubbes struck the first chord, and the pandemonium started. They were dancing about and making a racket, much to the amusement of some, although others in the audience weren't happy with this rabble of uncontrolled women acting like delinquents. Normally the theatre staff would have a word, but not tonight – there was nobody brave enough to confront this lot.

Now it was Dinky's turn and he was shaking in his boots as he hit the stage. At just over five and a half foot and sixteen stone he looked an unlikely pop star, but Dora and her lot, who must have been from St Dunstan's, were shouting and screaming at him. Every button on his white suit was near breaking point and the sweat was pouring from every pore as he tried to hit the high notes, without too much success. But he was now lapping it up and was prancing about on stage like something possessed.

He then committed the cardinal sin. He went over to Dora's crowd and sat on the stage in front of them. He looked like a gnome sitting there. Then it all kicked off big time. They groped him and pulled him off the stage.

Dora was bellowing out, 'I love you Johnny, I love you Johnny!'

They wouldn't let him get back on stage and he was shouting out for help. Nobody was going to chance their luck with Dora's mob until the cavalry in the shape of Big Al and a couple of the roadies turned up to rescue him. What a night! Poor old Dinky was never the same after that.

♫ 14 ♫

On the road from Colchester to Torquay

Next stop was the military town of Colchester, and the scourge of the mobile phone. Nearly every band that's ever played a gig has had the problem. We're just about to play a number when a mobile goes off in the front row. The ring tone yells out, 'Alert it's the wife, alert it's the wife!'

Why he answered the phone I don't know, bearing in mind it's his missus.

He shouts up to us, 'Don't play anything yet, guys – she doesn't know I'm here.'

A bird in her forties sitting next to him curls up with embarrassment.

He finishes his chat with the wife, telling her a load of porkies, and reckons he's got away with it. Then he switches the phone off and puts his arm around this bird. Then a woman shouts out from the back row and puts the fear of God into him.

'You lying git, Ronald!'

His head snaps round to see who's shouted out, and spots the woman. I'll never forget his words.

'Oh no, it's only the feckin' wife's sister!'

Steve and I were still sick as parrots about not meeting up with Anita and Jenny. Rick's mickey-taking on stage had backfired. The girls must've thought they didn't want to get involved with us two again. They probably just wanted a friendly chat, and instead saw us as a couple of clowns that just hadn't grown up.

The next show was a town just outside Ipswich, which was near Ray's place. All his family except his missus turned up, including his sons, who were great lads. Of course, Liz was there looking very tasty. But it all fell apart when Ray and Liz were having a chat outside the venue after the show. Out of nowhere Liz's husband appeared and lamped him one from behind. Ray fell to the floor, hitting his head on the pavement. Within minutes the police turned up and arrested the guy. Ray was rushed to hospital and ended up spending a couple of days there.

Ray was out of action for the next five venues and Rick took over the singing. Ray came back on board at Exeter. He was still playing a dangerous game, as Liz came along as well – she'd now left her husband.

The tour was now nearing the end. After Exeter tonight we had the final gig at Torquay.

For Big Al and Wayne the tour had been a great success – on most nights the venues were packed. The merchandising side of the tour had also been very lucrative and we'd earned a good few bob out of it. Even though we were having a great time we were all knackered. Robin, as usual, was still a cocky little bastard and was still full of himself. Then he dropped a bombshell.

'I wanted to know which one of you is my father so on the tour I've collected DNA from all of you.'

'You've done what, you little shit?' said Rick.

'And tomorrow I will have all the results back. So sleep tight.'

He rushed out of the dressing room before we could catch him. As you can imagine our performance on stage that night was well below par and none of us slept a wink.

The next morning we were all sitting in the hotel awaiting Robin, who sauntered in without a care in the world.

'This is the day we've all been waiting for. We'll know in a minute which one of you is my Dad.'

'You say that word once more, Robin,' said Ray, 'and I'll personally punch your head in.'

Suddenly there was a knock on the door.

'That's the courier delivering the DNA results,' said Robin.

We all looked at the door like condemned men awaiting execution. It opened and a man in his mid-seventies holding an envelope walked in. There was something about him that looked familiar.

'Long time no see, gentlemen.'

As soon as he spoke we knew who he was. We hadn't seen him for over thirty-five years.

'It's great to see you after all this time, TJ, but what are you doing here?' I asked.

'I've come to see my son.'

'What are you on about?'

'Didn't Robin tell you?' he said with a grin.

For a minute nothing registered.

'You're saying that Robin is your son?' said an annoyed Steve.

'Don't you remember the years I managed Modern Edge? There wasn't a day went by that we didn't have problems with girls, police, drugs, fights and God knows what else. I had to sort them all out. When my son told me you had got in contact with him I thought what a great wind-up. I looked after Penny financially but she wouldn't marry me. Yes, you lot had flings with her and she did live life to the full. She was a great girl and I loved her very much.'

Everybody was speechless until Steve said, 'But I thought those years with you were great, TJ.'

'They were, but I seem to remember that when she got pregnant you all seemed to say, "Not me, Guv," and distanced yourself from her. Penny told Robin all about her life with you lot, so he was quite happy to go along with the deception.'

'Too right he was,' said Steve. 'He enjoyed putting us through hell.'

'Sorry, guys, that was one for my Mum,' said Robin. 'She liked you all and there was never any bad feeling. She loved playing in the band and all the touring.'

Robin was now trying to be one of us, perhaps feeling slightly guilty about the last couple of months. Mind you, we think he really enjoyed putting us through the mill. TJ was coming with us to Torquay and we were going to have a beer with him.

We were in Torquay for the last night, then it was home. After an early-afternoon sound check we all did our own thing. Steve and I had a walk along the sea front for some fresh air and to clear our heads. It was a really beautiful day. We bought a couple of ice creams and sat on a bench opposite the sea reminiscing about the old days.

We still enjoyed playing and tonight was no exception. It would be a challenge over the coming months to see whether the band could continue touring. We were sitting there letting the world go by when, simultaneously, two voices spoke.

'Hi, Nick.'

'Hi, Steve.'

Steve and I looked up. Anita and Jenny were standing in front of us. What a shock, and for once we were lost for words.

'Can we join you?'

'Of course you can, Anita,' I said.

'What are you both doing here?' I asked.

'First, Jenny and I apologise for not showing up in the hotel bar. We've just been to where you're playing tonight and we saw Rick and he told us you'd gone for a walk. He also explained that you two had nothing to do with embarrassing us at Southampton, by making us stand up in front of all those people. We know what you two are like.'

Steve grinned. 'We've changed, Anita.'

'Changed? I bet you two are still chasing the ladies and getting up to no good,' laughed Jenny.

'We can't catch them now,' grins Steve. 'What're you two doing here?'

'Well, we retired here about ten years ago with our husbands. We sold the salons in Reading, made some money and we're enjoying life.'

'Sounds like you've got it about right. Where are your husbands now?' I asked.

'They've gone to a steam rally weekend in Brighton.'

'That sounds exciting, Anita.'

'Don't be facetious, Nick.'

'Do you know that's the word you used way back when I first went to your flat and asked where your dickhead of a boyfriend Simon was? I think I called him "The Saint" – Simon Templar, from that television programme.'

'I do remember that, Nick. Simon is now my husband.'

'Yeah, I forgot about that.'

Steve got me out of trouble. 'How about some coffee, guys?'

We found a coffee shop and ordered our drinks. I looked at the two girls. They were our age, but looked only about fifty. They still had their looks and were smartly dressed with immaculate make-up and manicured finger nails. They both had the same hairstyle and looked very Twiggy-like. They had an air of class about them. Steve was looking at me and thinking the same. We were scruffy; hair looking like something was living in it, unshaven and wearing old trainers.

Over coffee we laughed and enjoyed each other's company. It felt as if we'd just picked up where we'd left off in the early seventies. Jenny left to put some more money in the parking meter. Steve went with her.

'You don't know how good it is to see you again, Anita.'

'Same old Nick,' she said with a laugh.

'Sorry. So what's happened to you over the years?'

'I've had three children. Paul, he's a solicitor, Toby's an actor and Lucy has kept hairdressing in the family – she's got a number of salons all over the South West. I have three grandchildren and they're lovely. Simon retired ten years ago after he sold his accountancy business. He's captain of the local golf club and I'm the secretary. I also do a lot of charity work, we love cruising, and we're always away. As you can see, Jenny and I are still close friends. She has twin girls, and they're friends with my three kids. Her husband, Jonathan, and Simon get on very well. What about you, Nick?'

Brighton band The Rockits seen here in the sixties with ace singer Herby Boxall leading the line. *Herby Boxall collection*

A rare photograph of seventeen-year-old Cliff Richard with drummer Terry Smart and guitarist Ian 'Sammy' Samwell of The Drifters at Butlins, Clacton-on-Sea, 21 August 1958. *Joan Saunders*

Dave Berry performing at the Carre Theatre, Amsterdam, 1965.

Manchester indie rock band No Brakes were well known on the Northern circuit in the 1990s. From left to right are singer Anthony Leach, drummer Mark Brady, bass guitarist Mark Escott and lead guitarist Chris Ross. With the name No Brakes plastered all over their gig van they often got stopped by the police! *Chris Ross collection*

A close-up of lead guitarist Chris Ross with bass player Mark Escott playing a gig in Manchester. *Chris Ross collection*

Seen here playing at the Grey Horse, Kingston, South London, in the 1980s are Croydon-based country blues-rock band Speedo. The line-up was Roger Fullilove (guitar/vocals), Ray Homewood (guitar), Bill Aedy (bass guitar) and Paul 'Pinky' Floyd (drums/vocals). They were heavily influenced by Delbert McClinton. *Ray Homewood collection*

Essex band Quota Plus, with which the author played in the 1970s. Standing are lead guitarist Dave Buthlay (left) and bass guitarist Alan Hammond. Drummer Brian Rowland is in the middle, and sitting on the floor are keyboard player Dave Hughes (left) and singer Dave Moore. *F. W. Tyler*

Another shot of Quota Plus all in a tangle. *F. W. Tyler*

A great close-up shot of Ronnie Wood and Rod Stewart performing with The Faces on 3 December 1973 at the Worcester Gaumont cinema. *Chris Nicholson*

A classic shot of Rod Stewart in full flow at the Worcester Gaumont. The bass player of The Faces on the left is, I think, Tetsu Yamauchi, who took over from Ronnie Lane. *Chris Nicholson*

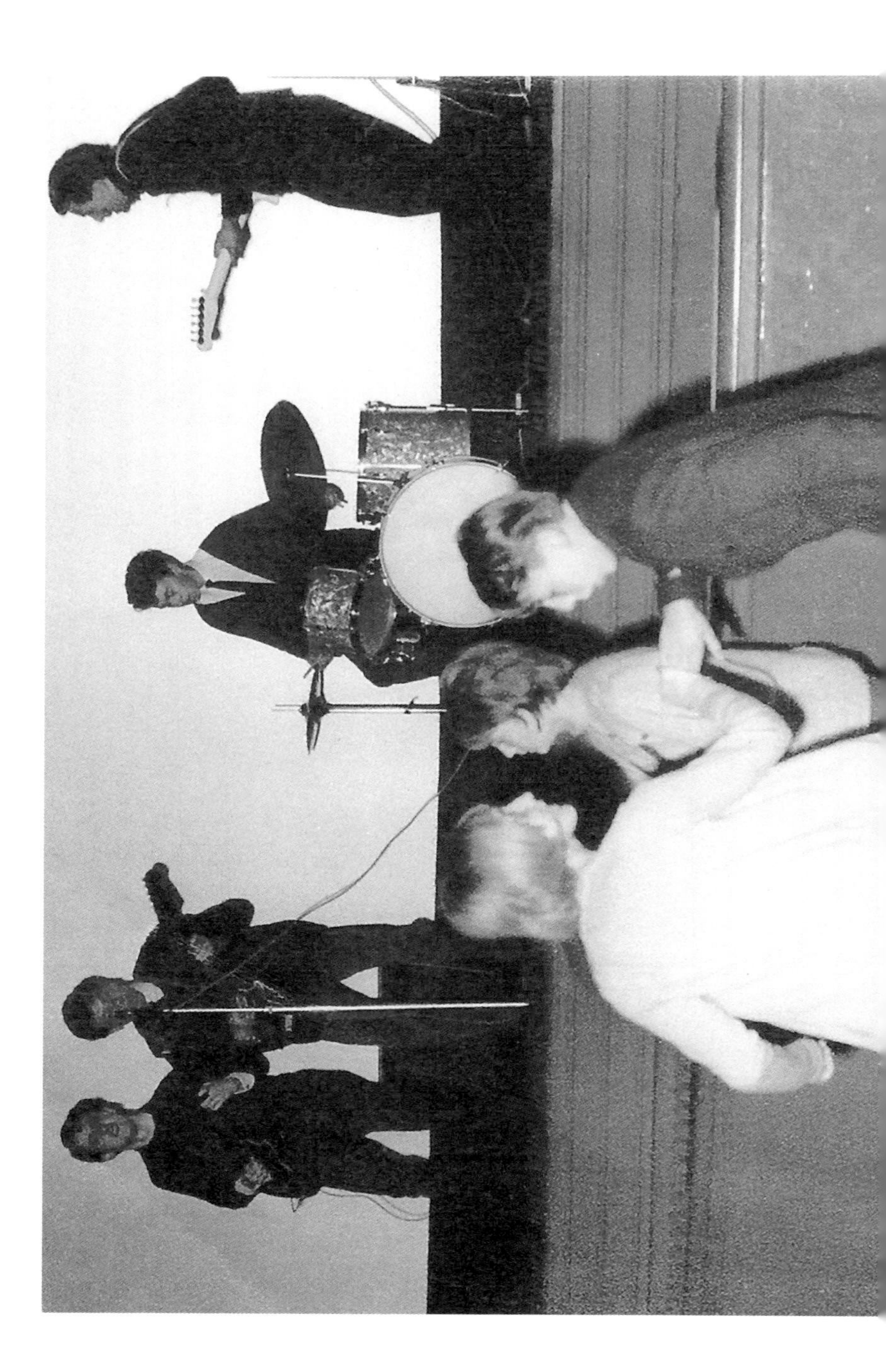

Opposite: Dancing to The Henchmen at the Hornchurch Odeon on 24 December 1962. On the right is lead guitarist Ron Saunders. *Ron Saunders collection*

Above: Top Somerset band The Storm are seen here in 1968. Left to right, they are Paddy Perry, Alan Bull, Paul Conibeer, Bob Conibeer, Mervin Howell, John Tingay and fourteen-year-old bassist Grahame Darch. Note the paisley shirts! *Grahame Darch collection*

A dance ticket for a gig by Essex band, Quota Plus, which the author played for in the 1970s. *Alan Hammond collection*

From the sixties we go to 2012, with Wellington-based band Homebrew, who have three family members in a line-up comprising Hazel Chard, Grahame 'The General' Darch, Tony Paisley, Gary Chard, Stuart Upton and Alan Chard. They play a lot of gigs for charity and have been playing since the 1970s. *Grahame Darch collection*

Mod Mick Phipps is seen here at Cheshunt in 1964 on his two-tone Vespa GS 160 with his friend John Langham and his girlfriend Joan, later to become his wife. *Mick Phipps collection*

Mods on the plot outside the Kings Oak pub in Epping in the mid-sixties. In the foreground George from West Ham is sitting on a white Vespa GS 160. *Mick Phipps*

What a great photo of Mods in the sixties suitably attired with their parkas. Centre stage is a Lambretta series 3 TV200, resplendent in chrome and dark red. These Mods came from Cheshunt, Waltham Cross, Harlow, Enfield and East Ham. *Mick Phipps*

Mods 2011-style at Paignton, with a fine array of classic scooters. *Lyn Mitchell*

Seen in 1964 is La Roulette coffee lounge in Loughton, Essex, an iconic scene of the Swinging Sixties. There are a number of Lambrettas and Vespas on show while their Mod owners enjoy their frothy coffees. *Mick Phipps*

Sixties lads Pete Davies, Glyn Grainger and Brian Atkinson enjoy cream slices in the back of a Morris shooting brake outside the Bath Pavilion in 1965. After their feast they are going inside to see Tom Jones. *Glyn Grainger collection*

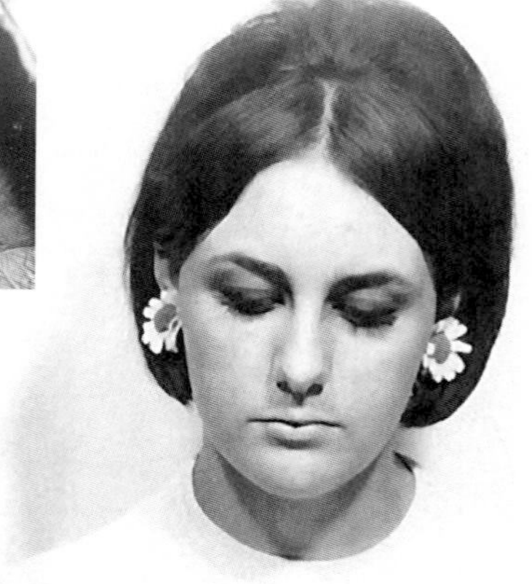

Teenage Mod Chrissie Hughes, with the hairstyle of the day, photographed in 1964. *Chris Hammond collection*

This could be a scene from TV's *Heartbeat* as sixties teenager Jill Bluffield poses for the camera in an Austin A40 Farina just outside Taunton in 1965. *Ivan Bluffield*

Three Mods on holiday at Little Canada, Isle of Wight, in the mid-sixties: from left to right, they are Ivan Bluffield (wearing his Fred Perry shirt, jacket from Harry Fenton's and hand-stitched winkle-pickers), Graham Cole and Martin Gale. Note the old suitcase and regulation football. *Ivan Bluffield collection*

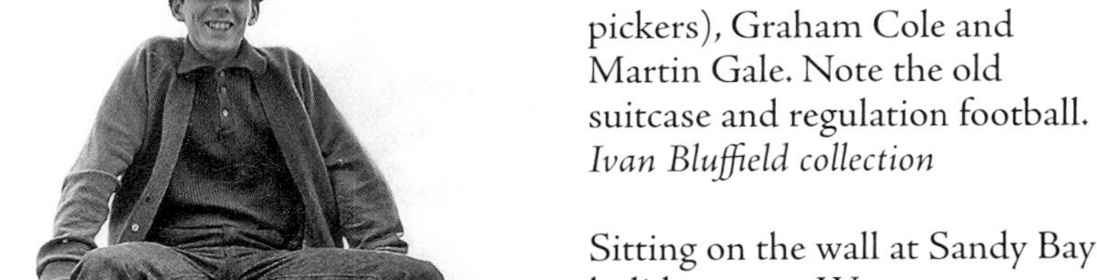

Sitting on the wall at Sandy Bay holiday camp, Weston-super-Mare, in the early sixties is teenager Ivan Bluffield wearing his pork-pie hat. *Ivan Bluffield collection*

It's mayhem on the track at Minehead in 1964 as the Beatles come to town. They are here for the filming of *A Hard Day's Night,* which was shot on what is now the preserved West Somerset Railway. *R. Kingsley Tayler/ Peter Lockwood collection*

My mate of more than 50 years, Terry Page from Dagenham, was, like me, a Mod. He is seen here in 1967. *Terry Page collection*

Mods get everywhere! *Author's collection*

Thank goodness Steve and Jenny came back. My life had been a nightmare compared to hers.

'Why did you come and see us play in Southampton?' Steve asked Jenny.

'We still love sixties music and we saw the ad in the papers advertising your tour. Knowing you both and liking your music, we came to watch. We're also coming again tonight to see you play.'

'We'd better go, Jenny,' said Anita. 'I've got to babysit for Lucy in half an hour.'

'Perhaps we can have a drink in the theatre bar after the show,' I said.

Anita laughed as she got up from the table. 'Do you know, you two never miss an opportunity, do you? We might, but don't bank on it. We're happily married and the past is the past.'

As Steve and I walked back to the venue we stopped off to have our hair cut. We wanted to at least look half decent before we met them.

Later we were having a quiet moment in the dressing room when Steve commented, 'Nick, for two happily married women, why would they come and see us play twice and maybe have a drink with us? It doesn't add up. I reckon they're bored out of their brains. Jonathan and Simon sound like a couple of pipe-and-slipper blokes. They're looking for some excitement and a bit of rough, and we just happen to fit the bill!'

There was a buzz in the dressing room as the bands and singers got ready for the last performance of the tour. In some ways we didn't want it to end as we'd had such a great time. On the other hand we were knackered and wanted a break before we went back on the road in a few weeks time.

Ray had been in touch with his previous drummer, Billy, about maybe joining the band. He'd also been busy on the house front. He and Liz were now an item and were setting up together. He'd rented a house in Ardleigh Green, Hornchurch, and got a two-bedroom flat for Steve and Rick in the same area. He'd paid six months' rent up front for them – hopefully they would manage after that. They were very grateful to him for doing that for them. It meant the band was living in the same area, which made life a lot easier. So things were looking up and we now had a purpose and were looking forward to a new era in our lives.

Torquay was a great night and when it came to our turn to play we were ready for it. Anita and Jenny were in the front row and we could clearly see them. Steve and I were like new pins. We'd really scrubbed up well and we were like teenagers trying to impress the girls, two grown men acting like dickheads. Our music went down well with the crowd and the two girls were really enjoying themselves.

For the last number the whole audience either stood up or danced in the aisles. Ray and Rick were on top form with their vocals and, if I say so myself, I was playing well, as was Steve. At the end of the show, as it was the last night, all the acts went into the large bar for a good drink and a party. TJ came in and we had a laugh with him. He apologised for the wind-up about Robin's parenthood.

We talked about the old times. It was good to see him again after all these years. I was just getting a refill when I saw Anita and Jenny walk into the bar. They looked gorgeous. Steve saw them first and took them over to a table, while I took the drinks order. They looked a bit nervous and not as confident as they had been that morning.

'This is a nice surprise, girls.'

'Yeah, it's a surprise for us as well,' said Anita. 'We were nearly home but decided to come back to see you both.'

This was not the time to be clever or act the fool. You could see they were feeling guilty about being here. Steve had sussed this out as well, so it was gently, gently.

'We're glad you've come,' said Steve. 'Did you enjoy the show?'

'We thought it was a great night,' said Anita. 'It brought back so many happy memories for us both.'

'Do you know it was well over forty years ago that we first met you,' said Jenny.

Steve then took Jenny over to the bar to get some refills, which gave me time to talk to Anita. We both looked at each other and were lost for words. We were once close, very close, and just for that moment we both went back in time. Steve brought our drinks over, then went to sit at a nearby table with Jenny.

Laughing, Anita said, 'You two haven't changed one bit.'

'What do you mean by that?'

'This is what you used to do before, split us up so you could chat us up and spin us a line.'

We both laughed. Anita added, 'You haven't told me about what's happened in your life since we last met.'

After I gave her all the nitty-gritty she didn't know whether to laugh or cry. She probably thought to herself, thank God I didn't end up with him.

'It's been an eventful life then, Nick?'

We then both burst out laughing.

'You had a narrow escape,' I said.

She didn't laugh, but just looked at me and said quietly, 'Maybe, or maybe not, Nick,' which I thought was a funny thing to say.

Steve and Jenny joined us and they seemed quite happy. It was just like old times when the four of us used to go out together. They never mentioned their husbands and we never asked. On the outside, their lives seemed perfect, but I had my doubts.

It was time for them to go, so what do you do next? In the old days it was a quick snog and a few suggestions as to where they could spend the night. We walked back to Jenny's motor and said our goodbyes.

'It was great to see you again, Anita, and I'm glad life has turned out well for you. I hope you don't mind, but I'd love to keep in touch with you. Have you got a mobile number?'

'I don't think so, Nick. It's been nice meeting up with you again after all this time.'

'I understand. Sorry about that – just old habits. Oh, by the way we've just got a new CD out. I've brought one along for you. I've put an inscription on the sleeve.'

I took it out of my pocket and gave it to her. She read what I'd written: 'Anita, memories are made of this, Nick.'

She looked at me for what seemed ages and said, 'That's sweet of you, Nick. You take care of yourself.'

She kissed me on the cheek and got into Jenny's car. They both waved to us as they left, and that was it, gone.

Steve piped up, 'Giving them the CDs didn't work then. I thought we might get invited back for coffee.'

'Get real, Steve – would you jeopardise all they've got for us two?'

♫ 15 ♫

The dreaded hen party

As we came through the Dartford Tunnel we knew we were back in Essex when a couple of police interceptors rushed past, pulled over this 4x4 and hauled two people out of it. With the radio telling us that there'd been a murder, an armed robbery, and the travellers were kicking off at Dale Farm, life was back to normal.

We had a few weeks before going back on the road, so we had some time to ourselves. The band was seeing Billy about joining us in a couple of days time. We got back home, dropped Robin off and wished him well.

I can't say I was sorry to see him go. He was from another era and he wasn't for us. Steve and Rick were going to sort out their flat, while Ray and Liz were doing the same with their place. We'd now signed a contract with Big Al and his son Wayne. We felt safe with them and we also knew that we wouldn't get ripped off.

Before I went back to my place I went and saw Des and Ruth. Des looked in good shape and it appeared they'd caught the cancer before it spread. They were now living together, and I was well pleased about that.

That's where the good news stopped. My kids were queuing up to see me again. They'd realised that with our new CD, which was rising in the charts, Dad must be earning some more money. I refused to see any of them until the next day.

I took my phone off the hook, locked the door, had a large scotch and slept right through to the following morning. The first knock on the door was Tracy. She had so much on show she looked like a bleedin' lap dancer. In her 'poor me' voice, and with moist eyes, she whispered, 'Dad, we're having trouble paying one or two bills.'

'That's unusual Tracy!'

'I know, Dad. You know I don't like asking you, but I've got nowhere else to go.'

'What about Mick? There's enough crime in London to keep him busy. He must be on bundles of overtime.'

'He's potless, Dad. My 4x4 needed some work on it and the new implants set him back four grand.'

'Sorry about that, Tracy. It's a tough life, girl.'

'I'll pay you back, Dad.'

'Yeah, and they've just found Lord Lucan living in a tent in Epping Forest.'

'It's only a thousand pounds, Dad.'

'Is that all, Tracy? What's it for then?'

'My Botox account is overdue and Zacharias's music teacher is owed two hundred pounds...'

'Christ, how many instruments is he learning?'

'And I've got to give the travel agent three hundred pounds tomorrow.'

'Going anywhere nice?'

'Amsterdam. It's Emma's hen party.'

'Hang about! That's not Emma who lives in Hornchurch?'

'Yeah, why?'

'This will be her third marriage and she's only twenty-eight.'

'So what? It's an excuse for a party. Do you know what, Dad, you're so out of touch with the real world.'

Next knock on the door was my son Rob.

'Dad, I don't know how to tell you this.'

'How much do you want?'

'No, it's not money.'

'That's a relief.'

'It's like this. I think ... I think ... I'm gay, Dad.'

'Have you told Zoe the good news then, and some of the finer details, like you won't be sleeping with her any more?'

'What do mean by that?'

'Well, think about it, son, if you're changing sides.'

'I don't understand.'

'You won't be having sex with her any more. And do you really want to stick your todger up some bloke's big hairy arse?'

'That's disgusting! What do you think I am?'

The next day my granddaughter Jade paid me a visit.

'How did the tour go, Grandad?'

She's now setting me up so I have to be on my guard. She could con for Britain.

'It went well, Jade – thanks for asking.'

'What's it like to be famous?'

Just then a mobile phone buzzes.

'Is that your mobile, Jade?'

'You're joking! That sounds like a right old rubbish phone. Nobody in their right mind would own one of those. It's got to be yours.'

She goes over to the table and picks it up in disgust like it's something under your shoe. She plays with it for a few seconds, then says, 'You've got a text.'

'What's that?' I said with a laugh.

'Do you know what, Grandad, you should be in a nursing home. It's a message – do you want me to read it for you?'

'Why send me a message? Everybody knows I can't text and only family and band members have my number.'

'I haven't got time to mess about. I'm off to an X-Factor show with the girls. Do you want me to read it or not?'

'Yeah, why not.'

She quickly reads it to herself, then says, 'Somebody likes you, Grandad.'

'What do you mean?'

'Just listen. "Hi, Nick, it was really nice to see you at Torquay, the CD you gave me is great. I've listened to it loads of times, it brings back all those great times we had together. All the best for the future and take care of yourself. Please don't ring as it could cause a problem, Anita x."'

'I'm gobsmacked! How did she get my number?'

'Take a tip, Grandad – she's smitten. She wants more than your pension. Do you want me to text her back for you?'

'Yes, please. Can you say it was great to hear from you and perhaps she could ring me on my home number, if she wants to?'

Jade's little fingers worked at speed.

'How does this sound, Grandad? "Hi Anita, thanks for the text. It was so nice to see you again. You looked really lovely, I'm glad you liked the CD. Like you, the memories flooded back when I saw you. Perhaps when you have a moment it would be nice to have a chat. Take care. God speed, lots of love, Nick xx."'

'You're going to have to change that, Jade, it's a bit over the top. And where d'you learn all the spiel? And what's all this about God speed?'

'That means good will, to someone who's maybe starting a journey into the unknown.'

'You've lost me, Jade.'

'If she's clever, she'll know exactly what it means.'

'We're going to have to change it.'

The little madam pressed a key and said, 'Too late – it's gone. Right, you know it's my birthday soon, Grandad…'

'Hang about! You've had three birthdays this year already.'

'Remember, Grandad, sooner or later someone will have to push you around in that wheelchair.'

'How much?'

We're all off to see Billy about maybe joining us. There was one reservation – the last time he played with us he was too heavy with the sticks. Hopefully age will have slowed him down a bit. While travelling to Billy's place in Southend I found out that Anita had gone back to the theatre in Torquay and found Rick, who gave her my mobile and home phone numbers. Steve was well annoyed that Jenny hadn't asked for his.

We turned up at a nice little semi just off the seafront. Billy opened the door. He looked well and he'd lost a lot of weight since I last saw him. As we walked into the lounge it was trashed. He could see we were not impressed.

'Don't ask how it got like this.'

Lying down in the corner was a black and white greyhound, looking right sheepish.

'See that horrible mutt over there. My missus got him a few days ago. He's just been retired from racing, and was going to get the chop. So when he comes into the vet's where she works she feels sorry for him and brings him home. About half an hour ago I'm watching the boxing on the TV and the bell rings to finish round one. As you probably know, just before greyhounds go into their traps to race they ring a bell. Well, Ace Flyer over there thinks he's back at the race track and takes off like a bloody bullet. He's belted round the room like a bleedin' maniac, and destroyed the place. I'm waiting for the missus to come home to show her what he's done. Ace Flyer is definitely due for the knackers' yard.'

We roared with laughter and took the piss, as you do. We then filled him in about the band and our need for a new drummer. He was up for it – he had plenty of time on his hands and would love to get back on the road. He'd owned a night club and sold it a year back, so financially he was OK. To keep his hand in he'd been drumming with a few local bands.

His missus appeared to do her own thing, so there wouldn't be any aggravation about him being away from home for a week or so. The next question had to be asked, and Steve, being Steve, delicately said, 'Billy, you're not still knocking shit out of them drums are you?'

'Let me put it like this, Steve. When I played with you, your bass playing was so bad I had to play over it so nobody could hear you.'

We heard Billy play in a pub and he was fine, so he was on board. Big Al got us a place in Elm Park to rehearse, which was just up the road from us, so we were ready to rock 'n' roll. He also set us up with a sound man and two roadies, and hired out a van. The money we were going to earn wasn't a fortune, but it was enough to make it worth our while.

Steve and Rick had settled into their flat nicely. But they knew they had six months to get their act together as Ray wouldn't be funding them after that. He and Liz were now full on and divorce proceedings with his missus and Liz's husband were ongoing. It all sounded a bit messy. I've had my fair share of divorce lawyers trying to screw money out of me, so I know.

Des was feeling much better now and he and Ruth wanted to come along. They were happy to run our merchandising stand at each venue for nothing. Money wasn't a problem as between them they were quite comfortable. All the profits on our stand were ours.

With lots of venues booked we made sure we had plenty of CDs. There was also the DVD of our last tour. Ray organised a photographer to take photos of the band, which now included Billy, so we had plenty of goodies to sell. Des and Ruth had bought themselves a camper van to travel around in. It was an American job and looked a real beast.

Modern Edge was now set to go on tour as a solo act after nearly forty years. We were all looking forward to it, but with some trepidation.

There was some good news and some bad news. Diane was back from America and I met her for a drink. I was hoping we could continue our relationship. Wrong. She'd met this bloke and she was well hooked. So much so that he was coming over to see her in a couple of weeks time. I had to listen to her for two hours telling me how Hank was her dream man. He was everything a woman wanted, good looking, lots of money, twenty years younger than her, and probably got an eighteen-inch dick! So it was home alone for me tonight.

I hadn't heard from Anita and, to be fair, I wasn't expecting her to contact me after Jade's text, which was a bit over the top. I did ask her where she got 'God speed' from.

'Oh,' she said, 'I saw an American film about a soldier going off to war and his girlfriend wished him God speed. Pity he got killed.'

I'm still none the wiser why that precocious little cow used it.

A couple of days later I was having a toasted cheese and onion sarnie when the phone went.

'Hello, Nick, it's Anita. Is it all right to talk?'

After choking on a bit of cheddar I finally got my words out.

'Of course, it's great to hear from you. I'm so pleased you rang.'

A bit hesitantly she asked me where I got 'God speed' from. I told her about Jade and she thought it was very funny. We just talked and talked, enjoying the conversation. I badly wanted to see her again, but did she want to see me? I took the plunge and said we were playing at Exeter soon and would she like to come to see us play again. She didn't say yes, but she didn't say no. It was left that we would speak again before then. The call lasted about an hour and we left on good terms.

We did some rehearsing with Billy before playing. He'd fitted into the band really well.

The first show was at Margate, one of our old stamping grounds in the early days. It's a lot different doing a two-hour set than the 25 minutes we did on the Mod tour that we'd just finished. The hall was nearly full and there was a great atmosphere. We made a few silly mistakes, but on the whole we played well. I must admit I really enjoyed being back with the boys again on a full-time basis.

After the gig Steve and Rick wanted to party. I just wanted a beer with the other guys, so they did their own thing. We were staying overnight at Margate in a B&B as we were playing at Bournemouth the following night. About three in the morning Steve and Rick came back. I was sharing a room with Steve so he made sure he woke me up. He brought some cans in with him so we had a drink. After we'd downed them we were too lazy to go to the bog up the hallway. On top of the dressing table was a pot of artificial flowers. They came out and we relieved ourselves in the pot and put it under the bed.

The band was having breakfast in the conservatory, all except Steve who was having a lay-in. I was just having a nice kipper when there was a splash above us and this yellowish water came cascading down the window. The owner came in and glanced up at the window but couldn't make it out as it was a lovely day and definitely no rain. I knew what'd happened. That lazy bastard Steve had lobbed the contents of the pot out of the bedroom window.

We'd now done about eight venues and so far so good – all was working well on the music front. On the domestic side it was all kicking off. Steve's second wife Karen turned up at Eastbourne and stormed into the dressing room, telling him in no uncertain terms that there was a shortage of cash coming into her household. Steve being Steve waffled and spluttered and tried to lie his way out of it. It didn't work because she'd brought her brother along, who was one big lump. Steve got his wallet out and gave her a few quid. As he was taking the notes out of his wallet the Queen blinked, as she hadn't seen daylight for a long time! Karen seemed to be following him from gig to gig. She also turned up at the venues at Crawley and Croydon. She was now getting a right pain in the arse.

Des was getting ruckings from Ruth as he'd started smoking again. Ray and Liz were being given hard times by their partners as the divorce action progressed.

Billy was also in the dog house! After the greyhound had destroyed his lounge, his missus said it wasn't the poor dog's fault and she was keeping it. Billy had other ideas and the day before he left for a gig he'd left the front door open. It saw its freedom and is probably now on its way back to Romford dog track! Unfortunately for Billy, his missus had had it microchipped. It was found and returned to her later that day. Only Rick and I were spared any aggro from the opposite sex.

Anita had kept in touch while I was touring – nothing heavy, just the odd phone call. She wasn't coming to the Exeter show, which was a shame, but we were going to meet up in Dawlish for a coffee. Her mother still lived in the town, so she was going to visit her as well. We had a few other gigs in the South West, our favourite part of the country to tour.

It doesn't matter where you play, there's always a place where they seem to let them all out just for the night! I was the first idiot to be let out. To give the driver a rest I drove the van from a booking in Swindon to the next venue, a seaside town near Exeter.

I'd been voted by the band and crew as the worst driver for reversing, which I thought was uncalled for until today. I was reversing into a tight gap in the car park at the venue when one of the concrete pillars moved! It's horrible when you hear that scraping noise and you know you've dropped a bollock. The piss-taking by the others was really cruel, so I disappeared outside for a fag. I was having a quiet smoke when this bloke, about my age, came up and kept staring at me.

'That's it,' he said. 'I know who you are now.'

Fame at last, I thought.

'You're that bloke with the big nose … what's his name? It's on the tip of my tongue … that's it … Barry Manilow! You singing here tonight then?'

After I told him to feck off it was time for a sound check.

Tonight it was cabaret style, which meant tables and chairs and a small dance area. These could be fun unless you got a few nutters in. Tomorrow I was seeing Anita, so I should've been in a good mood, but I had a feeling it was going to be hard work tonight.

We were all set up and ready to do our bit. There were about two hundred and fifty coming, which was pretty good. At fifteen pounds a ticket it wasn't a cheap night out.

We were only into the first few bars of our first number when this skinny old geezer, about seventy, got up from his seat. He was wearing a suit that was far too short for him and a flat cap. They'd definitely let him out for the night. He started dancing on his own and, as it happens, he had all the right moves. The trouble was that he was only a few feet away from us and you can lose a bit of concentration. He was floating about all over the place like a bleedin' butterfly. All the punters were eyeballing him and winding him up. He was relentless and wouldn't go away.

This sparked off another oddball to dance. She was in her fifties, and must've been the fattest bird in the South West. She was a whopper. Her tits were enormous and were bouncing up and down as she started dancing with this skinny bloke. She wore a short skirt, which left nothing to the imagination. When she jumped up in the air the lights flickered! What a sight, as the odd couple did the twist to our last number of the first set! When we'd finished the number the crowd cheered them both – bollocks to us, we were just the side show to these two clowns.

In the second set it didn't get any better. The dreaded hen night reared its ugly head again. Most times the girls have a great night and we all have fun. A dozen or so old girls got onto the floor and were dancing a bit of rock 'n' roll. A few blokes got up to dance with them. They looked a bit lairy and had obviously had too much booze. After a while the wives of the blokes took exception to their men getting too close to the women. Within a few minutes there were women trading punches, and the men laughing their heads off. Little and Large were still dancing around the hall, oblivious to it all.

What a night – but it didn't finish there. After all this we needed a bevy or two and went to the local pub. Steve got too friendly with the landlady and her husband got the ache. Another punch-up and we were thrown out of the boozer. I was glad to get to bed that night. I'm far too old for all this aggravation. Little did I know that this was just the start of it.

We used the services in our job a lot, and on our way to Exeter we stopped at one. I was dying for a number two. I dived out the van and rushed into the bog. As I came out of the trap I faced a woman who was washing her hands. She looked at me puzzled like and said, 'Welcome to the ladies toilet.'

What an embarrassment! I felt a right idiot. I wondered why I kept hearing heels clattering on the tiled floor while I was in the trap. I told the boys, who took the right piss out of me. Then big-gob Steve says, 'I'll tell you what, mate, if she complains about a perv in the toilet, they'll be scanning the CCTV looking for you.'

Do you know, he put the fear of God into me. I worried about that for days.

♫ 16 ♫

Randy Mandy

We arrived in Exeter early. Everyone was doing their own thing until the sound check at 4 o'clock. I caught the train to Dawlish to meet Anita. I made an effort to look good, close shave, haircut, fresh pants, the works. I was meeting her in the original coffee bar that we used when we first met in 1965, now an old-fashioned tea shop.

As it was a nice day I sat outside at a table overlooking the sea. Within a couple of minutes Anita turned up. She looked stunning and I'm thinking to myself, why is she seeing me, it doesn't make sense.

She broke the ice and said with a smile, 'Blimey, Nick, that aftershave is a bit heavy.'

'Yeah, not like the Brut I used to splash on, is it?'

'Do you remember sitting here when Big Al, his dog Sampson and Steve went by on that four-wheeler fun bike wearing "Kiss me Quick" hats?'

'I do! All of them were scoffing candy floss, and they were a menace on that bloody bike, running everyone over.'

'It was so funny. We were so young, Nick. Life seemed to be so uncomplicated in those days. There was no pressure on you.'

'Not like today. Sometimes I feel everybody wants a piece of me.'

'Where's the time gone, Nick?'

'Tell me about it. One minute you're seventeen and then, with a blink of an eye, you've got your bus pass.'

'You speak for yourself! I haven't got mine yet,' she said with a laugh.

'You wish!'

'Sometimes I wish I was back in those days when we didn't have a care in the world and enjoyed life to the full,' she said.

'But you've done well for yourself – three kids with good jobs, grandchildren, still married first time round, and still looking terrific.'

'Nick, don't you ever give up with the old Essex chat-up lines?'

We chatted for a couple of hours. She was really interested in the group. She thought that us going back on the road was a real cool thing to do. Time quickly moved on, and Anita was now going to see her Mum, then she was going to give me a lift back to Exeter.

With time on my hands I just wandered around Dawlish. It's a lovely place. I went past the hairdresser's where Anita had worked all those many years ago. It was now a charity shop.

She picked me up in her car and we were off to Exeter. After about five minutes she started laughing. 'Do you know, Nick, you're just the same! Do you remember when we went out in my Austin Mini in the sixties with Steve and Jenny to Weston-super-Mare and I wore a short miniskirt?'

'I don't know what you mean.'

'Every time I changed gears you sneaked a look at my legs to see if my skirt had ridden up.'

Well, I went as red as a beetroot and was completely lost for words. 'Did I? I'm sorry. That's all I seem to say to you.' I changed the subject quickly. 'Steve would've liked to have seen Jenny again.'

'No chance. She's a very happily married lady.'

Why I said it I don't know. I've got a big gob and sometimes I can't keep it shut.

'Aren't you then, Anita?'

'Nick, you're a friend, that's all. I've got a husband who'll do anything for me. I would like to think we're both mature adults, and that we can have a chat without any hidden agendas. Perhaps you should look at yourself, Nick, and consider where it all went wrong in your relationships. Even today, you're still acting like Jack the lad.'

She knew how to hurt someone and I went quiet after that. She could see she'd hit me below the belt and tried to make a joke of it. The problem was that she was right and there wasn't a lot more you could say after that. She dropped me off in Exeter and we said a quick goodbye and that was that.

Exeter and the other nights in the South West went OK, but Ray wasn't himself on this part of this tour. Something was up, and we found out what it was later when we got back to base. He wanted out of the band. Ray and Liz were getting a lot of hassle from their partners and intended to go to France to live. He was gutted, but they had no choice. He was really sorry because he was having so much fun.

It was a blow, but we all understood his reasons. He wanted to leave straight away so they could look for a place to live. We had a two-week break so we could work round it. Rick was the main singer when we first started out, so he would take on that role. We decided we wouldn't look for another band member – we'd just be a four-piece band again.

Ruth offered to pick up all the paperwork for the band from Ray and liaise with Big Al regarding the gigs. She was a girl who could hold her own in any company, so we knew we had a good replacement.

It was quite sad when we said goodbye to Ray. We had a great party to give him and Liz a great send-off. He was still going to fund Steve and Rick's flat till the rental expired, which was quite soon.

Out of the blue the taxman was after me and it was heavy duty. They wanted to know the ins and outs of a duck's arse. I thought it was my ex-missus stirring the pot and made contact with her, but she said not guilty. I believed her as we were still on talking terms. Anyway, the bloke she had married wasn't short of a few bob. I went and saw Solly, my accountant. He was as sharp as a razor. He looked at the letters from the taxman, and my so-called books, and scratched his head.

'My son, plead insanity – that's the only hope. You're either very unlucky or someone has put the bubble in to cause you mischief. They don't normally come after people like you unless you're earning big bucks. I've always made sure that the royalties from your records are declared. The last few years you've only been earning buttons so there's nothing there. The recent tour will be declared as well, of course. I'll write them a letter to find out more, but I would strongly advise you to keep every receipt pertaining to the band until it hopefully blows over.'

We played a local hotel, the first gig without Ray. It didn't feel right, but by the end of the night it all worked out well. Steve met up with a girl we knew from school called Carol. Within a month they were living together. She must've had a calming influence on him because he was not looking for anybody else.

I went out with randy Mandy from time to time. They call it friends with benefits nowadays, I'm told.

Rick was now in a relationship with Josie, who he'd met at a gig. She seemed a nice girl.

Rick said to me one morning, 'Do you fancy breakfast and a bit of shopping?'

As he was paying for breakfast I was up for it. We started off at Sammy's and had a full English. Sammy was working behind the counter and didn't look too happy. Rick wound him up.

'You fired everybody, Sammy?'

'Son, is that meant to be a joke? The only person I'll fire at will be you.'

'Sorry, Sammy, just polite conversation.'

'You was a cheeky little git when you was after my Carol in the sixties, and knowing what you did to her I'd tread very carefully, otherwise it could be an early bath, son.'

After winding Sammy up, it was off for a bit of shopping, which I didn't mind as I needed a few things. Once sorted, I said to Rick, 'What have you come into town for?'

'Just a few odds and sods.'

We kept walking up and down the same row of shops until he stopped, took a deep breath, closed his eyes and dived into this sex shop. Like a mug I followed him. Now I've never ever been into one of those places. What an eye-opener!

I said to him, 'What are we doing in here?'

'Josie wants me to bring a bit more to the party on the sex front, if you know what I mean.'

'Wouldn't it be a lot easier just to take a blue tablet?'

Rick was now hiding in the corner, like I wasn't there, looking at these vibe delights that came in all sizes and colours. Then a young girl of about eighteen came over to us and said, 'Can I help you, gentlemen?'

I've never ever been so embarrassed in my life. I said quickly, 'Him, luv, don't look at me.'

Rick is now looking at the floor and has gone purple. This sales assistant has been well trained and gently coaxes Rick into telling her what he is looking for, so much so that she's now demonstrating the virtues of each one of these quivering toys.

He has now decided which one he wants. It looks a mean beast and I wouldn't like that poked up my arse. He's now full of confidence and decides to investigate what else the shop sells. He buys one or two more gadgets and goes to the counter. Then he rushes back to the stand and brings back an enormous demo dongler.

'One of these as well, please.'

He's got this thing in his hand and he's waving it about like Herbert's baton on the Mod tour. There is now a queue of women looking at him and giggling. I did notice that there weren't any other blokes in there – I wonder why? The shop assistant is bagging them up and she says to Rick as she goes under the counter, 'How many batteries do you want, sir?'

That is too much for me and I walk out of the shop. Then my worst nightmare – my daughter-in-law Zoe walks in. She looks at me in astonishment, then laughs and says, 'Have you got a new girlfriend, Dad?'

The embarrassment didn't stop there. Rick is carrying his bag full of goodies. It must be a telltale sign that this bag has come from a sex shop as a few people are giving us the look and the grin.

It seemed a long time ago that Modern Edge would party and do most things you shouldn't. It had all changed now. We'd do the gigs, act normal and go home to our partners, except me. Sooner or later you have to grow up and this was the time to be sensible. It all sounds wonderful, doesn't it? How long will it last? Not long, I hope!

It was the day of my sixty-fifth birthday and the family were really pushing the boat out for me. Tonight they were taking me out for a meal at a Harvester! The presents consisted of a ten-pound W. H. Smith's book token, a book about grumpy old men and a CD from the seventies that I know cost a fiver, because two of our numbers were on it.

Little Jade turned up with a card and present, and said, 'Here you are, Grandad. Don't say I don't think about you.'

I undid the package. I couldn't believe my eyes. It was a 45rpm vinyl of Modern Edge's *Suburban Mod*. I'd lost mine many years ago, and was always looking out for a copy.

'See, Grandad, I do think about you. I heard you talking to Steve about trying to find a copy.'

'How did you find it?'

'I just kept trawling the net until I saw it. Dad paid for it on his credit card, and I pay him back out of my pocket money each week until it's all paid for. I do feel a bit guilty, though.'

'Why's that?'

'Well, some of the pocket money I've had from you this year went on buying the record. It wasn't cheap.'

Knowing Jade, I thought there'd be a catch. It appears there wasn't.

She kissed me and gave me a cuddle and said, 'It's great to have a famous Grandad. I love you. See you tonight.'

As the door closed I thought that this was one of the kindest thoughts that had ever come from a member of my family. I was still gobsmacked when the phone rang. I knew that voice. It was Anita. I hadn't heard from her since we met at Dawlish.

'Hi, Nick – happy birthday.'

'That's nice of you. I didn't think I would hear from you again.'

'Look, Nick, I'm really sorry – I was a bit cutting in the car. I was a real cow. I'm truly sorry. Hope you forgive me.'

'Of course. You were right, anyway. How are you?'

'Yeah, good. How's life with you on your sixty-fifth?'

'How did you remember it?'

'I don't know, Nick, I just did.'

We had a chat for a few minutes, then she said,'I'm down your way in a couple of weeks time for the National Women's Golf Convention. As the secretary of the club I have to attend. Is Upminster near you?'

'Yeah, just up the road.'

'Perhaps we can have dinner, Nick.'

'Yeah, I'd like that.'

I checked the diary and we didn't have a show that night. She was going to ring me a few days before she came down.

Then another phone call came from Mick, Tracy's husband. He'd phoned me up to wish me a happy birthday. He was travelling back in a motor with another CID colleague and two prisoners they'd picked up from Liverpool. I could hear the two scousers singing 'Happy Birthday' to me – in the end all four of them were singing. I thought that was well funny. This was turning into a great birthday until Des knocked on the door.

'You've been summoned.'

'By who?'

'Sammy. He wants to see you, now.'

'Oh, leave it out, Des. It's my birthday today, and by the way where's my card? Look, he'll have to wait.'

'Nick, we're talking about Sammy. He plays with sawn-offs. Remember Rick and his daughter?'

'What's he want?'

'Don't ask me. I'm just the bookie's runner.'

As we entered the cafe Sammy was sitting around a table holding court with four of his cronies.

'Nice of you to come over and see me, Nick.' Then he shouts out to his missus,'Get the boys a cup of tea, Eve. By the way, Des, I hear you've been a bit poorly. All right now, I hope.'

'Yeah, on the mend now, thanks, Sammy.'

'What can I do for you Sammy? It's my birthday today and I'm going out with the family so I haven't got much time to talk to you.' For a minute I forgot who I was talking to and backtracked a bit.

'How can I help you?'

'You've just said the very word – birthday. In a month's time it's my eightieth and I want your band to provide the entertainment.'

Again I forgot who I was talking to.'We charge two grand a night.'

At that moment Sammy was having a mouthful of tea. He choked and it went everywhere. Des went white and looked at me as if to say, not a good move.

After Sammy composed himself he said, 'Do you know what, son, for a minute I thought you said two feckin' grand. Tell me I'm wrong.'

I gulped. 'Only my little joke, Sammy. The only problem is we've a lot of gigs already booked, and we might not to be able to fit you in.'

'That's not a problem, son. If you've already got a booking on my birthday, you just cancel it. Do I make myself crystal?'

The tone of Sammy's voice was telling me that he meant business. He was not to be messed about with.

'Yeah, of course, Sammy, we'll be glad to do it for you.'

'That's more like it. Of course, it's a freeman's, innit?'

'Of course, it will be our pleasure to play, no problem.'

'Good boy. Now sling your hook. I've got a catering company coming to see me about sorting out the food for the party.'

Fortunately we didn't have a booking that day. When I told the boys that we'd got to play a free one, they all said bollocks until I told them who it was for.

Big Al had spread the gigs around nicely. We were averaging about three a week, which was just about right. In between playing, Rick was giving keyboard lessons at a nearby school, which brought him in a few bob, and Steve had somehow wrangled some session work, so he was sorted. Billy was well-heeled, so playing in the band was a bit of pin money for him.

The royalties for Steve and me from the sales of the songs we'd written were coming in regularly. After all the recent publicity about the band, sales had certainly increased. I could really enjoy playing now without too many financial pressures, which was a great feeling.

How wrong can you be? Solly had been in touch with the taxman and they were looking to collect a fair chunk of money from me. I've never earned big money so I didn't know where they were coming from. This was a worry and I didn't like it hanging over my head.

Des had now got us our own minibus to travel around in. He kept it round his place. Every time we entered the van there was a smell of fish and chips. I thought to myself, Ruth and Des certainly liked their fish and chips. We were off to Grantham to play, but the thought of smelling this horrible stench all the way there was going to get us down.

Steve shouted out to Des, who was driving, 'Can I suggest, Des, you don't have fish and chips the night before we go to a gig? The smell is doing us as all up.'

Des started laughing. 'I forgot to tell you, I've saved us loads of money on diesel.'

'What're you on about?' I said.

'Well, a mate of mine has got a sideline. He converts all the used vegetable oil from his fish and chip shop to sell as fuel.'

'You've lost me,' I said.

'The vehicle is now running on Eddie's fish and chip special.'

'You're jesting!' said Rick.

'Check it out on the internet – they're all at it.'

'Now we know why we've always got seagull's crap on the van,' said Ray.

Tonight I was seeing Anita, but I nearly never met her. We had a booking in Wales, and on the way back we nearly had a major accident. We'd done two gigs in Cardiff and were on our way back down the M4. Thank goodness Des was driving – he was the best driver out of all of us. It was early morning when suddenly a piece of metal from the back of a lorry hit our windscreen.

How Des controlled the minibus I don't know. For a few seconds I thought it was curtains. My life flashed by in front of me – it's a horrible feeling.

He pulled us over onto the hard shoulder and we got out of the vehicle. We were all shaking and thankful to him for saving our lives. If it hadn't been for his bit of smart driving I wouldn't like to think of the consequences. The windscreen was shattered and we had to call out for a replacement. The police turned up and they were great. They said we were well lucky as they'd been out to incidents like this before and others hadn't been so fortunate. After the windscreen was replaced we continued on our way back home. We all went very quiet at the thought of what could've happened.

We knew we'd had a lucky escape, and it's times like that that you reflect on your life. Back in 1964 I lost three of my best friends – Rod and Carol, who where brother and sister, and Jimmy were in a similar accident. I still lay flowers on their graves.

I was meeting Anita at a hotel in Upminster and I thought I'd take on board what she'd said about me acting like Jack the lad. I put on a smart suit with a shirt and tie, and the shoes were shining. Des was taking me down there so I could have a beer.

As I was coming out of my flat I had a funny feeling that somebody was watching me. A motor was parked across the road, and I was sure the geezer was eyeballing me. Anyway, Des picked me up and took me to the hotel. Again I thought I saw this guy pass Des's car in his 4x4, but thought no more of it.

I met Anita in the bar. She looked really nice. She kissed me on the cheek and said, 'Hi, Nick, great to see you again.'

'It's good to see you. Had a good meeting today?'

'It was a bit boring but had to be done.' Then she laughed and said, 'Like the suit and tie, Nick. This must be the first time I've seen you in one of those.'

'And it will be the last, don't worry about that.'

We had a drink in the bar then sat down for dinner in the restaurant. While we were waiting for the first course Anita took an envelope out of her bag.

'I haven't told you. Mum died.'

'I'm really sorry to hear that.'

'Thanks. She'd been suffering for some time so it was a relief in a way.'

'But it's still not nice when you lose your Mum.'

'While I was clearing Mum's house out I found these old photos of your band and a couple of me and you.'

She handed them over to me and I had a good look at them. 'We look so young and fresh in 1965.'

She started laughing and said, 'You were fresh, too fresh – you lot were on a crusade when it came to girls. No girl was safe with you lot around.'

I looked at the last photo, which was of Anita and me taken on a beach in Devon when we were about eighteen. I had my arm around her and we looked really happy together. I looked at her across the table and put my hand on hers. 'I wish we could go back to them days now.'

'So do I sometimes, Nick.'

It was the first time I'd seen her drop her guard. She realised what she'd said, and quickly took her hand away from mine. I got the impression, as the evening wore on, that her husband was old before his time and the spark in their marriage was missing.

She spoke about her kids with real pride. When it was my turn to go through my lot it was embarrassing. I always seem to talk to other people whose kids are wonderful.

After dinner we sat in the lounge drinking coffee. From the corner of my eye I just couldn't believe who was coming towards me on a mission. I tried to get up quickly and go to the bar, but she was on to me like a bloodsucker. It was Mandy, dressed like a tart and well pissed. It was my worst nightmare. Anita was absolutely dumbfounded and looked at her in disbelief as Mandy spluttered out her words.

'Nick, you haven't rung me lately. I've been missing your body.'

I couldn't say anything I just froze with embarrassment as this man-eater started to feck everything up.

She added, 'Is this my replacement? She looks a bit stuck up to me. You never wear a suit for me. Ain't I good enough?'

She wouldn't stop talking and I wished the ground would open up and swallow me, then she blabbed out, 'Anyway I'm with my sugar daddy tonight – he knows how to show a girl a good time.'

This eighty-year-old bloke stumbled out of the toilet, his zip undone, saw Mandy and came over. He was having difficulty walking and he'd clearly had too many.

'Come on, girl, time to get you home to bed.'

He slapped her bum and she said, 'Hang on, Arnold, you ain't paid me yet.'

Surely it couldn't get any worse, but it did when she said to me, 'You get it for nothing, Nick. You don't charge mates.'

As Mandy staggered away, falling over and showing her knickers, I looked at Anita.

'Look...'

'Nick, don't say a word. Incriminating evidence comes to mind. I can see she's a homely girl and she certainly likes you...'

'Please, Anita, she's...'

'I'd keep quiet and put it all down as a bad day at the office if I were you.'

She looked at me but I couldn't face her. Then we both burst out laughing and couldn't stop. Thankfully she'd seen the funny side of it and it wouldn't be mentioned again. It was time to go. I called a taxi and we stood outside together waiting for it. I could see it driving up to the hotel entrance and quickly said, 'Please keep in touch, Anita.'

'Of course, Nick. It's been great seeing you tonight and I've really enjoyed the cabaret!'

I took a gamble and pulled her towards me and gave her a cuddle, which she didn't object to. I kissed her lightly on the lips and left it as that. We looked at each other, and as I got into the taxi I clumsily said, 'I still love you, Anita.'

The taxi was away, and I was wishing that bloody Mandy would disappear off the face of the earth. Probably the last time I'll hear from Anita now, I thought.

♫ 17 ♫

The Godfather

Tomorrow we were doing Sammy's party, who we now nicknamed 'The Godfather'. He'd been in touch and given us a list of some of the numbers he wanted us to play, half of which we'd never even heard of. It was a worry that we wouldn't be able to play what he wanted.

We were also a little bit concerned about Des. He was overdoing it with the band and wanted to be involved in everything we did. It was great having him on board but his health had to come first.

Sammy's party was being held in a large expensive hotel in the Essex countryside, and we were playing in the ballroom. Fortunately there was an entrance at the back of the room so we could hump the gear in.

Sammy's son, Ben, was in charge and was barking out orders to everyone. We only took notice of him because he was a brute, over six foot, eighteen stone of muscle, earrings and tattoos. Des handled him for us as he knew him well. Mind you, he made his presence felt early on by saying with a growl, 'You might think you're the stars, but there's only one star tonight, and that's my Dad. You'd better be on top form or you'll have me to answer to.'

He walked over to Rick, who was now shitting himself. He looked at him eyeball to eyeball, and spat out, 'As for you, my son, if you sniff around my sister Carol tonight your band will be playing at your funeral next week, know where I'm coming from?'

Shaking with fear, Rick replied, 'Yeah, of course, Ben, it won't happen.'

'Good. Now you lot tune up or do whatever you need do, and be ready to play when I give you the word.'

As he disappeared to give some grief to the catering people, I thought to myself, what a great motivational talk just before you start playing. I've played in arenas to thousands of people but tonight I'm bricking it in front of a couple of hundred.

Steve warned Rick, 'Don't go near or talk to that Carol tonight.'

'Leave it out, Steve – it was over forty years ago when I was having a nibble with her.'

'Good. If you feel the urge, have a nibble on a sausage roll instead, eh?'

We'd done a sound check and had an hour to spare, so we sat down and had a beer, watching the other gangsters and their molls arriving. It was like a scene from *The Godfather*. Everybody was wearing dress suits. Des was giving us a running commentary on who was who. I've never seen so many bent noses, bald heads, no-necks and bling in one room.

Then I couldn't believe my eyes. I'd recognise that crombie anywhere. It was only Eddie Tucker, my first boss. He had a car lot down Seven Kings High Road, a real tuck-up merchant.

I remember one punter asking him, 'What's the guarantee on this Ford Zodiac, Mr Tucker?'

He replied, 'Guaranteed to get you off the pavement, mate.'

I went over to see him. He was now in his eighties, and a bit stooped. He was wearing his trademark dark glasses and still looked a smart man. He was on his own and I said laughingly, 'I bought a motor off you – poxy thing broke down after a day.'

He looked at me, trying to suss out who I was. Then the penny dropped.

'It's young Nick! How you doing, son?'

'Yeah, fine thanks, Eddie.'

'What're you doing here?'

'I'm playing in the band tonight.'

'You'd better play well for Sammy or one of his sons will be playing a tune on you.'

We had a nice chat and I found out that he was living in a flat not far from me. One of his sons was selling the motors, and he was now a sleeping partner in the business. I made a mental note of where his car lot was. I didn't want to buy a motor from there.

We were now back on gangster watch with the boys when Des said, 'Hey, see the geezer with the black suit who's just come in? He did more pavement jobs in the seventies and eighties than Wimpey. He's a legend – no security van was safe while him and his gang were active.'

A pavement job was a security van robbery committed when the money was being transferred to or from a bank, the guard having to cross the pavement to enter the building.

A few soap celebs came in and some well-known footballers. Des reckoned that people could rest easy in their beds tonight as most of the villains were here.

Another familiar face appeared at the door. Ronnie 'Iron' Dicks was a bloke about our age. We knew him well – he was a right wheeler and dealer. The stories about him are endless. He'd got the nickname 'Iron' because one day he was having his once-a-week bath, and when he got out he shouted out to his Mum to iron a shirt for him. She was already ironing one for him at the top of the stairs when there was a knock on the door. She went downstairs to open it, leaving the iron unattended. Ronnie called out again, and his younger brother thought he wanted the iron. Ronnie bent over to pull the plug out of the bath just as his brother walked in holding the iron, and branded his arse.

There was another time when he told us that his mate worked in a stockbrokers. He had red-hot info that a share was going to make a lot of quick money and they were cheap to buy at that moment. So all the boys raided their Post Office accounts and Steve's Dad bought the shares for us. The first week they went up, then dived and finally crashed. It took weeks to find Ronnie, and the question had to be asked: 'Ronnie, what's your mate's job in this stockbrokers?'

'Well he doesn't actually work for them as such. He's an electrician, and while he was replacing some sockets in their office he heard the rumour going around about these shares.'

We were ten minutes from starting when Sammy entered the ballroom wearing a white suit. Everybody stopped talking, stood up and clapped him. He was like royalty and loving every minute of it as he bowed to his public.

Ben came over, growled at us and said, 'Play "Happy Birthday" now, and make it good.'

We did as we were told and continued playing for another forty-five minutes. It was now nosh time, and it was a banquet fit for a king. He'd certainly pushed the boat out. Whether he'd paid for it was another thing. We were sitting by our gear having our grub when Carol walked over and started talking to Rick.

'Hi, Rick, long time no see.'

'Yeah, you're looking really good, Carol.'

'You're not bad yourself.'

This is what we didn't want to hear, with big bad Ben on the plot. Carol was looking quite tasty, as it happens. Rick couldn't help himself and was oblivious to Ben's threats. They went outside for a breath of fresh air.

Ronnie came over to us. As soon as he saw me he started snorting and grunting – only I knew why he was doing this. When I think about it now, we must've been mad in the sixties.

Ronnie knew this dodgy butcher, who would supply him with

meat that wasn't exactly kosher. One night unbeknown to me I went pig-rustling. We drove to a place in Rainham. Ronnie disappeared for a moment, then I heard an animal squeal. He called me over and said he wanted a hand. Under a blanket was a dead pig with its throat cut. He wanted me to lift it into his Ford Anglia, and like an idiot I did as I was told. The bad news was that it was too big to go into the boot, so we put it on the back seat with a blanket covering it. We then moved off at speed. A mile later Ronnie came to a sudden halt by a bus stop where two girls were standing.

'Want a lift, girls?'

They didn't need to be asked twice. Because it was so heavy, the pig had gone right down on the springs of the seat. The girls, who fortunately were quite small, sat on the back seat on the blanket covering Mr Porky. Ronnie pulled up sharp at a zebra crossing, the blanket came adrift and the pig's head was now on show, with blood oozing from its mouth and its tongue hanging out. I've never ever forgotten the words uttered by those girls as one said to the other, 'What the feck's that?'

With a loud scream the other yelled, 'We're only sitting on a feckin' dead pig.'

Today Ronnie was wearing a suit with one of those long jackets. He looked like a teddy boy from the fifties.

'Nick, my son, I see they've dug you up again and put you back on stage. You're brave doing this one. You know Sammy plays with sawn-offs?'

'Ronnie, how'd you get an invite here – and by the way, we want a refund on that bleedin' Kraut satnav you tucked Des up with?'

The satnav complaint went straight over his head. He said, 'I'm family. I'm married to June, Sammy's eldest daughter.'

'How'd you worm your way in there then?'

'I was doing time with Ben in the big house. When I came out I visited Ben, met June and the rest is history.'

Just then Steve and Carol came back into the room laughing like a couple of school kids.

'He's got to be out of his mind,' said Ronnie. 'Ben still treats Carol like his baby sister, and he doesn't like Rick, that's for sure.'

Out of nowhere Ben appears and, seeing Rick with Carol, he says with more venom than a rattlesnake, 'What did I say about him?'

Carol turns on Ben like only an Essex girl can and gives him both barrels.

'You can keep your gob shut, Ben. My so-called husband left me three months ago for his twenty-five-year-old boob-job secretary. If you think I'm sitting at home like the good little woman waiting for him, you've got another think coming. I'd look in your own back yard if I was you, Ben.'

'What're you on about, girl?'

'You know your Kathy's got the hots for that Joey. Just look over there. He's all over her like a rash.'

Ben was on his toes straight away to give someone else grief.

They must've liked our music as everybody was dancing and obviously enjoying themselves. Then there were a couple of presentations to Sammy. It was just about to start when we heard loud music and laughter coming from another room. Sammy just looked at a few of the chaps, and they disappeared next door. The music suddenly screeched to a halt and the disco unit appeared to suffer a malfunction going through a window. There was no more laughter or noise coming from next door as the chaps come back into the room.

Sammy actually thanked us for the night while we were packing the gear away. He gave us a monkey and said to have a drink on him. A good night all round.

♫ 18 ♫

Rampant rabbits

There was a bit of order in the band's love life now – sooner or later it's time to grow up. Steve and Rick were still with their partners and Des and Ruth were having fun together. We still kept in touch with Ray – maybe at a later date he might rejoin the band. He seemed well happy with Liz. They had rented an apartment in the South of France and were enjoying the sun.

We had a good few gigs booked and everything was working out well. The only problem was me. I had no special lady in my life except Jade, who, for whatever reason, was getting closer to her Grandad. I was hoping it wasn't a financial reason.

A couple of days after Sammy's birthday bash I got an urgent phone call from Big Al. A well-known band from our era that Al looked after had got a problem. The lead guitarist's Dad had died, and of course he had to organise his funeral.

They were booked for a big show in Plymouth and didn't want to cancel it. Would I fill in for him? I knew most of the numbers that the band played, so I said of course I'd help out. I had to be in Plymouth early the next morning so I could rehearse with the band.

I thought, hang about, Anita doesn't live a million miles away. Perhaps I could see her. It was always agreed that I would never phone her – she'd always get in touch with me. Texting was out of the question, as I always messed it up, so I thought I would give her a bell. Wrong move. When she answered it she went ballistic.

'Don't you ever do that again!'

The phone went dead and that was that.

That night my neighbour in the flat above, a guy in his mid-twenties, knocked on my door. Michael was very shy and wouldn't say boo to a goose. He wore these National Health glasses that we used to wear when we were younger. He said very quietly, 'Do you fancy a drink, Mr Sheldon?'

As I had a night off I said, 'Why not? And the name's Nick.'

So we shot into Ziggies for a swift half, and it was only a swift half.

As soon as he'd finished his drink he went into the bog. Then we were off to the next pub, the Royal Oak, which was only a few hundred yards away. Same procedure, half pint, a leak and off to the next pub. I was dizzy with it all. He was paying, so why should I complain? We got to the fourth pub and he went into the bog for his usual pee. Then I heard a banging noise and him shouting out, 'Poxy machines – not one of them works in any of these places.'

I rushed into the bog to find him banging the shit out of a French letter machine.

I said to him, 'What're you doing, Michael?'

'All I want is a condom. Can I get one? No I bloody can't.'

I'd never heard him swear before. I said, 'What are you on about?'

'My girlfriend Nancy is at home waiting for me to perform, but she'll only do it if I'm wearing something. I've never had sex before and I'm desperate.'

The poor git was too embarrassed to go to a shop and buy some. I took him straight round to Mr Patel's newsagent, which is about a hundred yards from our flats, and bought him a couple of packs. It must've worked, as I heard a fair bit of banging coming from above all night.

I arrived in Plymouth in good time and met up with the lads from the band. They were top boys and could they play. They still used Vox 30 amps and were the ultimate pros. We had a good morning session and I felt comfortable about playing with them tonight. We were having a short break when the mobile went off. It was Anita.

'Hi, Nick, sorry I couldn't speak to you yesterday. Simon was in the next room so it was difficult.'

To be honest, even though I thought the world of her, I'd had enough of the cat-and-mouse relationship and said, 'I do understand. Look, you're a happily married lady and I'm making it awkward for you, so let's call it a day.'

It all went quiet at the other end of the phone, then she said, 'But Nick, I don't want to. I still want to speak and see you when I can.'

'Look, Anita, so do I, but unfortunately it's not going to happen, is it?'

'Why did you ring me, Nick?'

'I'm playing a one-nighter in Plymouth tonight and while I was down this neck of the woods I thought maybe we could meet up.'

'I would really love to, Nick. Look, can we meet at the same cafe in Dawlish, say about eleven tomorrow?'

The Plymouth venue was fantastic. It was a great night and I don't think I let anybody down.

The next morning I made my way to Dawlish to meet Anita. On arriving at the cafe I found that she was already there. It was obvious that she was pleased to see me. We skipped coffee and had a walk along the beach. How it happened I don't know, but we held hands and at that moment we became very close. It started to rain so we went back to the cafe. We had our coffee and just looked at each other until Anita said with a grin, 'How's Mandy?'

'Please don't go there...'

'Only teasing you, Nick.'

After a few minutes of chatting, she said, 'What're we doing, Nick?'

'It just feels right to be with you, Anita. When things happen like this it's normally a sexual thing. After a month or two the novelty wears off...'

'Do you do this all the time then?'

'Of course not. What I'm trying to say is of course you are sexually attractive, but this is so much more. As I've already said, if only I could turn the clock back, I should've held onto you and not been such a prat. You really were the only one for me.'

'At that time in your life you wouldn't have been true to anyone, Nick.' Then she laughed and said, 'As I've said before, you and that band of yours used to chase more girls in a month than most guys would do in a lifetime. Do you remember what the girls used to call you lot in my salon? Rampant rabbits, because you were always burrowing for holes.'

'I remember it well. I couldn't believe you said it then and I can't believe you've said it again now.'

'Nor can I.'

We just looked at each other and laughed.

'You know how I feel about you. Is there something not quite right at home?'

'You could say that. I stopped loving him about ten years ago...'

'And for him, does he feel the same?'

'Simon's oblivious to it all. He still thinks we've got a loving relationship, and everything is fine.'

'What about your kids with all of this?'

'They've got no inkling anything is wrong, and it would break their hearts if they knew how I felt.'

'Have you broached the subject with Simon?'

'No, he wouldn't listen. It would just go over his head. He can get quite aggressive and nasty, so I've said nothing.'

'He doesn't hit you?'

She went very quiet and a tear dropped down onto her cheek. 'He has in the past.'

'How'd you cope with all that?'

'It can be difficult so I just try to keep the peace and not upset him.'

'That's not on. Why haven't you left him?'

'It's not that easy, Nick. Can we just leave it for now, please?'

'I don't like hearing all this, Anita – it's not on. How can anybody want to hurt you?'

'I'm going to have to go, Nick.'

She went outside while I paid the bill, then I joined her. She was crying, and after wiping away the tears she said, 'It was lovely to see you again, Nick.'

'We can't just leave it like this.'

'Look, I'm going to have to go. I'll ring you in a couple of days.'

'You promise?'

'Yeah, promise.'

She gave me a peck on the cheek and quickly left. She looked back before she turned the corner and gave me a wave.

I was totally gutted to hear her story, that her coward of a husband had used violence against her.

As I made my way to the car park I thought I saw that bloke again, the one in the motor that was outside my house a while back. I must be seeing things. What a changing world we live in! I can never recall any bloke hitting a woman when I was younger, and now two ladies I'm fond of have both suffered violence from their partners.

What was hard to understand is that both of their partners came from different sides of the fence. I suppose violence has no class barriers. I still couldn't get my head around it as I made my way home. I felt full of sadness for her. Little did I know there'd be bucket-loads more to come…

♫ 19 ♫

A shock

On arriving back home I found out that Steve and Rick had both got major issues with their partners. Probably something to do with the other ladies! They were now back renting a flat together, so time to grow up didn't work for them. I knew it wouldn't – Steve and Rick can never say no. They still think they're teenagers.

Anita didn't ring, which was a shame, as I really wanted to speak to her, but I did get an urgent phone call from Diane. Her American hunk had gone back to the States and did I fancy a drink with her? We met up at Ziggies. There is me thinking I'm back in the frame when she tells me she's off again to America to see him, and she'll be gone for a few weeks. I thought, what has this got to do with me? Then she says, looking worried, 'I need to warn you, Nick. Neil is back around here and he could be looking for you. He blames you for his beating and having to disappear for a while.'

When I got home Des was on the doorstep and said he needed to talk to me urgently. I poured us both a nightcap.

Des looked pale and gaunt as he said, 'That head-case Neil is back on the manor and there could be trouble for you.'

I explained about my chat with Diane, who'd also warned me. 'I'm grateful, Des – I'll have to keep an eye out for him.'

'You do that. If you need any help, mate, just let me know and I'll be there for you.'

'I appreciate that. Are you coming up to the Midlands with us for the three gigs?'

'Nick, I'd love to, but I've got to have some treatment over the next couple of days, but we'll come on the next gigs down in Sussex.'

I told him about Anita, who of course he knew well. He was upset, like me, especially about her husband being handy with his fists. We finished our brandy and I was just about to say goodnight when he said quite emotionally, 'You know I love you like a brother.'

He gave me a quick hug and he was on his way. I thought he'd had too much brandy and thought nothing more of it.

I went to bed thinking about Anita. I was really upset about her. On top of that I'd got this maniac on the loose, who wants to tear lumps out of me. I wonder if that bloke who was outside my house had anything to do with this Neil. What a night's sleep! It didn't help that I had to have four pit stops through the night.

We were playing two nights in Birmingham and the third on the way back was in Northampton. For whatever reason Steve and Rick were now best mates, where, once upon a time, Steve and I were inseparable. I had no problem with that. Perhaps I'd slowed down and they'd gone up a gear.

Billy had one vice, which we knew about – he did like a bet. Wherever we were he was always in the betting office or on the phone to the bookies. Later he would come unstuck and owe money to the wrong people.

The first venue was at an arts centre. It was like playing in your front room. It had a small dance floor and some steps leading up to about fifty seats. What an atmosphere, and what a night! It was like being back in the old days when we did a lot of venues like that. We couldn't have made much money but we did have some fun.

The next gig was an all-seat job in a big theatre and it was full, so Big Al had got his maths right with this one. They were nearly all our age and they really gave us a warm welcome when we hit the stage.

The next night it was hard work getting any response from the punters. There was no reason why, it sometimes happens, and you just have to get on with it. In the end we did win them over and everyone went home happy.

We left that night for the journey home in our minibus with Joe, our sound engineer, driving. I was nodding off after a gut full of kebab when my mobile went off. Half asleep, I answered it.

'Who wants me at this bleedin' time of the morning?'

I listened to the person at the other end of the phone intently.

'No, no, I don't believe it, Ruth. I'm so sorry. We'll be home in a couple of hours. I'll be round straight away.'

I was totally stunned, really upset, and started crying.

'What's wrong, Nick?' said Steve.

Sobbing I said, 'Des is dead. He died a couple of hours ago.'

'Not our Des? I can't believe it! What happened?' said Rick.

'Ruth said he wasn't feeling very well and went to bed. She went to wake him up but he was dead.'

'Des is one of us! We've known him all our life. I can't believe we won't see him again,' said Steve.

No more was said until we reached home. No one wanted to talk any more, everybody was too upset. The boys agreed that just I would go and see Ruth.

We just held onto each other and cried.

'I think he knew he didn't have long,' said a tearful Ruth. 'He just kept telling me he loved me. He said that this was the first time in his life that he had found true happiness with a woman.'

'I know he thought the world of you.'

We talked a little more and I said I'd come back in a few hours and help her with the arrangements.

I'd known Des sixty years. Steve and I lived down the same street as him and went to school with him. His early life wasn't easy. His Mum died when he was about six and his Dad was in and out of prison. He lived with his Aunty May when he was young, and tragically she died when he was seventeen in an accident at the top of our street.

Kids can be cruel and his nickname at junior school was 'Orphan'. He'd worked for our band as a roadie, driver and Mr Fix-it. He could repair anything and many a time he'd sorted our amps out when we'd had a problem at a gig.

When we disbanded he went back to working with his Dad, repairing and selling motors underneath the arches at Romford Station. From about 1980 I saw or spoke to him nearly every day except when I was touring. He would do anything for you.

He was a top mate and I couldn't believe I'd never see him again. I'd always remember him giving me that hug a few days earlier and telling me I was like a brother to him.

The night before Des's funeral all the boys came round to my place. We were going to have a Des night. There were so many stories about his exploits that we were going to recall some of them and celebrate his life. He would've loved to have known that we were doing this. Perhaps he was looking down on us right then.

All the band were there, including Ray, who'd come over from France. Terry Sherman and Ronnie came over and so did Alec, who was once king of the Essex Mods. Big Al was there and Roger, who was a mate back in our coffee bar days at La Nero in Hornchurch.

We had Jade to thank for tracking down Alec and Roger, using one of the social network sites. The fags were lit and the beer was flowing as we remembered Des. I recalled when he was cleaning his Ford Zodiac outside his house. On the outside it looked a nice motor but it was a real rust bucket. I suggested that he take it down to the scrappy.

'Bollocks,' he said. 'It's a nice motor, just needs a right good shine because I'm taking my new bird out in it later.'

Next day when I saw Des he had a broken arm, cuts and bruises and was walking with a limp, and there was no motor outside his house.

'What's happened, my son?' I said.

'What happened? I'll tell you what feckin' happened! I've got my new bird in the motor when this Morris Minor pulls out in front of me. I swerved and hit a Ford Anglia. It was unreal after that. After I had hit the Anglia the motor splits in half. I see my bird in one half of the motor – she sails past me and hits a Mini. My half of the motor goes along for another few yards with me in it, then veers off and hits a lamp post. My bird's in traction in hospital and the motor's a write-off.'

Well, we all roared with laughter. His motor was a cut-and-shut, with no tax or insurance.

Steve reminded us when Des used to cultivate cannabis plants in his greenhouse. For a laugh he entered some in a local gardening competition as a new vegetable that was all the rage. He won first prize and told everybody that they were nice and tasty. He even got them to pull a leaf off a plant and have a chew!

The stories kept coming. The MOT one was a classic – Sammy had brought it up when we were in his cafe a while back.

Des had bought us a fogger and wind machine off a scrappy in Bolton. We played a working men's club there and what a laugh that was. The club chairman wanted his son to sing three numbers. We didn't want him to, so Tony and Des hatched a plot to make sure he didn't. Des put the fogger on. The guy was just about to sing when the mist from the fogger engulfed him, and he couldn't see anything. Then Des activated the wind machine, which was an industrial job – it was like the feckin' launch of an Apollo rocket! What a noise! The bloke shit himself and shook all the way back to the bar. He didn't sing that night.

There was a load more stories but it was getting late and we had the funeral in the morning.

Des had already planned his funeral, knowing he had advanced cancer. In fact, he didn't die of that – his heart just gave up and he died in his sleep. It was a sixties-themed funeral. A Ford Zodiac estate carried Des's coffin, while the mourners rode in Cortinas, Minis, Anglias, Consuls and an Austin A40. Big Al was riding a big Norton in his Rocker gear while Alec, wearing his parka, rode his Vespa, complete with loads of mirrors and lights. The band had flowers made up of the Mod target sign, which was placed on top of the coffin. There were about two hundred people there including Sammy, plus loads of local faces that had turned up to pay their respects. I gave the eulogy – how I kept it together, I don't know. This was the most nerve-racking ordeal that I'd ever been through. As his coffin disappeared out of sight and the curtains closed, all the band members had tears in their eyes.

Outside I held Ruth's hand as we looked at all the flowers laid out in the gardens of the crematorium.

Des was the original loveable rogue who would do anything for his mates. He was loyal and if you were in a tight corner he'd be first up to help you. I was going to miss him big time. Rest in peace, Des.

A couple of weeks after Des's passing, Mick, Tracy's husband, turned up. He looked more like a villain than a policeman. After a cup of tea he said, 'That guy Neil could be on your case.'

'Well, can't you take him off my case? You are the Old Bill.'

'It's not as easy as that.'

'Why not?'

'Well, he hasn't done anything wrong yet and it's only hearsay at the moment.'

'Have I got to have a leg broken before you act?'

'We'll keep an eye out for you, don't worry.'

This was just what I needed on a Monday morning, some nutter trying to do me damage. I hadn't got Des now to fix these things for me. I really missed Des – it was like losing my right arm. I was lost without him.

Our next booking was three days away in Canvey Island, so I had time to sort a few things out.

Solly, my accountant, rang me and reckoned that somebody had definitely caused mischief with the taxman. They were trying to delve into every aspect of my life. But he was confident that it could be sorted. He said he was on the case with the tax people and reckoned he could do a deal with them.

The last bill I had for Solly's services was bigger than the feckin' national debt!

Later little Jade came to see me. Was it a call to see how I was, or was she having another birthday?

'Grandad, it's about time you got a Grandma. You don't want to be on your own for the rest of your life. You can get yourself fixed up on the internet now. There are loads of sad people like you looking for love, so

I've marked up a few likely sites for you. So when you're ready I'll bring my laptop round and we'll get started. Let's be honest, you ain't got long so the sooner the better.'

She was off as quick as she came, saying as she left, 'Love you, Grandad, and don't take too long – time is marching on.'

I couldn't believe a twelve-year-old was trying to sort out my love life. Was I really that sad?

I met the band later and we spent a few hours rehearsing. Afterwards we went to Big Al's office to see him. He had some good news. We'd been asked to appear on one of the breakfast shows. It had something to do with a Mods and Rockers programme that they were showing later that evening. They wanted us to kick it off with our record *Suburban Mod*. At last something to look forward to.

The next day Ronnie phoned me up. 'That head-case Neil is back and could be trying to make a comeback with another firm who're trying to get involved in the club scene again. Sammy's not happy, as this encroaches on his territory, so don't worry about this geezer Neil – it will all be sorted. Before Des died he spoke to Sammy and asked him to keep an eye on you. Be lucky and I'll be in touch.'

I thanked him and got well upset to think that Des, who was struggling with a serious illness and in a lot of pain, would still worry about me. Fortunately there was no comeback by this Neil. It all went quiet and I never heard any more.

♫ 20 ♫

How did her husband find out?

The band hadn't been on television since the seventies, so we were looking forward to it. It was quite daunting, as you were playing live to a few million people. We got there in plenty of time, set up and were ready to play. I wasn't quite sure that at our age we should be wearing target tee-shirts, but Big Al thought it would be perfect.

The four of us came out of the green room and picked up our instruments. The presenters gave their spiel and introduced us to the viewers. We were ready and we went straight into *Suburban Mod*. It doesn't matter how many times you've played it, you still do something different every time. The boys were on top form and we played it as well as we'd ever done.

After we finished we sat around on the settees and answered questions about the pop music of the sixties. Sometimes you say stupid things on air, but Big Al had marked our cards so that if we played it right we could get a load more bookings off the back of this.

We handled ourselves well except for one question, when this young woman presenter said with a laugh, 'I suppose you met loads of girls on the road?'

Big-mouth Steve had been quiet but he jumped in with the answer and said with a snigger, 'Yeah, we were crumpeting every night.'

Well, this girl had no idea what this term meant and she was stuck for words. She got no help from the other presenter, and said innocently, 'Oh, didn't you get fed up eating crumpets every day?'

The other presenter was a bloke much older than her. He roared with laughter as he knew exactly what we meant. He could've helped her out, but didn't. He just fed her to the lions.

That night I was at home having a quiet drink when the phone went. I picked it up.

'Is that what you used to call me, a bit of crumpet?'

'Anita, it's great to hear from you! Yeah, sorry about that, Steve can't help himself.'

She'd seen the show that morning and just wanted to touch base, as they say. I told her about Des. She was well upset as she'd met Des many times when we were youngsters. She seemed friendly enough and for that reason, or more probably with Jade's voice in the background warning me about being on my own for the rest of my life, I said to her, 'Anita, I really want to see you again. I know it's all wrong and I'm probably making a fool of myself asking you.'

It all went quiet and I thought she'd hung up on me until she said, 'I want to see you again too, Nick.'

For a minute I was lost for words, then I said, 'I've got some time off soon. Perhaps we can meet up with each other. I can come up to your neck of the woods and perhaps we can have a meal together.'

After that we spoke to each other a lot.

It was getting near the end of the year and Big Al called a band meeting to discuss the New Year. We sat in his office and Sampson was by his master's side.

Rick said to him, 'Al, do we have to have him in here? He gives us the willies. He's not customer friendly, is he? He just keeps eyeing us up all the time.'

'He's a pussycat. Right, let's get back to business.'

Al outlined where we were at the moment and where he thought we should be going. The TV slot had been good for us. First of all *Suburban Mod* was now an unlikely chart hit again. Second, Al had a lot more bookings in place if we wanted them.

We gave ourselves till the end of the year, which was now just a few weeks away, to decide what we all wanted. We'd already had one chat about it. Steve and Rick wanted to do as many gigs as possible. Billy was sitting on the fence, as I was.

I didn't want to be one of those bands that lived out of a suitcase and did bundles of shows a year. I'd been there and had got that tee-shirt. I liked playing as much as anybody, but at sixty-five I wasn't going to kill myself. I also felt like writing a lot more material for other people. In fact, one of Big Al's acts was recording a number that I had written, so it would be interesting to see how it fared.

After a second meeting it was agreed that we'd continue as we were for the next six months and look at it again the following summer. I now felt like my own man again. A lot more royalties were coming in and financially I was looking quite secure. Saying that, I was now off to see Solly again about my tax problems. Solly was a wily old bastard of about seventy, and his clientele included a number of high-profile villains and celebrities from the East End of London.

'My boy,' he said. 'I think it's sorted. They're looking for a gesture…'

'A gesture, Solly? I know the country's in the shit but can't they pick on someone else to help them out?'

'Look, they ain't got a lot on you because over the last few years you've been earning peanuts. Yes, you've got royalties coming in a lot more now, but that's this financial year and we're on top of that. So I've suggested two grand.'

'Two grand? You're having a feckin' laugh! With your fee that's no change out of five K.'

'If it eases the pain, I've just had a cheque from your record company for ten thousand…'

'What?'

'Yeah, big bucks. That record *Suburban Mod* and some others that you wrote are selling well. You'll never have to worry about money any more if they continue to sell like this. But one word of caution – I'm pretty sure somebody out there who knows about this business has tipped the wink to the Inland Revenue. We'll have to be whiter than white now till they find some other poor bastard to hound.'

'Are you sure?'

'I'd lay money on it. You've upset someone out there so be on your guard. I would do a bit of digging to find out who it is, otherwise you'll have this monkey on your back for ever.'

When I got home I thought of all the people who might want to do me wrong. As I was thinking, which was hard now, the phone went. It was Anita. She'd told her husband that she was going Christmas shopping in Exeter next Wednesday.

That wasn't a problem for me as I had a couple of days off, so it was a date. I was like a big kid when I came off the phone. I was seeing my favourite lady and I wanted it to be special. I booked up a nice hotel and made sure we had the best table for lunch.

We still had a few more gigs to do that week, mostly corporate Christmas do's. One was out of this world. We were playing at one of the big five-star hotels in London. There was no shortage of money for this one. Big Al charged them three grand and they didn't bat an eyelid.

It was a Hooray Henry and thinking man's crumpet bash. It was dress suits and bow ties for the men and the women were wearing top-drawer clobber. There wasn't an ugly bird amongst them. Whoever had invited them had taste. We set up in the beautiful ballroom, which was decked out in the most expensive Christmas decorations that money could buy.

We wore suits and looked quite sharp, if you liked the seventies. The bell bottoms were so wide you could have put three legs in them! They were in a party mood and so were we.

There were buckets of champagne on offer and we had our fair quota of it. After the first set a few of the ladies came over to us. What surprised us was that they were in their forties, some even younger, and they were well chatty. Danielle was about forty-five, dark hair, and classy with it. She was nice and knew a fair bit about our band. Having been on the internet and checked us out she said, 'You were quite famous in your day.'

'We had our moments.'

'In fact, your band has been relaunched with the wave of the sixties music that's now on offer.'

'I wish my body had been relaunched,' I said with a laugh.

'You don't look too bad to me. Perhaps we can have a drink when you've finished,' she said, giving me a great big smile. I didn't need to be asked twice and the meet was set in stone.

Billy was a bit of a tealeaf – if it wasn't nailed down you were in trouble. There were plenty of bottles of Moet on offer, so he took advantage of the situation. He was filling up his drum box with as many bottles as he could cram in. Rick had to give him a lift to the van with the box in the break.

The night went down extremely well and everybody was happy. I saw Danielle afterwards and I had a feeling that it was going to be a busy night. I told the guys I might catch the train home tomorrow.

Billy was well happy, too – he had more bottles of champagne in the van than Tesco.

Danielle had a room at the hotel and it just seemed a natural thing to do after a great night. There was no drama, we just wanted sex. At my age I was just grateful that someone wanted to go to bed with me. She disappeared into the luxury bathroom while I sat on a chair marvelling at the beautiful surroundings. It must have cost a fortune. She reappeared in some sizzling underwear that clung to her slim body. Her make-up had been freshened up and she looked gorgeous.

It was now my turn for the bathroom. I stripped off. What a mess. Hair seemed to be growing everywhere, sagging bollocks, big gut and a dick that had shrunk so much I couldn't see it over my stomach. What a catch I was! I had a shower and fortunately there were all sorts of nice smellies. Thank God for the dressing gown behind the door. I could hide the lot behind that. I took a deep breath and said to myself, I hope you can still do the business.

She was in bed waiting for me. As I got in I saw three condoms on the small cabinet by her side of the bed. Three? She'll be feckin' lucky, I thought. I won't go into the nitty-gritty. All I can say is, I didn't let myself down, but it took its toll.

I was woken up by the maid knocking on the door. It should've been the other way round as I rushed to put my clothes on.

She'd left a note on the table: 'Not bad for an old un. Love, Danielle.'

She'd also left her phone number. I left the hotel quickly and headed for Liverpool Street Station. I got on the train but I was so knackered I slept right through to Chelmsford. So it was back on another train and then home. I could hardly keep my eyes open and went straight to bed.

It only seemed like minutes before somebody was knocking the shit out of the door. Bleary eyed, I opened it. There was Steve, full of himself.

'You look like death, mate. You want to leave it alone.'

'Tell me about it. I'm so tired you wouldn't believe it.'

'Well, you'd better wake yourself up. We're playing at Chelmsford in three hours time.'

'Oh, bollocks! If I'd known that I would've stayed there when I fell asleep on the train.'

It was a charity concert that I'd totally forgotten about.

We'd performed all our outstanding gigs before Christmas and tomorrow I was seeing Anita. I was really looking forward to it. The weather forecast wasn't too good for the morning – maybe some snow – so I left really early. I scooted up the M4 and M5 in record time and had breakfast in the hotel.

I was staying overnight. Fortunately they let me get into the room early. Anita was going to do her Christmas shopping in the morning then meet me for lunch. I bought her a present, which had to be something her husband wouldn't suss out. I bought her a CD called *You & I* by the Pierces. It had a great track called *You'll Be Mine*, which I thought was appropriate.

She was already there in reception when I came down from my room. I went up to her and gave her a cuddle. She didn't object and we held on to each other for a few seconds. We had a drink and chatted, then had lunch. I gave her my Christmas present. She was quite taken aback, as she hadn't got me anything, which seemed to embarrass her. We were getting on famously and were enjoying just being together. It wasn't until I went to the toilet that I saw the snow falling down in bucket loads. I quickly went back to tell her. She was now in panic mode. We quickly said our goodbyes and I took her to reception. There was a television on the wall and it was flashing up traffic reports. It was bad news: Haldon Hill on the A38, which is on the way to Torquay, was now at a standstill, and police were advising motorists not to travel. That spot is renowned as a problem when there is snow about.

We waited to see whether the conditions would ease, but they didn't, and it was clear that Anita wasn't going anywhere tonight. In the old days I would've loved an excuse for her to stay here. But I wasn't eighteen any more and she was really upset that she couldn't get home.

I said, 'I feel really guilty about this.'

'It's not your fault, Nick.'

'What's the next step?'

'I'm going to have to phone Simon and tell him that I'll get home as soon as the roads allow me to.'

It wasn't a pleasant phone call as he was really arsy with her.

'It's not my fault the road is blocked, Simon.'

He was really nasty and aggressive, and didn't once ask her how she was. I felt annoyed that somebody would treat her in that way. Mind you, I'm being a bit of a hypocrite as I'm here with his wife, but he's not to know that, so bollocks to him.

She came off the phone and said, 'You heard all that, I suppose. I get that most days. He really is a pig. All he was worried about was his tea, not me. OK, I'm with you, but he's not at all worried about how I'm going to get home.'

'I'm sorry I've put you in this predicament.'

'Nick, I'd arranged this Christmas shopping trip already. All that is different is that I am having lunch with you. Jenny was initially coming with me but she's taking the grandkids to a pantomime.'

'OK, it doesn't look like you're going to get home tonight, so I'll see if I can get you another room.'

While she went to the loo I went to reception to see if there was another room available. There wasn't. Because of the weather everybody was trying to get one.

When Anita returned her attitude seemed to change when I told her, 'I'm afraid there are no rooms. I can sleep in a chair downstairs and you can have my room.'

'Yeah, I'll believe that when I see it,' she said sarcastically.

'What do you mean?'

'Well, you love this. You've got me where you want me.'

I was a bit annoyed and said, 'As it happens, I'm here because I care about you, not because I want to get you into bed.'

'Sorry, Nick, I'm a bit uptight at the moment.'

We went to the coffee shop. Within half an hour all three of her kids were on the phone, making sure she was all right. You could see they really cared about her and she obviously cared about them.

In fact, all three of them were prepared to come out and collect her now. Of course that couldn't happen because the weather had worsened. She told them she was in a hotel on the motorway and that she'd stay there until the weather cleared.

Then her arsehole of a husband was back on the phone giving her more grief. She had a full-scale argument with him. He only expected her to go out and try and get home. I couldn't believe it.

'Sorry about this, Nick. As you can see, it's not easy.'

As we were here for the night I took her up to my room where she had a shower and freshened up. I made sure I stayed downstairs. I had no intention of trying to take advantage of the situation. Once upon a time I would've done, but not tonight.

Over dinner and a bottle of wine we both relaxed. I asked her whether her best friend Jenny knew about her seeing me.

'No, I haven't told her, but she knows something is going on. She's not stupid.'

Anita's husband rang up again and there was more hassle. She said, 'How can I get home tonight, Simon? I'm staying at a hotel on the motorway and the minute the weather clears I'll be home.'

When the call finished I said, 'He's persistent. What's his problem?'

'How long have you got.'

'Why do you put up with it?'

'I often ask that same question Nick. Any love we had between us finished years ago. He's a control freak and not a nice man now.'

'It's probably the wrong time and wrong place. I was really stupid. I should never have messed you about…'

'Please don't go there again, Nick.'

'I've got to say it. I've always loved you and I always will. I would do anything to make you happy. Come and live with me.'

'It's too late. I can't leave him. My children would be devastated. They think everything in the garden is still rosy, and it would break their hearts for the family to split up.'

'What about you? You've got a life. You can't be bullied for the rest of your days.'

She then got the right arse-ache and stuck the knife in by saying, 'It's all right for you. Your life's been full of broken romances, and look at your marriage. I've been with someone for a long time. So don't give me advice, Nick Sheldon, about what I should or shouldn't do, not with your track record.'

That put me in my place and I said no more. I let Anita have my room and I kipped on a chair in the lounge.

In the morning the weather had improved, making it possible for both of us to continue our journeys. I'd made up my mind after she'd volleyed me last night that there was no point in me trying to see her again. I was living in the past and she'd moved on and I hadn't.

I was being an old fool and I was embarrassing both myself and her. So while she had a shower I left, leaving her a note with words to that effect.

Driving back down the M5 I thought of what could've been. I didn't want to speak to anybody so I made sure my mobile was off. It was a long journey home and I had time to reflect on my life. I'd messed up my marriage. I was never faithful. I stupidly thought that Anita would give it all up for a poxy little flat in the back end of Romford. Dream on, get real, I'm saying to myself. These days I was talking to myself more than I talked to other people. More worrying, I even answered my own questions!

On arriving home to an empty cold flat, I was probably as low as I could get. My best mate Des had just died, I'd made a fool of myself with Anita and I'd run out of fags! I took the phone off the hook and gave the brandy a right hammering. I didn't want to speak to or hear from anybody for at least a day. In fact, it was two days before I put the phone back on, then it was Christmas Eve. Steve and Rick were having their Christmas dinner with Ruth. She'd invited them around; in fact, Rick was getting quite close to her in a nice sort of way.

I was having my dinner with Tracy, Mick and the kids. Rob was having Zoe's parents round. His mother-in-law was a right dragon, so he was in for a good Christmas!

I was just about to go and do my Christmas shopping when the phone went. I answered it, and what a shock it was.

'Sheldon, I will only say this once. We had a similar conversation back in the sixties and, as then, I'm warning you off. I'm Anita's husband and I'm telling you to leave her alone. I know everything about you. When she went with Jenny to your show in Southampton I knew you'd be sniffing around.'

I was in complete shock as I said, 'What are you on about?'

'Don't take me for a fool! I know every move you've made. I've had somebody watching you, from having dinner with my wife in Upminster to having coffee twice at that seafront cafe in Dawlish. She'll never leave me, so you're wasting your time. And by the way, I know you had a room at that motorway hotel a few days back. When she said she couldn't get home, I rang around the hotels. And of course there is a Sheldon staying at one of them. I'm too clever for you. She never goes shopping without Jenny, so I knew you were involved. And just to finish off, she doesn't know I know about you and her – it's our little secret, so she'll never know, otherwise I'll have to get nasty with her and you don't want that.'

'Yeah, do you like hitting women?'

'What happens between my wife and me has nothing to do with you. I don't expect we'll be having any more conversations. Oh, by the way, have you heard from the Inland Revenue lately? Enjoy your Christmas, Sheldon.'

The phone went dead. I couldn't believe what I'd just heard. I was totally gobsmacked and in shock.

No shopping got done today. They'd have to have money instead. I sat on the sofa thinking about what I'd just heard. It now all fell into place. I hadn't imagined it that somebody was sussing me out that night when I went to see Anita in the hotel at Upminster, and seeing the same bloke in Dawlish when I was with her confirmed that.

He, of course, was a top accountant, and knew what to say to the right people at the tax office. Solly was spot on that I'd been spiked!

I'd been outmanoeuvred and I had nowhere to go with this. Hopefully, Anita wouldn't ring me, and it would go back to the status quo before I came back on the scene. It didn't feel right and I was feeling a bit wimpish. I needed to think this out properly. It was Christmas Day tomorrow, so at least something to look forward to!

I'd only been around Tracy's a few minutes when she and Mick were at it, arguing about the presents he'd bought her. He then said to her, 'I've just bought you *The Only Way Is Essex* box set, Jordan's autobiography, Cheryl Cole's latest book, an X-Factor DVD and two hundred quid's worth of Botox vouchers – what did you get me? A feckin' book on West Ham's achievements over the last ten years!'

We sat down for the Christmas meal. Tracy's not the best cook in the world – when she stuck the thermometer into the turkey to test the temperature it broke. The poxy bird had rigor mortis. I've never had Christmas dinner at 10 o'clock at night before! It wasn't much better when I went to Rob and Zoe's on Boxing Day. Rob was arguing with

Zoe about how much she'd spent on the credit card, and she was having a pop at him about all the time he was spending down the gym. Then she had a go about him about using her smellies that she'd got for Christmas presents. She said, 'I'm sure you're bleedin' gay.'

That hit home. For a second I thought, oh no, don't tell her you think you're gay, on Boxing Day. Then Jade kept asking me how my love life was. I was glad to get home.

New Year's Eve I saw Rick, Steve and Ruth at Ziggies. I told them about Anita's husband and asked them about what I should do. Steve was first.

'Punch his lights out.'

Then Rick said, 'It sounds like a can of worms mate. I'd leave well alone and move on.'

Ruth had a more gentle touch and put her hand on mine. 'Nick, is she worth fighting for…?'

Steve then butts in. 'That's what I said – punch his lights out and…'

'Steve, go and get a round of drinks – mine's a gin and tonic,' said Ruth.

She looked at me and said, 'If you are really in love with her, then fight for her. She sounds very unhappy and she'll need time to make, probably, one of the biggest decisions in her life. She'll have so much to lose and, with your track record, will she be prepared to take that gamble? If she does, then you'd better make sure you treat her like a princess because at your time of life you'll probably never get another opportunity for true happiness. I found it with Des, and I'm so glad, for even the short period we shared together I knew what being in love was.'

♫ 21 ♫

Terry and his Shadows

It's seven in the morning and the phone goes. What idiot wants me at this time of day? It's Big Al, it's urgent and he's on his way round to the flat now.

When he arrived I was still in my dressing gown.

'What's the bleedin' emergency, Al?'

'How many Shadows numbers do you know?'

'Do what?'

'I know it's a stupid question to ask at seven thirty on a Tuesday morning, but do you know any?'

'Well, just the usual suspects, *Wonderful Land, Apache,* etc. They're the numbers we used to learn when we first started playing. What's this all about?'

'This Saturday I had my best tribute band playing at a top-flight gig – well, I thought I did until the lead guitarist found out that the drummer was giving his missus one. The shit hits the fan and overnight the band is no longer.'

'Do I see an Exocet missile coming my way?'

'Look, Nick, I'm in big, big trouble. I'll be straight with you. My band was playing at a Shadows convention...'

'There's loads of Shadows tribute bands out there – get one of those.'

The penny then drops.

'Al, I'm getting this funny feeling that you want Modern Edge to be a Shadows tribute band and do this gig.'

'I wouldn't ask...'

'Oh piss off; we're a main-line band, not a Sexton Blake. We're the real deal.'

'I know that, but I've put my reputation on the line and a considerable amount of money has been invested in this gig. By the way, is your passport up to date?'

'What are you on about?'

'The gig is in Stockholm.'

'Feckin' Sweden! You are having a laugh, Al?'

After the initial shock I felt sorry for him, but this was a no-win situation for us. Shadows fans are very critical when it comes to somebody trying to imitate their idols.

'Look, Al, it's not a goer.'

'Nick, I'm counting on you to get me out of trouble.'

'Sorry, but you're going to have to get somebody else.'

'OK, but I thought five hundred apiece to each band member in cash for about six or seven numbers would be of interest.'

'What did you say?'

'Fly in early Saturday morning, out again Sunday morning and Monday cash in hand.'

'Just a few numbers, no banana skins or something you ain't telling me?'

'Nick, how long have we known each other?'

'Too long – that's why I'm asking. What's the SP then?'

'Right, it'll just be you, Steve and Billy. Terry Sherman is going to play rhythm. This has got to be as authentic as possible so we don't need a singer, so Rick's not on this one. I've organised all the amps and the other kit with a local dealer in Stockholm. It will all be set up ready for you at the gig. You've got to learn the Shadows three-step walk…'

'Oh, feck off, Al – that's corny.'

'You'll be playing to an audience who love the Shadows.'

'As it's a convention I suppose there are other tribute Shadow bands playing?'

Al just glossed over that and I thought nothing more of it.

'I've booked Elm Park again for rehearsing so you've got a couple of days to put a few numbers together. I'll see you on Friday with the airline tickets and all the info.'

'Aren't you coming with us?'

'No, you don't need me there.'

I spoke to Steve and Billy, who weren't too enamoured about it, but money talks. Rick wasn't bothered about it; anyway, he didn't even have a current passport.

We met Terry the next day and got down to some serious rehearsing. He was an excellent guitarist and fortunately could play more Shadows numbers than me, so I suggested he play lead. There was a striking resemblance between him and Hank Marvin – he wore the glasses and had his grin, so we now called the band Terry and his Shadows! We all had a right laugh trying to play and learn the Shadows three-step walk. Steve's got two left feet and he was like Lance-Corporal Jones in *Dad's*

Army.

As we were only playing a short set we thought about eight numbers would do. So the next couple of days we got them canned and were pleased with the result.

We met Al on the Friday. He gave us the airline tickets and some money for expenses. He told us what hotel we were booked into and told us there would be somebody to pick us up at the airport in Stockholm. It was a short and sharp five-minute conversation and Al was off, which was very unlike him.

Next day a minibus took us to the airport. The flight went OK and we arrived on time. As we cleared customs there was a guy holding a card with 'Shadows' on it.

The taxi driver took as to a theatre a short drive away. There was a hoarding above the entrance. Terry said to the driver, 'What does that say?'

'World's Number One Shadows band playing here tonight.'

'Thank God they've got a real Shadows band playing! That makes it a lot easier for us,' says Steve.

As we walked in carrying our guitars, a guy in his sixties came up to us and said, 'Nice to see you, gentlemen. I'll show you the dressing room and stage.'

We reached the dressing room, which was a matter of yards from the stage. We had a peek inside the hall. It was a two-tier auditorium and looked impressive. I said to this bloke,
'Are all the bands changing in here?'

'I don't understand. There's only one band playing tonight.'

'What about the World's Number One Shadows band?'

'That's you, isn't it? The sound engineer will be with you shortly. We'll send in some food later.'

And he was off. The four of us looked at each other. We were shell shocked until Billy laughed and said, 'We're shadows of our former self!'

Terry shot off and had a word with the guy we'd just spoken to. When he got back he didn't look too happy.

'I can now confirm we're the World's Number One Shadows tribute band. Firstly, in a few hours time this theatre will be full of Scandinavians arriving to hear this great band. Secondly, this great band is on for two whole hours…'

'Two feckin' hours? We've only just enough material for about forty-five minutes, top whack,' said Steve.

'Thirdly,' said Terry, 'none of the kit on stage is set up…'

'Well, who's going to do that?' I asked.

'Fourthly, we are.'

A guy aged about thirty walked in, with long hair down to his shoulders, a bit scruffy and wearing round tinted glasses.

'Morning guys! I'm Harrison, your sound engineer for tonight. So you're the World's Number…'

Terry looks at him and says, 'Oh feck off…'

'Have I hit a raw nerve?'

'So you're English then, mate?' I said.

'Yeah, Catford, South London. I married a Swedish bird…'

'Lucky bastard.'

'They still moan, kick off and fart like all women do, mate.'

'We are going to have to be up front with you,' said Terry.

After we'd told him about the problems we had, he replied with a grin, 'Yeah, I can see the punters and management might not be very happy tonight. Have you got a getaway car ready?'

This guy was one of us and we felt safe that he wouldn't spill the beans. He then said, 'OK, let's get going – we can sort this out. First thing first, let's get the kit set up on stage.'

Within three hours we'd set up and had a quick sound check. Harrison was now in charge and over coffee he looked at Terry and said, 'How many numbers can you play?'

'At a push about ten…'

'Not enough, so let's work this out. Each number is going to have to last at least five minutes. Also, start off with *Apache* and *Wonderful Land*. At the end of the second set you ask the audience what numbers they want to hear again. I've done these Shadows gigs before and they always ask for those two numbers. Next, do you know any Jet Harris numbers?

'I think we all know *Diamonds* and *Scarlett O'Hara*,' I said.

'As we know, Jet played for the Shadows so the audience will buy into that. We're looking good – that's another two out the way. Now I have a little ace up my sleeve. To start the two sets off I always play a few minutes of film of the Shadows, so I'll extend that. Right – tips for tonight. They only want music. No jokes or pissing about, and the Shadows three-step walk is a must. I suggest you get out there now and go through the set list and brush up on Jet's two numbers.'

And that's what we did. Harrison was turning out to be our saviour, not like Big Al, who had a lot to answer for. We tried to get him on his mobile. Funnily enough it wasn't switched on.

The audience of a thousand or so were now settling into their seats.

Harrison came into the dressing room and we confirmed the set list.

We're suited and booted and ready to go on stage to a full house. Harrison is as good as his word and puts the film on before we start. It goes on for an age, which is handy. Now we're on. As we hit the stage we get a great reception from the audience. I look at Terry, and feck me he does look like Hank! He gives me a grin and for a moment I think I'm in the Shadows. Thank goodness he's playing lead.

We went straight into *Wonderful Land* and with the three-step walk we were on a roll. I don't know why, but the four of us kept grinning at each other. We had to remember to hang out the numbers for as long as possible. I think *Apache* lasted about seven minutes. At the end of the first set the punters seemed happy.

Harrison bounced into the dressing room.

'That was great, lads. The Shads would be proud of you.'

I turned round to Terry and said, 'I have to say, mate, you were top man on lead.'

Then Harrison said, 'OK, how many numbers have you got left in the locker?'

Billy looked at the set list. 'Not enough. Three Shadows, two Jet Harris, and hopefully *Wonderful Land* and *Apache*...'

'And with plenty more film, I think we're in business,' said Harrison.

As we're congratulating ourselves the promoter walks in. He's the equivalent of a Swedish Big Al. He has a look about him that you wouldn't want to mess with.

'That wasn't bad gentlemen. Some of the numbers went on too long, but everyone seemed happy. Harrison, don't show any more film, they just want music and plenty of it.'

As he goes out of the door, he suddenly turns and looks at Steve, grins and says in perfect English, 'I don't know whether you've got feckin' two right feet or two left feet.'

That was that and he was out the door. We're now crapping ourselves – we're going to come up short and he won't be happy. Then Steve says, 'What's he on about my feet? I was going to audition for *Strictly*!'

Harrison replies, 'Yeah, strictly out of step with everybody else – you were shit.'

The laughter stops as we realise we're in trouble. Suddenly the buzzer goes, Harrison rushes off and we walk back on stage. Then Terry says, 'I've got an idea. When we've run out of numbers, just look at me.'

We get a great reception and start the second set. The audience accepts the non-Shadows numbers and we've now finished. We've still got twenty minutes to play when Terry gets on the mic and shouts out, 'Who wants some rock 'n' roll?'

For a second there's no response, then Terry plays a couple of bars of *Shakin' All Over*. Then as if by magic the audience responds and we go for it. They love it, and so do we. We've somehow got out of trouble and are heading back home.

On the Monday morning we were in Al's office to have it out with him about dropping us right in it. He was adamant that he only knew as much as we did, but we didn't believe him. When he dished the money out and gave us an extra couple of hundred quid on top we calmed down and moved on.

♫ 22 ♫

Big Al, Sammy and trouble

Our website was now fully operational, with all our gigs and listed blogs of the band – we even had an on-line shop. We'd signed a new contract with Al in spite of the Shadows debacle. He had full control, but not on any future recordings we might want to do. We left this open as in the past we'd been tucked up; if we made any records in the future we wanted to handle these ourselves.

I still didn't know what to do about Anita, so for the moment I just let it ride. I made contact with Danielle from the corporate night. She lived in Kent so it was over the Dartford Bridge, which wasn't too far.

She'd broken up with her long-term partner and she just wanted some fun. I was starting to get a bit of a grumpy old man so she was good for me. I was still missing Des big time and there wasn't a day went by that I didn't think about him.

Steve was a bit lost. With Rick spoken for and Billy happily married, he was on his own until Sue found him on a social networking site. She was a girl he had gone out with in the late sixties. I used to go out with her best mate, so I knew her well. Sue was a buxom girl, who knew how to keep a man happy, but unfortunately the only drawback was that she had a gob as big as Blackwall Tunnel. They also used to argue all the time. On one occasion she thought she was pregnant by Steve, but fortunately it was a false alarm.

She was now divorced, so Steve and her decided to see each other. He tried to keep it a secret about where he was going to meet her, but Rick and I were in on the plot. He was meeting her at a little pub in Collier Row. Rick and I got there a bit early and made ourselves scarce. A very attractive lady came in, slim, well-dressed and looking as good as it got at her age. Surely it couldn't be her?

Then Romeo came in looking bright-eyed and bushy tailed, wearing jeans and trainers. He couldn't believe his luck. Could this be the big lump he used to know? Once they settled down Rick and I made ourselves known.

'Steve, fancy meeting you here! And who's this?'

'Can't I do anything without you two?'

Sue then said, 'Nick, after forty years I would've thought by now you'd have come up with a better punch-line.'

'I have to say, Sue, you look gorgeous.'

'Well, you don't. Now, on your bike you two,' said Steve.

So we left them in peace and, as it happens, they got back together. Nothing too serious – just feeling their way!

There were some massive shocks for all of us at the start of the year. When Des's will was read he'd left me a shed load of money. I couldn't believe it. He'd left Rick and Steve a good drink and looked after Ruth.

We'd talked about doing an album a while back, and he'd left us some money to pay for studio time. He was a great supporter of the band and we always treated him as the sixth member of the group.

We never knew what he had because it was nothing to do with us. We knew he owned land that his Dad had left him. How much of his estate was down to crime, I really didn't know. In the will he said: 'To my best mate who was always there when I wanted him…'

I welled up when I read it. You could never replace Des, he was a one-off. Now I had to make sure my family were unaware of my inheritance otherwise they'd be after their cut.

Within a few weeks Steve moved in with Sue. She owned a really nice place in Ingatestone. When she'd divorced her husband, a wealthy builder, he'd left her well provided for. I couldn't see Steve messing this one up – if he played his cards right he was made for life.

Rick moved in with Ruth and they were giving it a try to see whether it would work out.

As I've already mentioned, one of Billy's vices was gambling. We did a booking at a racetrack and he was in his element, so much so that the first three numbers we had to play without him, as he never showed.

I came home early one morning from a show in Newcastle and went straight to bed. I was really knackered and slept until late afternoon. I was woken by the phone. I crawled out of bed and answered it. A familiar voice said, 'Hello, Nick, it's Jenny. I'm sorry to trouble you.'

'That's OK, it's nice to hear from you.'

'Look, Anita doesn't know I'm ringing you. She's told me that you've seen her a few times.'

'Oh.'

'Perhaps I shouldn't have rung you, but she's my best mate and I feel I have to.'

'What's wrong?'

'She's having a bad time with Simon. He's really treating her badly. She doesn't deserve it.'

'I'm sorry to hear that. The last time I saw her she made it quite clear that I was, how can I put it, invading her space. You know I still have strong feelings for her, but what can I do?'

'She told me about the note you left, Nick. Look, she's got a new mobile phone and number that Simon knows nothing about. Please give her a ring. She'd love to hear from you, I'm sure. I know she's on her own right now – no one's in.'

I took a note of the number and put the phone down. I made myself a cup of tea and as I sipped it I thought, do I want to get involved? I was happy with Danielle at the moment, which was a no-frills relationship that suited us both.

What was I thinking about? Anita was the only girl I really wanted and I would do anything for her! I rang the number and she answered it quickly.

'Hi, Anita, it's big bad Nick here,' I said with a laugh.

'Nick, I'm so pleased to hear from you.'

'Jenny has told me that life isn't too good at the moment.'

'That's an understatement. I need to see you, Nick.'

'I'd love to see you, you know that.'

'Look, I've looked at the gig guide on your website. You're playing Bristol next Friday. Can I see you there?'

'Yeah, of course – we'll be up there early as we're playing Cheltenham the night before.'

That night we were playing a local venue at Southend when Billy's gambling habit reared its ugly head. The last couple of weeks his drumming hadn't been good. His mobile was always going off and he wouldn't answer it.

Billy lived in Southend, so we were worried when he didn't show for a sound check. His missus phoned up and she was one worried lady. He'd taken their dog out for a walk.
An hour later she'd got a phone call from a friend down her street to say that their dog was wandering about on its own, but there was no Billy. She asked if we'd seen him. We hadn't, and of course we were worried about him as well, but it also meant we had no drummer tonight.

We made a frantic call to Robin to see whether he'd fill in for us if Billy didn't show. I wasn't expecting any favours from him after we'd ditched him. Fortunately for us he hadn't anything on and said he'd love to do it. He only lived about thirty miles away, so within the hour he was setting up the drum kit.

He knew our numbers so we just gave him the set list. Billy never showed that night. He'd been beaten up and was now in hospital. He was off the road for a week and Robin filled in for another three shows, all local, thank goodness.

Billy had built up a gambling debt with the wrong people, and they'd administered their own justice. Billy's Dad paid up the debt and the hounds left him alone. From that day on, we don't think he ever made another bet.

We did the Cheltenham gig, which went down well – a good crowd and plenty of clapping, which always helps. That night I was having a mini-crisis with my playing. I had arthritis in a couple of my fingers and was having difficulty playing some of the chords. I forgot about it afterwards – a few brandies did the trick!

The next morning I left early with the roadies who were setting up at Bristol. They dropped me off at a hotel near the venue to meet Anita.

I really didn't know what to expect from her. I walked into the coffee shop and saw Jenny, who gave me a kiss on the cheek and we both sat down. She then said, 'Nick, I'm glad you could make it. She's a bit fragile at the moment so be gentle with her.'

Anita came out of the loo while Jenny made herself scarce.

She didn't look the same girl. She'd lost weight and that sparkle had gone from her eyes. She gave me a cuddle and said, 'Thanks for coming, Nick. I really wanted to see you again.'

I bought some coffees and took them to a corner of the lounge where it was quiet. Gently I said, 'Things not so good at home?'

'You could say that, Nick. The last couple of months have been really bad. Simon has been a real pig. He's hit me a couple of times.'

'What? That's well out of order – what a bastard! How could anybody want to hurt you?'

'Oh, it's not new, Nick. He's done this before, as you know.'

'Have you spoken to your kids about this?' I asked.

'Of course not. They wouldn't believe it anyway. They idolise their father. In their eyes he can do no wrong.'

She got upset and left to go to the loo again, while I pondered about whether I should tell her about her husband phoning me up. I also felt it was about time that we understood the reason why we were having these chitchats.

When she came back I took the bull by the horns and said, 'Look, please don't get me wrong, but where's all this leading to? You know my feelings for you. But let's be honest, there's no chance about us getting back together again, you've made that quite clear. But I'm there for you, any time – you know I love you to bits, but...'

She was taken aback, as I was more forceful in my conversation than before. She said, 'Part of me wants you, Nick...'

'And the other part...?'

'My children would be heartbroken if I left him...'

'Look, before you say any more I think I'd better tell you about a conversation I've had.'

'What do you mean?'

'Your husband phoned me up a while back and...'

'What?'

'I wasn't going to tell you as I thought we had no more to say to each other and it was best to leave well alone.'

I told her all about the conversation, including the private detective following us and him putting the taxman on my case. She was devastated, held her head in her hands and started sobbing, so I took her outside. Once outside I held her tight as the biting wind off the Bristol Channel cut through us. I felt so guilty about putting her through this. Was it entirely my fault or did her showing up at the Southampton gig begin this mess?

And it *was* a mess, as it was now affecting so many people's lives. After a few minutes we went back inside and I ordered some more coffees. Jenny joined us and I told her what I'd just said to her. Anita was all over the place. Fortunately Jenny was a calming influence. Anita went to, as they say, powder her nose, leaving Jenny and me.

'Where's all this leading to?' I asked.

'Well, their marriage has been on the downward slope for years. My worry is that if she left Simon for you...'

'Hang on. That's a big ask, isn't it? It's all very well talking about it, and seeing each other for a few hours chatting about old times, but then to go and live with someone twenty-four seven...'

'I know, especially with your track record...'

'Look, everybody talks about my track record. To be honest with you, Jenny, I've had enough of people pinning labels on me as if I'm some sort of ogre who goes around putting it about. When I was younger, absolutely, I couldn't get enough of it. Those days are long gone, so let's change the tune. I'm getting fed up with it.'

I was a bit over the top and was just about to say sorry when Jenny said, 'Sorry, Nick, but I can only remember you as you were. She's my best mate and she's very special to me. She wouldn't hurt anybody – she's got so much to give. At the moment she's being treated badly by Simon. He's a manipulating bully, who can't keep his hands to himself.'

'What do *you* think she should do?' I said.

'If I was her I'd leave him for a trial period and see whether he changes, although I doubt that he will.'

'What about me and Anita?'

'You two have always been made for each other but...'

'But my lifestyle blah, blah, blah...'

'Nick, change the record. You're getting boring.'

'Yeah, you're right – I do go on a bit, don't I?'

'If you two could somehow get together, I'm sure it would work out for both of you.'

Anita came back looking a bit calmer and said, 'Been talking about me?'

'Look, I'm going to have to go as I've got to do a sound check. What about seeing you after the show?'

'I'd love to, Nick, but we've got to get back to Torquay.'

'I can't leave it like this.'

'At the moment I need to be on my own, to think things through.'

As I left I said to her, 'I'm there for you, and if you feel that we have a long-term future together...'

'I know, Nick, but...'

I said with a laugh, 'Don't mention track record!'

'Nick, I really care about you, but it's a minefield at the moment and I need to clear my head.'

'I understand, but I'm not putting up with him hitting you. Even if we don't get it together, he'll have to be warned.'

'Don't be silly, Nick – you can't do anything about that.'

'Watch this space.'

She thought I was joking, but I wasn't.

When I got back home from Bristol the thought of her being knocked about was too much to bear. Something had to be done. I was having a chat with Steve over a coffee and told him all about this Simon bloke, and he said, 'Look, he has to be taught a lesson. We could go up there and duff him up – it's easy as that.'

'Yeah, he'll be well scared of us, I *don't* think. He needs the fear of

God put up him.'

'Sammy.'

'I was thinking along the same lines, Steve.'

'Be honest, Nick, we've known each other a long time. Do you really want to get back with Anita and all the baggage that goes with it? Danielle is a super lady and you get on well together. The past is the past, and with the greatest respect, mate, do you want all the hassle? It really isn't your problem, and to me it's best left well alone. It could get really nasty.'

'I know, you're probably right. To be honest I don't know what to do.'

When you're trying to sort out personal problems in your own life, work gets in the way. You can't phone the promoter up with a sickie. It's a demanding business and there's a lot of pressure to perform. People are paying a lot of money to see you – all they want is a performance from you that'll send them home happy.

I was still enjoying playing, but I was wondering how long I wanted to do this. We'd gone from just playing a few gigs to a lot more than I really wanted to. Big Al was a businessman and all he was interested in was his cut, so the more bookings we did, the more he'd earn. OK, he was a mate as well, but his business hat came first. This is where I missed Des. He would always tell it how it was – I could always get sound advice from him.

When we signed up with Al, he stipulated in the contract that we would have to give three months' notice if any of the band members wanted to quit. Whether it was the Anita thing or I was just plain tired I didn't know, but I now felt that maybe it was about time to pack the band in.

Financially I was much more secure now and, together with the royalties coming in on a regular basis, and with Des's money, I didn't need the gig money to live on any more.

I heard from Anita. She was quite calm, but hadn't yet said anything to her husband, but did mention that Simon was going to London for two days next week. He was meeting up with his accountancy pals. My brain was working overtime.

'I hope he's not at the same hotel in London that we're playing next week.'

'So do I. He's staying at the Grande Eclipse. You're not playing there are you?'

'No, thank goodness. I'd hate to meet up with him.'

We agreed to keep in touch to see how things panned out.

The next night we were playing at Barking, which was only a few miles from where I lived. That morning I said to Steve, 'Do you fancy breakfast?'

'Are you paying?'

'Don't I always?'

When we got to the cafe, Steve knew what I was up to. Sammy was in his usual spot with the chaps. He looked up and said, 'Look who's here – Sonny and Cher.'

'Morning, Sammy, can we have two of your large breakfasts?'

'Who do you think I am, the poxy waiter? See the girl behind the counter.'

After we ate his artery-blocking breakfast I asked him if I could have a word with him.

'Oh, no – what favour do you want now?'

'Sammy, I need a couple of your lads to put the frighteners on a guy.'

'If you want somebody frightened I know the very two. That Rick and his new bird came in here last week – they'd frighten anybody. He could rent her out as a scarecrow.'

I laughed just to please him.

'I'm happy to pay. All I want is him frightened – no violence. I just want to make sure that the message gets through.'

'What's he done then?'

'A lady friend of mine is being used as a punch bag by him. He's her husband.'

'Hang about! Didn't I do this before for you? What do you think I am – an extension of the battered wives association? Where's he live?'

'Devon.'

'Devon? Leave it out, Nick! My boys get lost if they go over the bleedin' Dartford Bridge.'

'He's in a London hotel next week. Look, all I want is for him to be warned off and to make sure that he knows the score. Can you help me out?'

'Nick, in all seriousness, it's not as easy as that. You can't go around threatening people all the time...'

Then big gob says with a laugh, 'You do it all the time, Sammy!'

He was not amused, and said to Steve, 'Son, I'd be very careful what you say. There's a new motorway being built up the road soon!' He continued, 'There are CCTV cameras on every corner. If he doesn't like the message we give him, he could go to the Old Bill, then they'll trawl the tapes looking for my two boys.'

'Is that a no?'

'I didn't say that. What we could do is have a trade.'

'What does that mean?'

'Well, Eve and I have our fiftieth wedding anniversary coming up soon. Your band can do the entertainment for the night. It's a dig for a gig or a gig for a dig.'

The three of us fell about laughing, then Sammy said, 'You give me the details of the hotel he's staying at, a photo of him and of course the date he's going to be there. Once I have that info I'll make a decision.'

I had an idea how to get his photo. Steve got on his computer and I asked him to look on the websites for golf clubs where they lived. Bingo, second hit we found him.

He was the captain of this golf club, and his photo was on the facing page together with the other hierarchy of the club. I thought I hadn't worn well, but he was like Billy Bunter with no hair!

We ran the photo off and gave the details to Sammy. I never heard from Sammy, so I thought it's not a goer, but a week later I got a quick phone call from Ronnie, who said, 'Job done. He was like a pussy cat. Nothing heavy, he just got a bit of strong verbal. Oh, by the way, Sammy's anniversary is 1 April, and no April fool jokes. The last bloke who did is still swimming the English Channel!'

We did have a booking on the night of the anniversary so I had to get in touch with Big Al, who wasn't happy. But once I told him who it was for he said, 'No problem, Nick, I'll sort it.'

Al was a Hornchurch boy and had been brought up on Sammy's exploits. He fully understood that if we didn't do it, the repercussions were unthinkable. I squared it off with the other lads and they were sweet about it.

There was me thinking that I'd really helped Anita out when she rang me up with a voice like thunder.

'What have you done, Nick Sheldon?'

'Done what?'

'You know what! Simon came back a day early from London. He said he'd been intimidated and threatened with violence.'

'I couldn't see you getting hurt any more so somebody had a quiet word with him about his behaviour, that's all.'

'That's all? You might do these sorts of things in London, but we don't do it in Devon. He's now really scared…'

'Hang about! Let me just get this right. So you and Simon have spoken with each other about us meeting up and his arsey phone call to me.'

'Yes, it's all come out – we've had a long chat.'

I raised my voice as I was getting really annoyed.

'Right, so there's no bleedin' pretending any more. He knows he's out of order in raising his hands to you.'

'Don't you swear at me! I'm not one of your Essex girls.'

'Oh, leave the Essex thing out, Anita – grow up! I've been trying to help you out. Domestic violence, that's what it's called. Look, I hate the thought of anybody hurting you and I really...'

'Well, you haven't got to worry about me any more. Go back to that scrubber Mandy!'

'It's not like...'

'Look, Simon and I are going to give our marriage another go, so don't bother to get in touch with me any more.'

And that was that, the phone went dead. I looked in the mirror and saw a great big banner, 'Mug'. I was lost for words. The Mandy comment just about topped it all. Was I wrong in trying to stop her from being hurt? Perhaps I was, I didn't know any more. I felt used and had now put them back in each other's arms.

Fortunately Steve came round, and after I told him about what had happened he said, 'I told you it would all end in tears. It's back-fired big time on you. You know what's happened, don't you?'

'I suppose you're going to tell me.'

'He's got back home and has given it the "poor me". Beaten up by London gangsters, and big bad Nick is no better than them, as he organised it. He's a two-bit musician with no class and...'

'Well, thanks, mate. I'll put you on my CV as a reference!'

'Look, Anita is such a nice girl, she wouldn't hurt a fly. She's got a heart of gold and that bastard is playing on it. You've got no chance of getting her back now.'

'Unfortunately, you're probably right. I need to take control of my life, and not let others control me. I need to see the band around here at 10 tomorrow and don't ask why.'

The band turned up on time, even Billy, who lived a few miles away from us. I made them coffee and said what I needed to say.

'There's no easy way to say this but I want to pack the band in.'

It all went quiet for a moment until Steve said, 'What's all this about, or need I ask?'

'It's nothing to do with Anita, Steve. I've had enough...'

'Don't do this, mate,' said Rick. 'We're as popular as ever – we're having a great time.'

'I have to be honest, Nick,' said Billy. 'I need the money. I'm still paying off those gambling debts.'

'I'm sorry about that, Billy. Look, we started off doing a few gigs and that was fine. We've gone from just over half a dozen bookings a month to well over double figures and rising. I've had a gutful of living out of a suitcase, travelling up and down motorways and Travel Inns and B&Bs...'

'Be fair, Nick, we've done more Premier Inns,' he said with a laugh.

'I don't care if it's the Hilton every night – I've had enough.'

'Let me just get this straight, Nick, said Rick. 'You're not falling out with us?'

'Of course not, mate.'

'If we cut the gigs down to what it was before, would that suit?'

'Well, yeah, I love playing with you guys. I still get the buzz.'

'If Steve and Billy agree, I've no problem with that. To be honest, I've been finding it tough going myself. It would mean Ruth and I could spend more time together. What about you, Steve?'

'Yeah, fine, my new lady would be happy with that. And another thing – now we're all together, I was thinking maybe we should put an LP together...'

'Christ, Steve, where did you get "LP" from? That's a blast from the past!' said Rick.

'Yeah, sorry about that, I meant an album, of course. We've got a lot of material we've written over the years. I thought it would be great to get back in a studio and see what we can put together.'

'What about you, Billy? Where's that leave you?'

'I'm not sure, Nick. I like playing with you lot, but I need as many bookings as possible, so I need to think about it.'

'OK, we understand, but let us know as quickly as possible.'

'Cool. I'll do that.'

'Who's going to break the good news to Big Al?'

'I'll do that, Rick. Except for Billy, are we all happy about doing fewer gigs?'

Rick and Steve nodded, so I made arrangements to see Al the next day. As I entered his office, his mutt by his side, he said, 'I ain't got long – I've a meeting in the West End.'

'OK, I'll keep it sweet. The band wants to do fewer bookings.'

'Do what?'

'We don't want to be criss-crossing the country doing loads of venues.

We ain't youngsters any more…'

'Oh, bollocks, Nick, don't give me that old chestnut! There are thousands of guys doing it at your age who'd be only too happy with all the work I get you.'

As he raised his voice Sampson growled, and I said, 'Do we have to have that poxy dog in here every time we talk? It's really off-putting – it's like he's sizing you up for his dinner.'

'Tough – he stays. I've never had anybody in here before who's asked for less work. Your band is on a roll, you're flavour of the month at the moment. Tomorrow you could be yesterday's fish and chip paper.'

'Look, Al, you know and I know all we are to you is pounds, shillings and pence. Less gigs, less money for you. I understand that, but we're not in it for you. We're in it for us, and that's what we want. If you don't like it, then we can tear up the contract and move on.'

I'd never spoken to Al like that before and he was quite taken aback, but it had to be said. I was adamant.

'We don't want any more bookings without us knowing about it first and agreeing to them.'

'What are you now, the agent?'

'All we want is fewer shows, that's all. Other than that it's business as usual.'

'Well, it ain't business as normal for me. I don't know whether I want to represent you.'

'Fine, if that's what you want, we'll finish off the fifteen gigs that are booked and we'll go our separate ways.' I stood up. 'Let us know what you decide so we can make alternative arrangements.'

I walked out. Big Al's mouth was wide open. I don't think anybody had ever spoken to him like that before.

I knew Al from old. He could twist you round his little finger. I had to be strong. Perhaps I was too strong, but that's how it was. I told the guys what I'd said and they were fully supportive of me. Deep down I think they wanted what I wanted, so there was no rift between us.

I think I must have been on a roll, as when my daughter Tracy came round on the cadge, I said to her very firmly, 'There's no more money. You're an adult, and it's about time you stood on your own two feet. How did I get my money? Simple, I worked hard for it all my life. Now I am going to enjoy my semi-retirement and hopefully keep some of it for me.'

'Are you all right, Dad? I'm a bit worried about you.'

'In fact, I've never felt better, Tracy. You can tell your brother and all the kids that Grandad has locked the safe and thrown away the key. If you want to come and visit me, only come because you want to see me and not my wallet.'

Steve, Rick and I went to see Terry Sherman. He had a recording studio and was now producing and recording albums.

When we entered the studio he looked up and said, 'Look who's here, my Shadow friends! How can I help you, lads?'

We explained what we wanted and asked him if he would produce our album.

'Well, I'd like to work with you guys, but it doesn't come cheap. There's the hire of the studio, at least two weeks, my time and lots of other incidentals. It all mounts up.'

'We understand,' I said, 'but will you do it for us?'

'Yeah, I can do it. It should be some fun. We might have to get some session players in, Nick,' he said with a laugh.

'Bollocks!' was the response.

He checked his diary out and gave us some dates when he was free. It was agreed that he'd come back with a price and we agreed to let him know how many tracks we were thinking of. We went to the nearest cafe and plotted our next move.

We had Des's money, which would cover it in full. We still had our records being released by our previous record company, and we weren't under contract to them, so we were leaving our options open. This was our project and we didn't want any interference.

'Do we ask Ray if he wants to be part of it?' asked Rick.

We all looked at each other and we all agreed it would be great to have him back on board.

♫ 23 ♫

A special lady in Great Yarmouth

Things were happening fast. I rang Ray in France and updated him about the album. He was well chuffed that the band had asked him back. He was well up for it and made it quite clear that he would pay his whack towards the costs. Big Al came back and agreed to what we wanted. He wasn't happy, but that was tough – it was our band, not his. I was still thinking about Anita; even though she'd kicked me into touch I was hoping she was OK and things were working out for her.

Danielle and I were coming to the end of our relationship. I wasn't really bothered. She'd worn me out and she was now looking for a younger model. It had been fun while it lasted, but now I would just concentrate on my music.

Little Jade came round and said, 'Are you OK, Grandad? Aunty Tracy is really worried about you.'

'I'm fine. How are you?'

'Cool. I'm off to a concert at the O2 to see my favourite boy band tonight. They're awesome, especially the lead singer.'

'Well, have fun and I'll see you soon.'

She walked away slowly, turned around and said with a silly little grin, 'Grandad, is the safe really locked?'

I rolled up with laughter and said, 'Do you know, I've just opened it to take some money out of it...'

'Have you locked it back up yet?'

'I was just going to and, do you know what, I've just found this ten pound note that must've fallen out of it.'

I pulled it out of my pocket and she was on it like a flash. As she rushed out the door she shouted, 'Love you, Grandad.'

I felt really in control of my life. I was now calling the shots and it felt good.

Billy still wanted to stay with us, but said he would play with other bands as long as it didn't impact on us. He added that if a band wanted him full time and there were more gigs on offer, he'd have to look at it, as he needed the money. Ray came over for a couple of days to discuss the album. All of us, except Billy, had written various numbers, so we had to choose about fourteen of them. Some we were already playing, but others needed some work on them. Luckily we all agreed on the songs that we wanted on the album. The dates were set with Terry and we couldn't wait to start recording.

Big Al heard about what we were doing and said he wanted to help. We had no problem with his input, but we would make the final decision. I did feel guilty and had probably gone a bit over the top with him in his office, but he was fine about it and understood, and we remained mates.

We were in Great Yarmouth for two nights, where we loved playing back in the sixties. You could get bed and breakfast for a pound a night and a pint for one and sixpence. We were playing at the same venue as we'd played all those years ago. It was a real nostalgic journey for us.

We got there early, had a wander round and treated ourselves to fish and chips and a pot of tea each – we knew how to live! Then it was back to set up and a sound check.

The ballroom still had lots of photos of bands on the walls from those early years. We were lucky as both nights were nearly full, which is a bit of a result when you consider how the economic climate had hit people.

I felt much more relaxed now that I'd sorted out my life in the way I wanted it to go. I think it told in my performance that night. In fact, all of us played really well and the crowd were right behind us.

It was a great night, and after the show we went to the foyer to speak to our fans and also flog some merchandise. Ruth was at all the shows now; she was an ace sales lady. Before we came to Yarmouth, Ruth had wanted a word with me. She was really worried that I would think badly of her as she was now living with Rick so soon after Des had passed away. I made it quite clear that Des would have wanted her to be happy, and getting together with Rick was good for both of them.

As I walked down the stairs to the foyer, it was pleasing to see so many people there. Out of the corner of my eye I noticed a lady in a wheelchair who had a friend with her.. She was about my age, but didn't look well. I could see she wanted a chat so I went over to her.

'You don't remember me, Nick,' she said.

You get this all the time. Over the years you meet so many people at gigs.

'I'm sorry, I don't.'

'Cast your mind back to 1967 when you and Steve met two girls in the Acropolis coffee bar after your show.'

'Keep going, this sounds interesting.'

I called Steve over and we're both now listening.

'My name is Kay...'

The lady with her now chipped in.

'I'm Val. Now Steve, you must remember those sand dunes...'

'And Nick,' said Kay, 'you came round my house. We were enjoying a teenager moment on the settee when my Mum's dog kept barking and I had to let it out into the garden. It then escaped and we went chasing after it...'

'Bloody hell! I remember it like it was yesterday. We caught it and as we went back in to your house, your Mum and Dad turned up and there was no more settee! What about when we threw water bags over Steve and Val while they were in the sand dunes and...'

'Well, we won't go there, Nick. I don't think my husband would be too happy,' said Val.

'Look, Nick, I know you're busy but would it be possible if the four of us could have a coffee tomorrow. I would really like that,' said Kay.

I looked at Steve and he didn't seem to have a problem with that.

'Yeah, that'll be fine.'

'Oh, that would be great! Say about eleven outside the pier.'

'You're on, Kay. We'll look forward to that.'

As they left Steve said to me sadly, 'That Kay looks very poorly.'

'Yeah, not good. We don't know how lucky we are.'

Next day, the girls were outside the pier waiting for us. Kay had really tried to make herself look nice, but you could see she was struggling. Why I did it I don't know, but I started pushing the wheelchair as we made our way to the coffee shop on the pier.

We sat there having our coffee. Steve and I couldn't help ourselves and had two large doughnuts, the ones with the holes in the middle covered in loads of sugar. Before we started talking Kay brought out a photo of the four of us standing outside the Regal where we'd played the gig in 1967.

'Wasn't I good-looking in those days...?' said Steve with a giggle.

'You still wear those rose-tinted glasses, then,' said Val, grinning.

We were enjoying each other's company and talked about what we'd all got up to over the years. Kay had got married and had a couple of kids. Sadly her husband, who was older than her, had died a couple of years back. She explained that she had a wasting disease and was now unable to look after herself. She now lived in a nursing home, which was really sad. Val was married with one kid and saw Kay most days – they'd been friends since schooldays. They were really interested in the band. They'd followed us since they'd first seen us and were pleased that we had got back together again.

Kay reminded me of when we were walking along the beach one morning. Out of one of the beach huts came a dishevelled Tony with a girl called Alice, whose nickname was Slack Alice, so called because none of the bands were safe from her clutches. She'd read on our website that Tone had died but was unaware that he'd married Alice.

Kay was now getting tired and asked me to push her up to the end of the pier and back. I'd only met her for one weekend, but we talked like we'd known each other all our lives. I bent down and looked at her. She held my hand and said tearfully, 'Thanks for meeting me, Nick. The sixties were the happiest time of my life and meeting you again has really made me feel young again. In those days we didn't have a care in the world and enjoyed life to the full.'

'Kay, I'm so pleased we've met as well. You're right, I would love to go back to those days when we all seemed to have so much fun. Look, would you and Val like to be our guests tonight and come and see the show – that's if you can stand it again.'

'You try and stop me! We'd love to.'

With difficulty she lifted herself up from her chair and gave me a kiss on the cheek.

'Nick, thanks for making me feel happy again. I'll treasure this moment for the rest of my life.'

It was a touching moment and I realised how lucky I was.

That night we really made a fuss of the two girls and managed to get them two front seats. They really enjoyed themselves. They were about to leave when Kay said, 'Nick, would you mind keeping in touch with me? I'd be so happy if you would.'

'Of course, I'd love to.'

I rang her each week, but sadly during the third week she died. She must've known she didn't have long to live. She was a very brave and lovely lady and I felt honoured that she had remembered me after all those years. Steve and I went to the funeral to pay our respects and to remember a lady much braver than we could ever be.

Ray came over a couple of days before we started recording on the Monday. On that Saturday we played a pub in Dagenham – we used to go there quite a lot. They used to have more fights there than the Albert Hall. We knew the governor, Jack – he was the son of Larry, who used to run our local pub, the Queen's, now called bleedin' Ziggies. They had live music every night and it was one of the few pubs that I knew that didn't sell food.

We thought Ray might be a bit rusty after not playing with us for a while and it would be a good opportunity for us to get back in the mix as a five-piece again. I'd been to see Jack a couple of weeks before and said, 'What about a spot up here?'

'What? I can't afford you lot! What you charge for one night is more than I pay for all the bands for a whole year!'

'All we want is plenty of beer.'

'Are you saying this is a freeman's?'

'Yep.'

'You're on. What night?'

It was like old times as we lugged the gear in. It was packed out, which always helps when you're playing, so we were well happy until we saw the terrible twins, Mandy and Viv. Steve was crapping himself because Sue, his partner, was coming with Ruth later. The girls looked like they'd just come back from Soho. Their make-up was so thick they must have used a trowel to put it on. Their miniskirts were like belts and their boobs were on show. They were so big they reminded me of a couple of cows that hadn't been milked for a week. They came straight over to us.

'Long time no see, boys!' said Mandy, licking her lips. 'Don't you love us any more then?'

'Love you any more, Mandy?' I said. 'You were well out of order at that hotel in Upminster, acting like you were on the game. That was a special friend I had with me – or I did have. That was well over the top even for you.'

'Sorry, Nick, I was a bit pissed.'

'Pissed? You were out of it.'

'Look, Nick, I was only kidding. Would you pay me for sex?'

My face must have said it all.

'See, you know I was only messing about.'

Then Viv, who was clearly off her head, went up to Steve and grabbed his bollocks. Steve winced as she said, 'What's the matter? You used to like me grabbing them, Steve!'

'Yes Viv, but not that hard.'

She let go and said, 'Steve, maybe I'll see you later – we can have some fun!'

They both cackled like a farmyard of chickens. As they went to the bar Mandy said, with a big grin on her mush, 'Nick, I'm all yours tonight and I'm feeling hungry.'

When they went, Billy, who was listening to all this, said, 'Who are those monsters?'

'Yours if you want them. I'll introduce you to them.'

'You're joking! They're scary…'

Mandy and Viv plonked themselves on two bar stools in front of us with their drinks. They swung round and crossed their legs, giving us a full view. As the punters came in, it blocked them out, thank God.

What a night we had! We were well up for it. All we could see was the faces of everyone having a great night. Jack topped us up with lager and we were well on our way to getting pissed.

After a couple of numbers Ray had settled in and we were rocking like the old days. The sweat was pouring off of us – this was what music was all about. We played for three hours with a couple of short breaks. Viv had pulled, so Steve was safe.

You know the saying that when you've had a lot to drink everything looks a lot better than it is? When I woke up in Mandy's bed the next morning my head was throbbing. I looked over at her and she looked a wreck. I looked at myself in the mirror on the wall. I looked gruesome. Then she woke up, pulled me towards her and said, 'Well, we're both still here then. The way you were going I thought I was going to have to give you the kiss of life.'

'I don't remember.'

'Well, that's nice.'

'Sorry, Mand, but you know what I mean.'

'Do you know, Nick, we've been shagging on and off for nearly fifty years.'

'It's a wonder I can still do it. I always used to wake up with a stiffy, now I wake up and can barely see it.'

Thank goodness I had a day to recuperate before going into the recording studio. I was just in to my second cup of tea when there was a banging on the door. It was just like the old times as Steve, Rick and Ray came steaming in. The piss-taking started, with Steve first.

'I'll tell you what, Nick, that Mandy looked great…'

'Yeah, in a farmyard,' said Ray.

'No, she's all right; it's just her nickname that puts me off,' said Rick.

'What nickname is that then?'

'They call her B&Q, Nick.'

'Where did you get that from?'

'You can always get a knob in there!'

'Funny, funny… What're you lot here for anyway?'

'Well, coffee first of all,' said Steve. 'Then we need to make sure we're all singing from the same hymn sheet for tomorrow.'

After a couple of hours chatting we'd confirmed the numbers. Afterwards they all went down the pub. I didn't want to go, so I arranged to see them tomorrow at the studio early. After they'd gone I had a nice power nap, as Mandy had done me right in.

We were all there at the studio at 8 o'clock sharp. Terry explained what was going to happen and what he wanted. He had another guy with him who sat at one of the decks all of the time. We spent ten days there, working twelve hours a day, sometimes well into the night. In between this we had to fit in two bookings at St Albans and Maidstone.

We had no hang-ups about how we should play each number and none of the band was trying to outdo each other. We all respected each other's opinion and I have to say Terry knew his stuff.

Big Al came in a couple of times and gave his thoughts on some of the arrangements. It was a more subdued Al – Sampson wasn't with him, but nobody liked to ask him where he was. I later found out that he'd died a couple of days before. I felt a bit rotten as I'd had a pop about the dog a while back.

When we eventually finished, Terry was going to put it all together and contact us to hear the results of our efforts.

It was an exciting time for all of us and the band was as close now as it had ever been. We'd done so much together. Our only sadness was the loss of Penny, Tone and Des.

Ray indicated that he wouldn't mind coming back in the band full time. His and Liz's divorces were going through and they had both had enough of France. That would affect Rick more than anybody else, because he was the main singer now. But he didn't have a problem, nor did anybody else.

Ray was a good guy and he'd helped Steve and Rick out when they were skint. In fact, it would be great to have him back on board again. Once he'd sorted his affairs out in France he'd be straight in.

Big Al asked us if we'd do a cabaret spot and back one of his singers. It wasn't our scene, but we said we'd do it for him. It was a classy club up west. We found out what numbers the guy wanted to sing and we made sure we knew them. We opened first with some fairly light material, then the singer, Adam, came on stage. He was in his fifties, a bit portly, and slightly camp. But he had a good voice and the crowd liked him. He was on a roll but committed the cardinal sin and asked the audience if they had any requests, which you just don't do, because you look a complete prat if you don't know them.

It had happened to me once. I was playing for a band called the Five Dice Boys, a poxy name for a band. We were playing at a football club dance in the East End of London. We were on a roll and we said the same thing. Half a dozen young geezers came out of the crowd and confronted us. This was the era of punk rock and one of them said, 'We want Johnny Rotten and the Sex Pistols.'

We indicated in the nicest possible way that we didn't know any of their numbers. That triggered it and the same guy mouthed out, 'You're a feckin' useless band then.'

Then one of his mates added, 'Yeah, load of wankers!'

The dance came to a standstill and it was a stand-off. These blokes thought they were big-time Charlies and were going to mess up the evening until our drummer, Josh, stood up. He was built like a brick shit-house. He went over to the two blokes giving the verbal, got hold of them and banged their heads together. Their eyes started spinning round like reels in a fruit machine and they slumped to the floor. He then walked towards the other four, but they all ran off. Josh lifted the two blokes off the floor, put one under each arm and dumped them outside.

Back at the cabaret, Adam had shouted out to the audience, 'Any requests, ladies and gentlemen?'

This old biddy gets up and says, 'Yes, please – could you sing *Love on the Rocks* by Neil Diamond?'

Well, Adam went from a picture of happiness to one of abject misery, then ran off the stage. We found out later he'd split up with his fella the day before.

A couple of days later I had the shock of my life. My younger brother Arthur contacted me. Now, I hadn't seen or heard from him for over forty years. I didn't get on with him when we were younger and we drifted apart. He wanted to have a meet. I wasn't bothered but I suppose it wouldn't hurt.

I met up with him and his wife at a hotel he was staying at in Upminster – the same hotel where I'd met Anita, so it didn't bode well.

He was now living in Canada and was over here to bury his wife's mother. I thought I'd aged, but he was well overweight, bald and looked like he'd had a hard life. I shook his hand, which was all clammy, and nodded to his wife, who didn't look too friendly. She then went to the loo and I said to Arthur, 'How did you find me?'

'They've been playing your records recently in Canada and I looked up your band's website. I got in touch with your manager and he gave me your phone number...'

I said with a laugh, 'Bastard – I'll get him when I see him!'

That didn't go down too well, but I quickly added, 'What do you do over there?'

'I work in the office of a transport company.'

'Any kids?'

'No, we've been unlucky in that department.'

'You've done well, Arthur. If I'd known what I know now I would've had the op at eighteen.'

He was just about to introduce his wife, who had just joined us again, when I said, 'Do you remember your first girlfriend? What a dog she was! What was her name now? I always think of *Coronation Street* when I think of her ... that's it, Deirdre! She was one weird bird! She was as flat as a runway and always wore that red beret. She looked like Che Guevara! What about her hair? She had a flick-up hairstyle. The flick-ups were so high it looked like she'd been electrocuted. Whatever happened to her?'

'I married her.'

I nearly died on the spot as I tried to say sorry, but she said, 'I hated you then and I hate you even more now. You were rude, uncouth, common, and had a mouth like a sewer. I see nothing's changed with you. If you think I'm sitting here with this moron, Arthur, you've got another think coming.'

That was that, and I left. I suppose I was out of order, but I didn't know he'd married her. I did manage to contact them before they went back and I think he took my apology on board.

I was feeling guilty about a lot of things. Big Al had been a mate since we were at school. Being our manager was difficult at times as we still classed him as a friend and it doesn't always work in business. With him losing his dog I suggested to the band that we buy him an Alsatian puppy, and they were well up for it.

We spoke to his son, Wayne, and mooted the idea with him. He thought he'd be well chuffed, so that's what we did. We looked around, went to a top breeder and found what we were looking for. When we gave Al the pup he was well choked up.

'Thanks, guys, that's really thoughtful of you, but don't think the rate is coming down!' That was Al – ever the businessman!

He called it Sampson, as he had with all the other dogs he'd had over the years. The good thing was that it was a puppy and wouldn't start growling at us for at least a year or two.

We did Sammy's anniversary bash. All the usual suspects were there and he seemed happy with our performance. Ronnie came over and spoke to me.

'Has that bloke we put the frighteners on been behaving himself?'

I explained that the relationship between us was now finished and I hadn't heard from her, so thankfully, in one way, we had done her a favour, although it hadn't helped me.

Then Ronnie started talking about a scam he was up to and did I want in? It was speak to you later, Ronnie, and I was away.

Terry gave us a bell about the recordings and said to come over and listen to what he'd done so far. We were blown away with some of the tracks, but others needed a bit of fine tuning and maybe we'd have to do one or two of them again. Overall we were really pleased. He said he'd keep us in the loop and by the end of the month it should all be finished.

We did have to go back in for a couple of days to redo two tracks, but felt that what we'd done was some of our best work and we were looking forward to hearing the completed recordings.

Everything was on the up and it was a real buzz, especially when Ray came back in. Also all the personal relationships seemed stable in the band, which helps a lot. Diane was back from America – unfortunately she'd been dumped by the hunk and needed some TLC. So we picked up again, and that was going along nicely.

The first night with Ray back in the band was in Brentwood, home to TV's *The Only Way is Essex*. When I was about eighteen I used to play football for Brentwood, who were a professional club. We used to play teams like West Ham's 'A' team and Wimbledon in the Metropolitan league, so I have fond memories of the town.

Tonight a lot of our friends, partners and family members would be coming. It was one of those nights that if you didn't have to go out you didn't. There was a storm and the rain was lashing down, so it was pleasing to see so many people at the venue. The girlfriends of the band were in the dressing room and it was a great feeling. It felt like a family, and in a way it was.

The buzzer went and there were hugs from everybody as we left the dressing room. As we made our way onto the stage and picked up our guitars, I looked at all the other guys.

We'd known each other for well over forty years, and we'd all been round the block a few times and survived. It was great that we were still playing music together and our friendships were still as strong. We'd started off with *Suburban Mod,* which was the record that had set us off on this journey. It was a great night and the crowd really appreciated our music.

After the show Steve, Sue and Diane came back to my place for a nightcap. I was hoping Diane might stay the night, but the TLC didn't cover that! Steve was going to drop Diane off for me. Sue was driving as she hadn't had a drink. We all said our goodbyes.

It was still pouring with rain as they rushed to the car. I had only just shut the door when I noticed Diane's scarf. I picked it up and quickly went to the front door to try and catch her. I was just about to open the door when the bell went. Diane must've missed it as well.

I opened the door and had the shock of my life. It was Anita. She was standing there soaked to the skin. She looked so sad and dishevelled. Neither of us could get our words out. I quickly let her in. She grabbed hold of me tight and started sobbing.

'Nick, I've always loved you. I'm so sorry for what I said. I didn't realise how much I cared about you. I want to stay with you, Nick...'

'Of course, you can stay as long as you want...'

'I don't think you understand, Nick. I want to stay with you for ever.'

♫ 24 ♫

The end of the journey

The journey of our band, Modern Edge, started way back in 1964, as described in *The Sixties Boys,* and continued with *Sixties Boys Unzipped,* and finally *Sixties Boys on Tour*. So much has happened since then, so I'd better update you.

Anita did stay with me and we're now living together in a lovely flat overlooking the sea. We're really happy and enjoying being together every day. Once her children found out why she'd left their Dad they fully understood. I've met them and they are a credit to her. Her husband didn't go without a fight. He tried every trick in the book to get her back, but none of them worked.

The divorce is nearly finalised and it can't come soon enough for both of us. My family have met her; they can't understand what such a lovely lady sees in me. Jade adores her and they are best mates. We see Anita's best friend Jenny quite a lot – she's a great girl.

My kids are now a few miles away so I've got more money in my pocket! My son Rob must have had a change of heart as Zoe is now expecting a little boy.

Modern Edge is still performing, but only a few gigs a year, which suits all of us. The album was picked up by a record company and has performed well. We still see Terry and always wind him up about Terry and the Tanks.

Steve is still with Sue and we're still close mates. The girls get on really well together, which always helps. Rick and Ruth are now happily married, as are Ray and Liz. The band keeps us all together, so we never lose contact. Billy is still drumming with us.

Big Al's son Wayne is now running the business. Al is reliving his youth as a Rocker. He's got a couple of motorbikes, is well leathered up and meeting up with mates at the local motorbike club.

Robin, Penny's son, is now working with a band on a Mediterranean cruise liner.

TJ, who was our first professional manager, sadly passed away, as did my first boss, East End car dealer Eddie Tucker, a real rogue – I'll never forget him.

Alec, King of the Mods, is now going out with Diane. Ronnie is still ducking and diving, knocking out CDs and DVDs at boot fairs – all legit, of course!

Sammy is still going strong, although his pins are a bit dodgy and he's now in a wheelchair. They call him 'Ironside', but not to his face!

I keep in contact with my brother, Arthur, with a Christmas card and an occasional email.

People often ask me what it was like being a teenager in the sixties. I always tell them, 'The sixties was the start of a fantastic musical explosion. Anyone who could play a chord felt they could make the charts. We were part of an incredible decade in Britain, one that changed the world.'

It doesn't get any better than that.

Further memories of the 1960s
A small selection from THE RECOLLECTIONS SERIES

VOLUME 5: 1964
ISLE OF MAN

Peter Townsend & John Stretton

In this volume we travel back to 1964, a time when the railway lines to Peel and Ramsey were still open. Ray Ruffell spent several days in August 1964 photographing the railways and tramways of the island. Now, more than 40 years later, these rare and previously unpublished pictures provide a fascinating window on life. In the tradition of the series, key events of life in general in 1964 provide context to the period.

978 1 85794 278 1 Paperback £4.99

VOLUME 9: 1961

John Stretton & Peter Townsend

1961 was to prove to be a significant year on Britain's railways - the appointment of Dr Richard Beeching was set to have far-reaching effects on the railway network. This was the year of the A6 Murder, the Nuremberg War Crimes trial of Adolf Eichman and the first man in space. The Swinging Sixties were under way, while the decline of steam on the railways was set to gather pace. This volume includes a wide selection of subjects from around the railway network.

978 1 85794 292 7 Paperback £4.99

VOLUME 10: 1963

Chris Harris

1963 will be long remembered for its harsh winter, and this volume includes dramatic scenes of the railways in the atrocious conditions. The cold winds of change were to blow through the railway industry during this year with the publication in March of the Beeching Report, which was to reshape the railways in the years that followed. In the wider world this was the year that President Kennedy was assassinated, National Service in Britain ended and the Great Train Robbery took place.

978 1 85794 296 5 Paperback £4.99

Available through all good booksellers or:

The* NOSTALGIA *Collection

The Trundle, Ringstead Road, Great Addington, Kettering, Northants NN14 4BW
Tel/Fax: 01536 330588
email: sales@nostalgiacollection.com Website: www.nostalgiacollection.com